THE CROWS

THE CROWS

MARIS SOULE

FIVE STAR

An imprint of Thomson Gale, a part of The Thomson Corporation

THOMSON

GALE

Detroit • New York • San Francisco • New Haven, Conn. • Waterville, Maine • London

THOMSON

GALE™

LIBRARY OF CONGRESS CATALOGING-IN-PUBLICATION DATA

Soule, Maris.
 The crows / Maris Soule. — 1st ed.
  p. cm.
  ISBN-13: 978-1-59414-605-3 (hardcover : alk. paper)
  ISBN-10: 1-59414-605-5 (hardcover : alk. paper)
  1. Women accountants—Fiction. 2. Michigan—Fiction. I. Title.
 PS3569.0737C76 2007
 813'.54—dc22   2007030667

First Edition. First Printing: December 2007.

Published in 2007 in conjunction with Tekno Books and Ed Gorman.

Printed in the United States of America on permanent paper
10 9 8 7 6 5 4 3 2 1

Dedicated to
Mario Chirone
August 15, 1913–June 14, 2006

ACKNOWLEDGMENTS

I would like to thank Detective Richard Matteson of the Kalamazoo County Sheriff's Department for his assistance with this book. He took time out of his busy schedule to read the manuscript for procedural errors. If there are any mistakes, they are due to changes I made after his reading.

Also, my thanks to Dr. Jori Reijonen for her help regarding the symptoms and behavior of schizophrenics. The information Dr. Reijonen provided and the articles I read about schizophrenia gave me a greater appreciation of those who suffer from this illness and those who have to live with them.

And my everlasting thanks and appreciation to my friends and fellow writers who diligently looked for errors in my work, willingly offered advice and information, and constantly encouraged me. (Eat & Critique; WAG; Second Tuesday Writers; Kalamazoo Mystery Writers; and MMRWA.)

Finally, most of all, thanks to my husband, son, and daughter for their unerring support. They make it happen. For instance, when I needed a poem for this story, I turned to my son for help. "The Messengers" is by Deryk (Dirty) Soule and used with his permission.

Ladybug, ladybug, fly away home . . .

ONE

The crows cawed a warning. Then came the gunshots. Three in succession, a pause, then two more.

The sound was close—too close—and a shiver of fear slid down my spine. Those shots had come from somewhere in my woods.

I immediately stopped walking and listened. This was April, not September. The wrong season for hunters to be shooting. At least, the wrong season for hunting deer.

As birds flew from treetop to treetop, a sickening, giddy sensation invaded my stomach. On the winding path ahead was my four-month-old Rhodesian Ridgeback pup, a potential show dog that had set me back fifteen hundred dollars. If some idiot poacher was playing Rambo and shot him, the guy was going to be mincemeat.

"Baraka!" I yelled.

Branches snapped over on my left, and I looked in that direction. All I saw were tree trunks, brambles, and junk . . . and maybe the dark, shadowed figure of a man.

Another shot sounded.

I quickly got off the trail and crouched behind a tree, all the while yelling, "Hey! Stop! This is private property."

The next shot whistled above my head, and I ignored the mud and rocks on the ground and dropped to my stomach, making myself as flat as possible. A poacher might mistake a Ridgeback puppy for a deer, but not a screaming, twenty-eight-year-old woman wearing a bright red-and-blue nylon jacket.

I was trying to decide what to do next when a reddish-brown blur came lunging through the underbrush, ears flapping and brow all wrinkled. In a few months, Baraka will be a graceful, medium-sized hound. But at four months, his feet are too big, his ears too long, and his coat too loose.

Nevertheless, I was happy to see him. If any of those shots had been aimed at him, Baraka had survived unscathed.

He pounced on me, licking my face and whining with excitement. He was getting mud all over me, but I didn't care. I was just glad to see him alive.

I wrapped an arm around his chest and held him close, then tried to hear if anyone was coming toward us.

I knew I couldn't stay where I was. First, I didn't want whoever was shooting to stumble over me, and second, the frost wasn't completely out of the ground. I was getting cold, and Baraka was wiggling and twisting to get free. He might be just a puppy, but I couldn't hold him.

Once free, he bounced around me, growling fiercely and ready to play. When he started barking, I knew hiding was impossible. My best bet was to make a run for my house. There I could call the police.

I rose to my feet awkwardly, my mud-soaked jeans clinging to my legs, and an equal amount of mud was on my face, hands, and jacket. I was shaking all over, a combination of anger and fear pumping adrenaline through my body. I'd moved out of Kalamazoo because I thought living in the country would be safer. Now I was being shot at . . . literally in my own backyard.

"Come on, Baraka," I said and made a dash for my house.

Running through my woods was not an easy feat, not with all of the junk my grandfather dumped here over the years. In addition to trees, brush, and rocks, half-buried tires, chicken wire and rusted car parts created a hazardous obstacle course.

With every step I took, my anger increased. Someone had come into my woods and started shooting. Blindly shooting. In addition to the sheriff, I was going to call the DNR. The Department of Natural Resources should do something about this. My woods were posted No Hunting. I had my rights.

My anger monopolized my thoughts, and I barely noticed when Baraka put his nose to the ground. Ridgebacks are sight hounds, but there's nothing wrong with their tracking ability. They can pick up smells thousands of times better than any human. He sniffed the ground near the old chicken coop, then near the woodshed. From there, he traveled up the crumbling concrete steps that led to my back door.

He stopped at the storm door and looked back at me. My eyes were focused on the bloody hand print on the door's aluminum frame. As I came closer, I could see another print on the handle.

Now that I was looking, I saw spots of blood on the concrete landing, the steps, and the ground. A trail of blood. Someone had come along the same path I'd taken and had gone into my house. Someone who was bleeding.

Baraka whined to get inside, and I wished I hadn't so easily gotten into the habit of not locking my back door when I went for a walk. I stood at the bottom of the steps and debated what to do.

Both my cell phone and cordless phone were in the house. To call for help, I either had to go inside or to my neighbors. John and Julia Westman, who live the closest, are a quarter of a mile to the northwest of my house, and both work. Howard Lowe, my next closest neighbor, lives a half mile to the east, on the opposite side of the road from my house. Lowe and I haven't hit it off that well, not since I put up No Hunting signs all around my woods. He would probably shoot me if I stepped on his property. After those two houses, I'd have to go at least a mile before I reached another one, and my car keys were in the house.

I had only one option.

I opened the storm door, being careful not to touch the blood. Baraka immediately pushed against the wood door, and it swung open. It had been latched when I left.

Cautiously, I followed my dog into the house.

"Hey!" I called out, looking around my kitchen. "Who's here?"

More blood spotted the linoleum—bright red drops on a faded and worn pattern of tan and brown. Baraka headed straight for the dining room, and I followed . . . then came to an abrupt stop.

A man lay on the floor, not more than two feet from my telephone. I saw a small hole in the back of his nylon jacket. He was face down on the linoleum, a pool of blood spreading out from under his body. Baraka licked his face, and the man's hand moved. Just barely. I hurried to his side and pushed Baraka away.

"Are you all right?" I asked, then realized how stupid the question was. The man had a hole in his back near his heart and lungs. He was bleeding. Of course he wasn't all right.

"Shh . . . et," he said.

I wasn't sure I'd heard him right. "Did you say shit?"

He said it again, slurring the word, his voice weak. Then his hand relaxed.

Dead or unconscious? I wondered and checked the side of his neck for a pulse. I tried two spots and didn't feel any sign of a heartbeat. It was then that a new smell reached my nose, and Baraka began sniffing around the man's pants. In death, more than just the man's hand had relaxed.

I stood up to escape the stench and stared down at the man, my entire body trembling. He was clean shaven and dressed in casual work attire. The collar of a blue-and-gray plaid flannel shirt showed above the black nylon jacket and mud covered his jeans and work boots, but they were fairly new. His build was lean and wiry, and I guessed him to be around forty. He looked familiar, but I wasn't sure why. He wasn't someone I knew.

Baraka started barking, and I looked away from the body. My dog was standing at the window that faced the woods, his body tense and his tail held straight out. I walked over, grabbing my cordless phone along the way. I couldn't see anything or anyone outside, but I didn't question Baraka. He'd seen something.

I punched nine-one-one on the cordless phone's keypad, my hand shaking as I did and my heart beating a staccato. As soon as the phone began ringing, I looked back outside.

I couldn't see anything. No shadowy figure, no movement in the woods. Nothing.

And then I heard a voice.

TWO

I nearly dropped the telephone when a woman said, "Nine-one-one. What is your emergency?"

Shaking, I stammered out my message. "Someone is outside of my house . . . and . . . and a man is dead."

"How do you know a man is dead?"

"Because he's not breathing. I can't feel a pulse."

"And where is this man?"

"On my dining room floor. Someone shot at me. I came back to call the police and found him. Now my dog is acting like someone is outside. I don't know what to do."

"Are you alone in the house?"

"Yes . . . I mean, except for my dog and this man, the one who died."

"Do you know the man?"

"No." I looked down at the body. "He looks kinda familiar, but I don't know why. I'm sure I've never met him."

"How did he get into your house?"

"Through my back door. It wasn't locked."

"Is that door locked now?"

The moment she asked, I realized I hadn't locked the door behind me. "No. It's not." I started toward my kitchen. "I'm going to go lock it now."

"Good." Her soothing tone helped. "I've alerted the sheriff's department. Help is on the way. Don't touch the body. Don't touch anything."

"I won't." I locked my back door and returned to the dining room. Baraka had lost interest in whatever he'd seen outside and was sniffing the body. Quickly, I grabbed him and put him in his crate in the living room, all the while answering the dispatcher's questions.

I assured her that there were no weapons in the house and I couldn't see anyone outside. I couldn't tell her how many shots were fired, just that there had been lots and that the shooting had occurred in the woods behind my house, not in the house.

She told me her name was Martha and asked me mine. "P.J.," I said. "P.J. Benson."

"How do you spell that?"

"Initial P, like Paul. Initial J, like Jack. B like—"

She interrupted. "Just the initials?"

"Yes, just the initials."

If Martha had any opinions about a woman using her initials as a name, she didn't express them. She simply went on with her questions. "You live south of Zenith. Right? On RS Avenue?"

"Right." I guess they know that information when you call.

"Is this a one- or two-story house?"

"Two-story. It's an old farmhouse that belonged to my grandfather. I moved here a few months ago."

"Is the body near an entry door?"

"Yes. The front door opens right into the dining room."

"And where are you from the body right now?"

"About ten feet away." I had gone back to the window so I could scan the outbuildings for any signs of movement. "Should I be farther way? I have a cordless phone."

"Farther away is better."

"I'll go into the kitchen. Oh, I hear sirens."

The first truck to pull into my yard belonged to a volunteer firefighter. Behind that pickup came another, then the Zenith

Village fire truck. They all parked a distance back from the house. Martha told me to hang up and unlock the front door, which I did. No one, however, came inside until a Kalamazoo County Sheriff's Department patrol car arrived.

I met the two deputies outside and told them what had happened. Assured that there was no one in the house with a gun and no one had been shooting near the house, they sent the paramedics in. The two deputies then went around to the back of my house, guns drawn.

I followed the paramedics inside. I think I hoped the man lying on my floor would still be alive, that somehow these skilled professionals would find a sign of life that I'd missed. But as they checked the body, I knew that wasn't going to happen.

Fighting back tears, I headed for my bathroom and closed myself off from the reality of the other room. I took several deep breaths in an attempt to calm the giddiness in my stomach. Only when I saw my reflection in the mirror did I groan.

Even though I keep my hair cut short, it was a tangled mess of brown curls, mud, twigs and dead leaves. More mud, just about the same color as my eyes, covered the right side of my face from my hairline to my chin.

Seeing how I looked brought me out of my temporary shock. I grabbed a washrag and went to work on my face and hands, combed the debris out of my hair, and tossed my muddy jacket into the laundry area. The mud on my jeans had begun to dry, and I decided to hose off the worst before tossing them into the washing machine. That objective in mind, I headed outside.

The firemen and paramedics were gone, and one of the uniformed sheriff's deputies now knelt over the body on the floor. He didn't look up when I scooted by, and I didn't stop to say anything. In truth, I simply wanted out of the house. I needed fresh air and a moment to clear my head. The events of the last hour were too macabre to fathom.

★ ★ ★ ★ ★

I'd rinsed off most of the mud and was standing on the cement landing of the back steps, wringing the excess water out of my jeans, when a tan Jeep Cherokee pulled into my yard. I watched the driver get out. He stretched, then started for my front door.

I guessed him to be in his mid-thirties. Good looking if you like the tall, dark, and handsome type . . . which I do. He wore brown cowboy boots, chinos, a white turtleneck and a brown bomber jacket. His short-cropped brown hair reminded me of my dad's haircuts, and I wondered if he might be in the military. There is an Air Force National Guard base in Battle Creek, about fifteen miles from here. On the weekends they do maneuvers, but this was a Friday afternoon, and this man wasn't in uniform.

He must have sensed my presence, because he suddenly looked my way, changed direction, and headed toward me. He had a rolling walk that covered the distance between us with seemingly little effort. He also had a nice smile.

"You the one who lives here?" he asked, and I nodded. "So you made the nine-one-one call?" Again, I nodded. "And now you're leaving?"

"No." The idea, however, did sound appealing. Maybe if I left, then came back, this would all go away. "I'm just rinsing some mud out of my jeans."

"Oh, okay." He stopped at the base of the steps and glanced at my legs.

Actually, he glanced at all of me, and when his gaze finally met mine, I didn't know what to say. It's been a long time since a good-looking man gave me the once-over.

So long it took me a moment to shake off my stupor. When I did, I asked, "And you are?"

He reached into an inside pocket of his jacket, removed a leather holder and flipped it open to show a badge and ID.

"Detective Sergeant Wade Kingsley. Homicide."

Ah, homicide. That explained the lack of a uniform. "The body's in my dining room," I said. "There's another officer in there."

"That would be Deputy VanderPlough. He, evidently, was the first officer on the scene and put in the call for a homicide detective. I was the closest."

It didn't sound as if Detective Sergeant Wade Kingsley was excited about being the closest, but I figured that was his problem, not mine. I edged back on the landing so he could pass and go inside, but he made no effort to come up the steps. Instead, he glanced around the area, his gaze finally focusing on the bloody prints on the storm door. "Those the victim's?"

"Yes."

"So he was outside when he was shot, came up these steps . . ." Detective Kingsley stepped up on the landing beside me. "And went inside."

"I guess so." The man beside me suddenly seemed gigantic, probably because I'm only five-feet-two, and he had to be at least a foot taller. I shivered. I'm sure from my wet jeans and not because he frightened me.

He looked down at me, a concerned expression on his face. "Are you cold?"

"A little. My jacket got all muddy, and I tossed it in the laundry room." Now I wished I hadn't. "And these jeans are wet."

"You say the body's in the dining room? Where's this door lead?"

"My kitchen."

He nodded. "I think we can let you inside where it's warmer, but you'll have to stay where I tell you. This is now a crime scene."

"No, it's a where-he-died scene. That's where the crime occurred." I pointed toward the woods.

He looked that direction, and that's when I noticed his eye lashes. Why is it men always get the beautiful blue eyes and the long, thick lashes? It's just not fair. I did notice a few crow's-feet at the edges of his eyes, but they only added a rugged quality to his features.

His gaze came back to the door. "Did you go in this way when you found the body?"

"Yes, but I was careful. I only touched the end of the handle, below the blood."

"Good." He pulled a latex glove out of his jacket pocket and slipped it on. I noticed he wore no rings. Neither hand. Not that it meant he wasn't married or had a significant other . . . or that I should care.

Using his gloved hand, Detective Kingsley held the door open. I walked past him into my kitchen, glad for the warmth of my house. Some days in April can be quite warm. This wasn't one of them.

Now, I'm not a great housekeeper under the best of conditions; I absolutely drove some of my coworkers nuts at Quick Sum Associates. And at tax time, you can forget me playing Martha Stewart. Dirty dishes filled my sink and covered my counter, and I needed to dump the basket of old coffee grounds by my coffee maker and toss the empty soup can that sat on the stove. I would have gotten around to doing those things if I hadn't found a man dying in my house.

"The body's in there," I said, pointing toward my dining room. "Along with the other officer."

Detective Kingsley nodded, but didn't move, other than to pull the latex glove off and stuff it in another pocket. He then took a notebook from his jacket pocket, along with a stub of a pencil. "Your name is?"

"P.J. Benson."

"And what does the P.J. stand for?"

"It stands for P.J." He gave me a look of disbelief, so I explained. "That's the name I use. Officially. You can check with the Department of Motor Vehicles."

"P.J. Benson." He lifted his eyebrows, but wrote it down. "Your age?"

"Why do you need that?" Not that I'm sensitive about my age. I just wondered why it mattered. I wasn't the one who'd died.

He glanced up from the notebook. "For my records."

"Twenty-eight. What's your age?" The moment he frowned, I smiled and added, "For my records."

I didn't get an answer. He merely went on with his questions. "Time of the shooting?"

"I'm not sure, exactly. One-forty-five. Two o'clock. I didn't think to look at my watch, but Baraka and I had only been walking for a while."

"The victim's name is Baraka?"

"No, that's my dog."

Again, Detective Kingsley looked up. "Your dog's name is Baraka?"

"Right."

"What's the victim's name?"

"I don't know. I didn't check for a wallet. I just called nine-one-one and waited for someone to show up."

"You shot someone, waited for him to die, then called for help?"

"No. I didn't shoot anyone." We were obviously not communicating. "Someone shot at me."

"Someone shot at you, you shot back, and—"

"Ah, you've arrived." The uniformed sheriff's deputy stood in the doorway. "You want to come look at this body?"

"Stay right where you are," Detective Kingsley said, pointing at me.

I suppose I should have, but I didn't. I followed him into my dining room. Beyond the body, in my living room, Baraka was whining in his crate, scratching to get out. I went over to his side to calm him down.

Standing beside the crate, stroking Baraka's head through the wires, I watched as the deputy and detective knelt beside the body. Detective Kingsley pulled on a new pair of latex gloves and poked around the hole in the dead man's jacket then made eye contact with the deputy.

I didn't think either man had noticed me, but both looked my way. Detective Kingsley did the talking. "What kind of gun did you use?"

Although I'd told him I didn't do it, he obviously thought I'd shot this man. I decided it was time to get that straight. "I didn't use a gun. I don't own a gun, and I didn't shoot anyone."

His expression didn't change. "Then who did?"

"I don't know who did. I only got a glimpse of the guy before he shot at me."

Kingsley frowned, rose to his feet, and glanced around my dining room. "Where exactly were you when this man shot at you?"

"Out in the woods." I pointed out a back window and realized my hand was shaking again. Just remembering the incident had me trembling.

"I was walking with my dog . . ." I indicated Baraka in the crate beside me. "We were about midway in the woods when I heard a shot. Several shots, actually."

"And you say you saw the shooter?"

"Just for a second." I tried to remember what I saw. "I'm pretty sure it was a man, but I couldn't be positive. Basically all I saw was a dark shadow."

"Dark because of his clothing or because of his skin coloring?"

"I don't know." I tried to bring the image back in my mind, but it was just a blur. "Everything happened so fast."

"Okay, tell me exactly what you heard and saw."

I repeated what had happened, ending with Baraka acting as if he saw someone outside. "I think the shooter followed me."

"My partner and I checked the area," the deputy told Detective Kingsley. "We didn't find anyone."

"Because he left," I said. "I certainly would if I heard a half-dozen sirens."

Detective Kingsley asked more questions. Did I know what kind of gun was fired? That was easy. No, just that it was loud. How did I know to come back to the house? I asked him where he thought I should have gone.

"Where, exactly, did you find the body?" Kingsley asked.

"There." I pointed to where the body now lay.

"And he was alive when you found him?"

"Yes, but barely and he didn't live for long after I found him. Basically, he said 'Shit' and died."

"That's all he said?"

"Yes. I mean, I think that's what he said. It was hard to hear him. His voice was weak, and he sort of mumbled. But I think he said 'shit.' "

"And you say you don't know him?"

"I've seen him somewhere, but I've never met him. Never talked to him." Which, in a way, was good. His anonymity made it easier to keep my emotions in check.

"Any idea why he came to your house?"

"No." But I wished he hadn't.

"How did he get inside?" Detective Kingsley asked. "Did he have a key?"

"He didn't need one. I didn't lock my back door."

Kingsley's raised eyebrows expressed his opinion of that habit. He obviously lived in the city. In Kalamazoo, I would have locked the door. I always locked my doors when I lived there. Doors, windows, cars, and bike. But the first thing my neighbors said when I moved here was you could leave your doors unlocked and not worry.

Well, they were wrong.

"The van's here," the uniformed deputy said, and I saw a van pull into my yard. I also saw a female uniformed deputy tying a wide yellow tape to the maple tree out front.

I know, from watching cop shows on TV, that everything within the yellow tape is considered the crime scene and off limits to non-police personnel. That the woman was sealing off my house and yard bothered me. "The crime scene was out there, in the woods," I repeated. "This is where the guy died, not where the crime was committed."

The two men just looked at me, then the uniformed deputy headed for my kitchen and Detective Kingsley came toward me, pulling off his latex gloves as he did.

Baraka wagged his tail and wiggled with excitement, banging against the sides of his crate. Kingsley looked down at him and frowned. "I can see why you cage your dog. Is he always this ugly?"

"Ugly?" I stiffened at the insult. No one, not even a sheriff's detective, calls my dog ugly.

He must have realized I'd taken offense. He pointed at Baraka's back. "Look at the way he's bristling."

I understood then. To some, ugly means vicious. And others have made the same mistake. They see the ridge and think the hairs on Baraka's back are raised in anger. "If he was mean, he wouldn't be wagging his tail," I said. "He's a Rhodesian Ridgeback. That's his ridge. The hair grows the opposite direction. It always looks like that."

Detective Kingsley looked closer. "Interesting."

"See how the two whorls at his shoulders are the same shape, and how the ridge tapers to a point at the hips, like a sword?" I indicated the line and proudly stated, "Baraka has a perfect ridge."

"I'll have to take your word on that."

I think Kingsley was ready to talk about something else, but I was on a roll. After all, I'd had to go through two interviews to buy this dog. I wanted to show off my knowledge. "Rhodesian Ridgebacks are good hunters and family dogs. They're a combination of the breeds the Europeans brought to South Africa and the native Hottentot's dogs, which had a ridge of hair growing the opposite direction on their backs. I saw my first one at a dog show last year and knew I had to have one."

"Interesting. Actually, very interesting." He looked me straight in the eyes, then smiled. "Thirty six," he said.

"Thirty six?"

THREE

"That's my age . . . for your records." Kingsley smiled, and I remembered my earlier question. Then he motioned toward the front door. "We need to get you outside. We've already contaminated the crime scene."

I glanced down at my wet jeans. "I need to change."

He frowned, and I'm sure he was going to come up with an objection, but I headed for my bedroom before he could say anything. The moment I closed and locked the door, I kicked off my shoes and pulled down my jeans. Which, being wet, stuck to my skin.

He knocked. "Miss Benson." Knocked again. "Miss Benson, come out."

"Just a minute," I said, and tugged at the resistant denim.

"Please come out."

"I will," I promised, slightly breathless from the exertion of standing on one leg, leaning over, and pulling on the material. But finally my jeans were off.

"I don't want to have to break this door down."

"So don't," I said. "I told you. I'll be out in a minute."

I grabbed a pair of jeans lying on the floor by the bed. They weren't exactly clean, but they weren't wet and muddy. The moment I had them on, I unlocked the door and turned the knob. I was zipping up my jeans when the door swung open and I caught sight of Detective Kingsley, his body at an angle to the door, his shoulder slightly lowered and his feet taking him directly toward me. He managed to stop his forward motion before he dashed through the doorway.

I said nothing, simply finished buttoning my jeans and stuck my feet in a pair of loafers. He straightened, glared at me, then looked down at my wet jeans. "We'll need those," he said. "For evidence."

"Whatever." I walked across the room and grabbed my navy pea coat from the chair by my dresser.

Coat on, I walked out of the bedroom. Kingsley—holding my wet jeans away from his body—followed. At Baraka's crate, I stopped. "How long will this take?"

"Quite a while."

"Then I'd better take him outside with us."

He eyed Baraka suspiciously, then shrugged. "If you'd like."

While Kingsley handed my jeans over to one of the officers in my dining room, I slipped on Baraka's choke chain, connected his leather lead, and let him out of his crate. With my dog close to my side, I made my way through my dining room and out my front door, being careful not to "contaminate" anything.

While I was changing, others had entered my house. A short, balding man with wire-rimmed glasses now knelt beside the body, continually making notes on a pad of paper, and a very attractive woman wearing a brown pantsuit wandered about the room taking pictures. The medical examiner and forensic photographer, Detective Kingsley explained as we stepped outside.

"The sheriff's department has its own photographer?"

"Yes. Marge's pictures have helped solve a lot of crimes."

I glanced back through the open doorway. Marge, the forensic photographer, looked more like a model than an officer of the law. Tall and slender, she had long brown hair that flowed past her shoulders with a natural wave. She aimed her camera at my cluttered dining room table, and I wondered if that picture would be used to prove I was a messy housekeeper.

Other deputies had also come inside and were scouring my kitchen and dining room, picking up bits of who-knows-what with tweezers and placing whatever they found in paper bags that they made notes on. The more they picked up, the more I regretted not vacuuming that morning . . . or even within the last week or two.

Baraka gave a tug on his lead, and I turned back to Detective Kingsley. "So what now? Do we just stand out here until they're finished?"

Kingsley glanced over at the cars and emergency vehicles parked in my yard. "We can sit in my Jeep. It will be warmer." He looked down at Baraka. "Is there somewhere you can put him?"

"How about your back seat?" Where I went, Baraka went.

In silence, Detective Kingsley stared down at my dog, then he looked back at me. "He won't bite?"

"Hasn't so far. But he does like to lick my ear when I'm driving."

Kingsley frowned, but said nothing and we went to his Jeep. Baraka willingly jumped into the cargo area, but immediately moved to the back seat. Kingsley watched him, shrugged and took me around to the passenger's side, then went around to the driver's side. As soon as he was situated, Kingsley pulled out his notebook . . . then said, "Yuck."

"Yuck?"

Leaning forward, Detective Kingsley looked behind him. "Your dog just licked my neck."

Baraka's tongue made another foray for his cheek, but Kingsley avoided it this time. I wanted to laugh, but decided not to push things. "Lie down," I ordered, making my voice stern and motioning with my hand.

Baraka looked at me, sighed, and then lay down. I had no

delusions that he would stay down for long, but I took advantage of the moment and looked back at Kingsley. "As you were saying?"

Kingsley had me repeat everything I'd told him, starting with my decision to take a walk. Once he had that information, he switched to more personal questions. "How long have you been in business for yourself?"

"About four months. Before that, I was working for Quick Sum Associates in Kalamazoo. But when my grandfather died, and I inherited this place and some money, I decided to start my own accounting and bookkeeping business."

"And how did your grandfather die?"

The way Kingsley asked the question, I could see his detective mind conjuring up a murder scenario. I decided I'd better straighten him out fast. "My grandfather had a heart attack. I was nowhere near him. In fact, I hadn't seen or talked to my grandfather for years. Basically not since my father died."

Kingsley's eyebrows went up a notch. "And how did your father die?"

That one he definitely couldn't pin on me. "He was killed in a terrorist bombing eighteen years ago, when I was ten years old. He was in the Marines when it happened. Oh, and if you're tallying them up, my other grandfather—Grandpa Carter—died when I was fifteen. He had Alzheimer's."

Kingsley glanced up at me, then went back to writing in his notebook. "I hope you understand, we have to ask these questions."

"Sure." And I had nothing to hide. Not really. "My Grandmother Benson died when I was eight, but both Grandma Carter and my mother are still alive. They live in Kalamazoo."

He nodded. "Now, getting back to your accounting business." Kingsley checked a previous note. "You said your office is here, in the house. Do you always take a walk at the same time each day?"

"Not the same time. If I get involved in my work, I'll go for hours before I realize what time it is."

"So it was simply by chance that you were out of your house and in the woods at this particular time?" He looked up from his notepad.

He really did have gorgeous eyes. Not the same color as the sky. More a sea blue. Maybe ultramarine. A touch of green with—

"Ms. Benson?" He was waiting for an answer.

"Yes," I said. "Simply by chance." A rotten chance. "And you might as well call me P.J. Most people do."

Kingsley scribbled something in his notepad that I assumed he could read, then glanced up. "Just the initials?"

"Just the initials."

"P.J. it is."

Baraka whined, and I glanced his way. "I think he has to go," I said. It had been quite a while. "With all these people around, I think I'd better take him, not just let him loose."

"Good idea."

Kingsley got out with me. I kept Baraka on the lead and walked him back and forth in front of the house, Kingsley stayed by my side. Baraka sniffed the grass, licked Kingsley's boots, tried to nip my hand, and found a chew toy he'd abandoned outside, but he didn't squat. He didn't even seem to be contemplating the idea.

On one of our passes by the house, Marge the photographer came outside. She smiled at Detective Kingsley and headed our way. "We're finished in there," she said. "I was wondering how much longer you'd be."

"I'm about done," Kingsley said and stepped away from my side. "You looking for a ride back to the station?"

"If you don't mind." She gave him one of those helpless, seductive smiles that men always fall for, and I knew I might as well forget Detective Wade Kingsley's beautiful blue eyes. Someone else had an interest in the man.

He remembered me then. "P.J. . . . . Ah, I mean, Ms. Benson, this is Sergeant Bailey. As I said, she's our best forensic photographer."

"Only forensic photographer," she said and nodded my way.

Kingsley pointed at Baraka. "You ever see one of these dogs, Marge? It's a Rhodesian Ridgeback. See that ridge on his back? The hair grows that way."

"That right?" Sergeant Marge Bailey stepped closer and glanced down at Baraka. Then she again smiled up at Kingsley. "Isn't that cute. It looks like a zipper."

She was being so sweet and coy, I wanted to barf. Baraka, being the unfaithful pup he is, wagged his tail, pulled on his lead, whined, and rubbed against her pant leg in an attempt to gain her attention.

His cajolery, however, was wasted. Marge Bailey wasn't interested in a dog. Her attention stayed focused on Kingsley. "Just let me know when you're ready to go," she said. "I do want to get these pictures back."

Kingsley looked toward the house. "You say they're clear in there?"

"The ME's finished and the body's out," Marge said. "I do think they want to take the storm door, but the house is clear. The woods will take longer. It's a mess out there."

She looked at me as if the junk in the woods was my doing. I didn't bother to correct her. All I wanted to do was go inside. Maybe Baraka didn't need to pee, but I did.

"So, can I go in?" I asked.

Kingsley hesitated, then shrugged. "I guess so. But stay inside until they take the tape down."

"No problem." The problem would be if I couldn't go in.

I was about to head for my front door when he touched my arm. "You're not planning on leaving the country any time soon, are you?"

"With April fifteenth only a couple weeks away?" I shook my head. "Did you see the stack of tax forms on my dining room table? If I want any clients next year, I'd better get those done on time."

"Good enough." He pulled a business card out of his inside pocket and handed it to me. "If you think of anything else, give me a call."

I took the card, but I doubted I'd be calling him. He'd asked me so many questions, there couldn't be anything I hadn't remembered. And if he thought I might call for personal reasons, he was mistaken. Marge Bailey obviously had her eyes on him, and, as good-looking as the man might be, I didn't mess with another woman's man.

I turned to say good-bye to Marge the photographer, but the words never came out. The expression on her face stopped me. Mouth open, she stared down at her shoes, and I saw the trail of yellow across her tan oxfords.

Baraka had finally squatted.

FOUR

I put Baraka in his crate, and I took care of my needs, but that was all I accomplished. The sheriff's deputies kept interrupting me. They asked me to retrace my walk through the woods as best as I could. Which I did. Then they quizzed me about all my neighbors. By the time they finished gathering evidence—including my back storm door—removed the yellow tape and left, the sun was setting and I was exhausted, hungry, and frustrated. Maybe I should have been sad, too. After all, a man had died. But I didn't know the guy, and the idea of having my work schedule disrupted, along with having to now clean a bloody mess off my floors and walls, really irritated me.

The floors, however, did need to be cleaned. I was given a list of agencies that did that sort of thing, but after several calls, I realize no one would come out until morning. I couldn't let Baraka run loose in the house with dried blood on the linoleum. Just the thought of him licking those spots turned my stomach.

Disgusting as the task might be, it was up to me.

I mixed a bucket of warm, soapy water and bleach, put on a pair of latex gloves, and began scrubbing the floor. I was on my hands and knees, sponging the largest blood stain, when the Westmans' red-and-silver Dodge truck pulled into my yard. I'd been expecting them. Not only are they my closest neighbors, they've become my best friends.

They're also complete opposites, in looks and temperament. John is a scientist and Julia is an artist. He works at B.C. Bio-

Tech in Battle Creek, and she has a studio in their pole barn.

Julia does beautiful work. In fact, I have one of her etchings, and she's supposed to do another one for me. One of Baraka. I figure someday I can invite a man to my place to see my etchings. That would be a nice twist on an old cliché.

Her complaint is artists don't make enough money, so she also works part-time as a teller at the bank in Zenith. One advantage of that job is Julia always knows what's going on. I know she was working today. She probably heard about a man dying in my house within minutes of my nine-one-one call.

Julia got out of the truck first, and leaving the passenger's-side door open, she half-ran toward my front porch. Petite, blonde, and blue-eyed, Julia's a bundle of energy. I barely had time to stand before she reached my door.

John came up the steps behind her, his expression serious. He's always serious. I suppose that's a positive trait for a research scientist.

The moment I opened the door, they stepped inside. Immediately, Julia started talking. "Oh, P.J., you poor thing. What a day you must have had. A sheriff's deputy stopped by and questioned us. Seems this whole incident started at our place."

"Your place?" For some reason, I hadn't considered that possibility. "Were you robbed?"

"Sort of." Julia stared at the blood spot on the floor. "Tell us exactly what happened. You can't imagine the stories I heard at the bank."

Except, I could imagine. In a town where nothing major ever happens, even a speeding ticket garners gossip. A shooting would be a bonanza. "What did you hear?"

"Initially, that you'd been shot. Then Bill Welch said you shot a man in the woods and dragged him into your house so it would look like self-defense."

I groaned. Leave it to old Bill Welch to come up with a story like that. The man doesn't hear well and refuses to get a hearing aid. What he does hear and repeats is usually wrong. The results are often comical, but I wasn't happy about him telling people I'd shot a man. "I didn't shoot anyone," I said. "I don't even own a gun."

"I know that," Julia said, but I could tell she wanted an explanation for the blood on the linoleum.

"That's where I found him. I think he was trying to get to my phone. I wouldn't have even known he was alive if he hadn't moved his hand."

"He was still alive when you found him?" John had been looking around my dining room. Now his attention focused on me. "Did he say anything? Tell you anything, before he died?"

"He swore."

"Swore? Like how? What did he say?"

"He said 'Shit.' "

"Shit?" John repeated, clearly puzzled.

"Yeah." I grinned, in spite of the gravity of the situation. "And then he did it. So maybe he was warning me."

"You're sure that's what he said?" John didn't look convinced.

"Well, he did slur the word, but I don't know what else he might have meant. Detective Kingsley thought it might have been a reaction. You know, 'Shit, I got shot.' That kind of re-action."

"Did he have a box with him?" Julia asked.

"A box?" I shook my head. "No. What kind of a box?"

"A cardboard box," she said. "Heavy cardboard. Sort of a creamy white. Not too big." She gestured with her hands. "About the size of a brick. And it would weigh about the same as a brick."

"I didn't see anything like that. And from what I understand, the only things the sheriff's deputies found on him were a Swiss Army knife, a set of keys, and some change."

"Did anyone find a box? In here or outside?" John asked.

"Not that I know of. What was in the box?"

"I, ah . . . We'd rather not say," Julia answered. "But it's important that we get it back."

"Very important," John added. "You're sure he didn't stash it somewhere?" He glanced around my dining room.

I also looked around the room. My computer, printer, fax machine, and telephone sat on a desk near my front door. Along the wall that divided the kitchen and dining room was a buffet, where a coffee maker sat next to a can of coffee, a stack of filters, and an array of coffee mugs. And the center of the room was dominated by my grandparents' old oak dining table, which was almost completely covered with tax forms, client files, and books.

If there was a box in that mess, I didn't see it.

Julia looked at John. "I think they're gone."

"We can't just assume that," he argued.

"What's gone?" I asked. "What was in the box?"

"We can't say," Julia said quickly.

"No, we can't say," John repeated.

I wasn't about to accept that. "Why can't you say?"

"We . . . We just can't." John kept looking at Julia.

Their attitude irritated me. "Well then, I sure can't help you."

"I'm sorry, P.J." Julia grimaced. "It's just . . . Well, what we had in the box was sort of illegal, and—"

John stopped her. "Don't say anything, honey. Not yet. There's still a chance we'll find them."

Their conspiratorial attitude irritated me. "Well I can't help if I don't know what you're looking for?"

"We know that." John sighed. "I was at work when Julia called and said there had been a shooting at your place. At the time, I didn't think it had anything to do with us. If anything, I thought it might have been Nora again."

"Nora?"

Nora Wright and her sister, Rose, live north of my place. Their two-story farmhouse is on a road parallel to mine. They have ten acres of woods kitty-corner to my woods. John and Julia's more modern ranch house, pole barn, and ten acres border both of our properties. Nora's as tough as a man, but to shoot someone?

Julia confirmed her husband's statement. "Nora's shot at trespassers before."

"You're kidding." I couldn't imagine shooting another human being. For that matter, I couldn't imagine shooting an animal. Which is why my woods are posted.

"But I knew it couldn't have been Nora," Julia said. "I saw Nora at one o'clock. She and Rose were on their way into Kalamazoo for a doctor's appointment."

As I said, Julia knows everyone's business.

"Which leaves Punk," John grumbled. "Or someone Punk told."

"Punk?" I was getting more confused.

"Punk McDaniels." John frowned at me. "You know him, don't you?"

"No."

"She never met him," Julia told John. Casually, she walked over to Baraka's crate. "He's the guy I recommended when you were looking for a carpenter. Did you ever call him?"

"No, a former coworker's brother is going to do the work."

Julia knelt in front of Baraka's crate and scratched his muzzle, but I noticed she glanced around my living room.

"There's no box in there, either," I said, upset that she hadn't taken my word for it.

"Oh, I wasn't looking for a box." Her attention came back to Baraka. "I bet this guy was a handful with all of those people around here? Weren't you, baby?"

"He wasn't happy being kept in there. He wanted to be outside with the officers going through the outbuildings and into the woods."

John looked toward my window. "I didn't think about your woodshed. Maybe, instead of shit, the guy meant shed."

"From the trail of blood spots on the ground, the sheriff's deputies think the guy came directly to my back door. If he was trying to say shed, he must have thrown the box in there. And if he did that, I'm sure one of the deputies would have found it."

"And you're sure they didn't?" John said.

"I think they would have mentioned it."

"I'm sure they would have," Julia said. She stood and came back to where I was standing. Her gaze followed the trail of blood spots on my linoleum. "So you figure, where there's blood is where he went?"

"I'd say so. The spots come up my back steps, go through my kitchen, and end here." I pointed at the blood stain I'd been working on. "Which nobody cleaned up, so now I have to do it."

Julia nodded. "The same thing happened to us when we had that robbery at the bank. The police and FBI left fingerprint powder all over the place. And being the lowest one on the totem pole, I was the one who had to clean it up."

"Actually—" I hated to admit it. "Except for the blood on the linoleum, this place is cleaner than it was this morning. They even vacuumed."

"They missed these." John bent over and picked up a dead ladybug. There were several on the floor.

This time of year, lady beetles are a nuisance. The temperature warms up and they come out of hibernation. Until they make their way outside, they're everywhere. Alive. Dead. Crawling over the walls and into light fixtures.

John turned the ladybug over, looked at its underside, then

dropped it back on the floor. "What did the guy look like? The one who died in here?"

"Familiar," I said. "I think I've seen him in Zenith once or twice. But I'm sure I've never met him."

"Describe him," Julia prodded.

"Lean. Probably in his forties, though his face was so weathered, it was hard to tell. He was wearing jeans, a flannel shirt, nylon jacket, and work boots. Basically what most of the farmers around here wear."

"It could have been Punk," John said, glancing at his wife. "Or, like P.J. said, it could have been half the farmers around here."

"But half the farmers around here wouldn't know what we had in the barn." Julia nervously rubbed her hands together, looked at me, then back at her husband. "Honey, we've got to tell her."

FIVE

"Are you serious?" John stared at Julia.

"Yes. She needs to realize this is a matter of life or death. So tell her about the ladybugs."

He frowned. "The ladybugs?"

"Yes, the ladybugs," Julia repeated.

"I don't know . . ."

Well, I did. "Look," I said and stepped closer to John. "A man died here. In my house. I was shot at. I deserve to know what's going on."

"I, ah . . ." Again, John glanced at Julia. "What do you want me to tell her?"

"That the ladybugs were stolen. We've got to. P.J. isn't going to go searching for a box without a good reason. So you need to make her understand how dangerous those ladybugs are. Then she'll understand why it's so important that we get them back. And," Julia added, "why she must not open the box."

"But if she does open it—?"

"Tell her what would happen and she won't."

John blew out a breath, wrung his hands, then looked at me. "Well, as you know, I have my lab in our pole barn—"

"Where he plays with his bugs," Julia finished for him.

I did know that much. They'd given me a tour of their pole barn a few weeks after I moved here. Whereas most barns house animals or farm equipment, John and Julia's was divided into two halves, one half set up like a scientific laboratory, the other half transformed into an art studio. I also knew Julia didn't think much of John's mutated fruit flies and centipedes.

"It's not play," John griped, then shrugged. "Of course, what I'm doing is never going to make me rich, either. Not with that form I had to sign when I went to work for BioTech. They hold the rights to any discoveries I make while employed by them, whether made on the job or at home."

Again Julia broke in, glaring at her husband. "But that didn't keep him from bringing one of his experiments home. One he shouldn't have had."

John turned to me, as if I would understand. "They stopped the project without finding an antidote."

"An antidote?" That didn't sound good to me.

"Yeah." He looked a bit sheepish. "We sort of came up with something we weren't expecting."

"What were you expecting?"

"A new species of *Hippodamia*."

"*Hippodamia?*" I wasn't following. "What's a *Hippodamia?*"

"A ladybug. Only this one would have been better than your common ladybug."

"Should have been, could have been, but—" Julia interjected.

"Something went wrong, when we introduced DNA from the Mexican bean beetle and made a couple of other genetic modifications." John gave a strained laugh. "We came up with a species that eats plants as well as aphids."

"Biggest problem," Julia said, again interrupting "is this species bites. And its bite seems to be deadly."

"Deadly?" I repeated. I'd had enough of "deadly" for one day.

She nodded. "Last fall one of John's lab assistants was bitten. She developed an infection and died within a week."

"Died from the bite?"

"They never came out and admitted that," John said, "but

they shut down the project twenty-four hours after she died."

"I can't tell you how nervous I've been, having those lady-bugs in the pole barn," Julia said. "Which is why John hired Punk to build a secure room so none of them could get loose."

"Oh, my gosh." I was beginning to understand the problem. "BioTech stopped that experiment, but you brought the lady-bugs home and today they were stolen?" I looked at John. "And the ladybug you just picked up—?"

"Not one of them."

I was relieved to hear that, but then Julia said, "It's the box we've got to find. The box with the ladybugs in it."

"Maybe the shooter got it." I knew that wouldn't be good, but I'd rather have these lethal ladybugs somewhere far far away.

"Maybe," John agreed. "I need to find Punk." He stepped toward my front door. "Julia, you stay here and help P.J. clean up. I'm going to Punk's place."

"Check with the sheriff's department," I said. "By now they may have identified the man who was shot."

John nodded. "I hate to think it was Punk. I rather liked the guy."

"But we know he needs money." Julia turned to me and explained. "Punk helps support his mother. In fact, she lives with him. Two weeks ago, she flew to Florida so she could visit her brother. Evidently it was a last-minute decision because Punk said he had to pay top dollar for the ticket. He told me that when he transferred money from his savings to his check-ing account. And I know there's not much in either account. Selling what's in that box would solve his financial problems."

"That is if he's still alive and has it," John said.

"So, go find out what you can," Julia urged with a wave of her hands.

"Yeah, go," I agreed.

We watched John walk back to his truck. Julia said nothing until he'd pulled out of the yard, then she sighed. "I'm sorry, P.J. This is all my fault."

"Your fault?" I didn't see why her husband bringing home a dangerous project should be blamed on her.

"I told Punk too much. You know me and my big mouth. I just never thought something like this would happen."

I didn't know what to say. I wanted to tell her it was all right, but it wasn't. Not with one man dead and those ladybugs missing.

"Is this what you're using to clean with?" Julia asked, pointing at the bucket next to the spot of dried blood on my linoleum.

"You don't have to help," I said, but Julia ignored my protest.

Leaning down, she pulled out the sponge. "I caused this. It's the least I can do."

I decided I wouldn't mind a bit of help and found her a pair of protective gloves. She worked on the floor area by the telephone. I tackled the smaller spots. For a while, we worked in silence, but I kept thinking about genetically altered ladybugs. Finally, I asked, "If those ladybugs did get out of the box, how long would it take for them to multiply?"

"The ladybugs are not going to get out," Julia insisted. "Not as long as no one opens that box."

"But let's say someone does open it. How long before they multiply?"

"If you find it, don't open it."

"I won't, but—?"

"Oh, I don't know." Julia wiped the last of the blood off her section of linoleum, sighed, and looked at me. "From what John's said, one female ladybug can lay a thousand eggs over a three-month period."

"A thousand eggs in three months?" Now I did hope the shooter got away with the box. I sure didn't want thousands of those lethal ladybugs around my place.

"Which is why," Julia said, "you mustn't tell anyone. We don't want to panic people."

"You told the sheriff's deputies, didn't you?"

"We told them . . ." Julia paused. "What they needed to know."

I didn't like the way she'd hesitated. "Meaning?"

"Meaning . . ." Again she hesitated. "Meaning they know what they need to know. It's you I'm worried about. All I'm saying is, if you find that box, don't open it. Call us immediately. And don't say anything about this, not to anyone."

I didn't like the way she was lecturing me, and I don't like secrets, especially ones that can hurt others. Besides, I didn't see how she could keep something like this quiet. "There's bound to be something in the news."

"About a shooting, yes. Not about ladybugs. Anyway, I watched the six o'clock news. Neither Channel Three nor Eight had anything."

I hadn't watched television, but now that Julia had mentioned it, I didn't remember seeing any TV cameras around my place when the sheriff's department was here. And I'd been glad. Julia might not want word of the ladybugs getting out to prevent panic; I didn't want anything in the papers or on TV because of my mother. If she saw I'd been involved in a shooting, she'd be sure aliens were involved . . . or that it had something to do with my dad.

Poor Mom, she's never accepted the fact that he's dead.

Six

Julia's more of a housekeeper than I am, and when we finished wiping up all of the blood spots, she insisted we mop and wax both the kitchen and dining room floors. The linoleum actually sparkled. She even touched up a spot after I let Baraka back in from a potty break.

My stomach growled as I fed him, and Julia asked, "Have you had dinner?"

"No." I glanced at my wall clock and groaned. It was nearly nine o'clock. No wonder I was hungry.

"I haven't either," she said. "What do you say we go into Battle Creek for a hamburger? I'll buy."

How could I turn down an offer like that?

Julia called John on his cell phone and let him know what we were doing. He still hadn't found Punk, but was going to check at the local bar. Since he had their truck, I drove.

Twenty minutes later, Julia and I sat in a fast food restaurant eating hamburgers and French fries, and drinking our drinks. "Every time I come to one of these places," Julia said, as she dipped a French fry into catsup, "I remember the six months I worked at one. How humbling to think you'll have a great career as a graphic designer, and end up flipping hamburgers."

"And then you met John." She'd told me this story before.

Julia looked at me, the French fry halfway to her mouth. "And now I'm a teller in a bank."

"A bank that exhibits your prints," I reminded her. I knew

she sold one or two a month. "Are you working on more?"

"I was." She sighed.

I thought I would be the one moping over the events of the day. Julia had me beat. But I supposed she was worried about those ladybugs. I tried changing the subject. "Think winter's finally over?"

"Winter?" She looked out the window at the cars driving by. "I hope so." Another dab at the catsup. "We just got our fuel oil bill. I wish John would put in a wood stove." Finally, she looked at me. "You use yours a lot, don't you?"

"Quite a bit since learning how to build a fire without start-ing one in the chimney. Our dear neighbor, Howard Lowe, won't let me forget about that."

Julia finally smiled. "He was the first one to tell me there was a fire truck at your place and a sheriff's car. He saw them when he drove by on his way to the bank. He figured you'd tried to burn the place down again."

"He probably wishes I would. He'd like to see me gone."

"He's just upset because you posted those woods."

"Upset?" The term seemed too mild. "He pounded on my door the day after I put up those signs and yelled that city folk should stay in the city. He scared the heck out of me."

Julia swirled the tip of another French fry in the catsup. "Did you know he was in Special Forces when he was in the army? The Green Beret or something. It was back about forty years ago. John thinks he belonged to the Michigan Militia before Nichols and the Oklahoma City bombing."

She stopped, an odd expression crossing her face. "I wonder."

"Wonder what?"

"I wonder if that organization still exists. A militia might be interested in what was taken from our place."

I could see where Julia was going with this. "My house is between your place and Lowe's. If someone stole the ladybugs and was taking them to Lowe, but that someone got shot while going through my woods, he might end up in my house."

"Exactly."

It was ten-thirty when I dropped Julia off at her place. Her house was dark, the garage door closed. We couldn't tell if John was home or not. "Doors aren't locked," Julia said. "So it doesn't matter."

I will never be that trusting again.

I was about to drive off, when Julia said, "Don't forget tomorrow night. We'll pick you up around ten to seven."

"Tomorrow night?" I had forgotten the neighborhood euchre party I'd promised to attend. "I can't go, Julia. I lost a half a day's work today. I've got taxes to get done."

"But Nora and Rose are expecting you."

I shook my head. "Nora doesn't want me there. I don't know why, but that woman does not like me."

"She's jealous."

"Jealous?" I laughed. "Of me?"

"Nora thinks Rose likes you."

"Well, I do like Rose." She was definitely the friendlier of the two women. "And if Nora wasn't so standoffish, I might like her, too."

Shaking her head, Julia laughed. "P.J., haven't you figured out yet that Nora and Rose aren't sisters?"

"Not sisters? But . . . ?" Julia was right. I didn't understand. Not immediately. Then it clicked. "You mean they're . . . ? They . . . ?"

"Yes." Julia intertwined two fingers. "At least they have been for the last ten years. But Nora told me Rose has been acting strange lately. Disinterested. She said it started sometime after you moved here."

Now that Julia was spelling it out, I did see how naïve I'd

been. I'd ignored Nora's short hair, lack of makeup, her wardrobe of bib overalls and clunky workboots. Lots of women—common, everyday, heterosexual women—dress like that.

"We all know what's up," Julia said. "But we go along with their story. If they want to pretend they're sisters, that's fine. But it's obvious to me that Nora thinks Rose is attracted to you. That's why she's jealous."

"Oh great." If Nora was jealous of me, that meant one thing. "So does everyone around here think I'm a lesbian?"

"Oh, no," Julia insisted. "But you do wear your hair short, don't wear makeup, always have jeans on, and aren't married. So when Rose said you were cute, Nora automatically jumped to conclusions. I'm sure you can convince Nora that you aren't a threat. Shall we pick you up at six-fifty tomorrow night?"

I agreed. It seemed I needed to go just to clarify my sexual preferences.

A minute after leaving Julia's house, I was at my place. I'd locked both of my doors, so I decided to go in the front. It took me a minute to get it open and switch on the lights. I figured the first thing I'd better do was let Baraka out for a potty break. The poor pup had spent most of the day in his crate.

I glanced in that direction and wasn't surprised to see him on his feet, his tail wagging in expectation. What did surprise me were the footprints on my newly waxed dining room floor. They were all over the place.

SEVEN

"So what did you do when you saw the footprints?" my grandmother asked when I called her Saturday morning.

I phoned early, before she would have gotten the paper and read about the break-in. I wanted her to know exactly what had happened Friday. As usual, the *Kalamazoo Gazette* had most of the facts wrong, including my name. I was now P. Jay Benson.

"I called the police," I said. Actually, it was the sheriff's department, but I didn't bother clarifying that detail.

"And did they find anyone?"

"No." The whole incident irritated me. "The way those deputies acted, I'm pretty sure they think the tracks belong to John, my neighbor."

I'd called Julia after I called nine-one-one. I wanted her to know about the footprints. John was home and came over right away. He was there when the deputies arrived.

"I explained to them that John and I only went into the house as far as Baraka's crate, so I could let him out. I showed them the impressions of our footprints on the linoleum. Told them that except for letting my dog out, John wasn't in the house after Julia and I left."

"So, if the prints weren't your neighbor's, whose were they?"

"That's the thing, I don't know. I just know someone was in my house while I was in Battle Creek."

"You didn't lock your doors?"

"Yes, Grandma, I did." And would from now on. Not that it

seemed to help.

"How about your windows?"

"Those were locked, too."

"So how did someone get in?"

"That's what those deputies kept asking. I told them I didn't know, that it was their job to figure that out."

"Probably not the best attitude to take, my dear." I heard the rustle of newspaper before my grandmother spoke again. "I found the article." She chuckled. "So how does Mr. Jay Benson feel about all of this?"

"I don't know about Jay Benson, but I'm pissed. I always thought living in the country would be safer than living in the city. At least in the city, if I found a man laying on my dining room floor it was because he'd had too much to drink, not because he had a bullet in his back."

"Says here," Grandma said, "that your back door wasn't locked yesterday afternoon."

"It wasn't." I would admit to that. "But it was last night."

"Do you want to come stay here for a while?"

I thought of my grandmother's house, of the smell of cigarette smoke and cigarette butts in the ashtrays. Both Grandma and Mom smoke. Mom's almost a chain smoker. An hour in their house, and I'm ready to gag. I always have to air out my clothes after a visit.

"No," I said. "I've got a stack of taxes to work on, and you know I can't concentrate with Mom around."

"Well then, why don't you come after dinner and spend the night? It's been a while since we've seen you."

"I can't do that, either. I'm supposed to go to a euchre party tonight. A neighborhood thing. It probably won't end until after midnight. How about if I come tomorrow? Just for a visit."

"If you think you'll be all right there . . . ?"

"I'll be fine," I said, as much to reassure myself as my

grandmother.

"Then we'll look for you tomorrow. And, P.J. . . ." She paused, and I knew what she was going to say. "You could sell that place and move back into the city. We'd love to have you living closer."

"I know, Grandma. But I kind of like this place."

I felt guilty that I had moved twenty-five miles from my grandmother's house. I didn't stop by as often as I used to, and there were days I could almost forget my mother and her problems. My grandmother didn't have that option.

Oh, she could put my mother in a home, and there were times when she had no say in the matter. Those were the times when the medical community felt institutionalizing my mother was necessary. And there were a few years when just Mom and I lived together. That was after my father died but before Grandpa Carter died and we moved in with Grandma Carter.

A silence hung between us as I tried to think of something else to say. Grandma spoke first. "I do believe someone broke into your house, P.J. no matter what those officers think."

"Thanks, Grandma." Knowing she believed me did help. "I'll see you tomorrow."

I washed my red-and-blue jacket. As it dried, I drank my second cup of coffee and thought about my decision to move into this house. When the lawyer told me I'd inherited the farm, I knew right away I wanted to live here. This is where my father grew up. He brought me here when I was a child. I never particularly liked Grandpa Benson, but I loved my dad and I loved this old house.

There's nothing fancy about it. It's a two-story rectangle with a small wooden porch in front and crumbling cement steps in back. The windows are old, single-panes and odd shaped. They let in a lot of cold, and need to be replaced, but it's not going to be easy or cheap.

Also, the house has little insulation and the ceilings are high, so I lose a lot of heat that way. I've gone through almost all of the wood that was in the woodshed, so I either have to get more or use fuel oil until the weather warms up. Fuel oil isn't cheap, either.

The furnace is in the cellar and makes noises before it comes on, which always spooks me out. Michigan cellars aren't much more than deep holes above which houses are built. They're a place for the furnace, water pump, and hot water tank. This one, like most, is damp and musty smelling, and I rarely go down there.

When I was little, I used to think monsters lived in the cellar. Grandma Benson poo-pooed my imagination and would make me go down with her whenever she needed a jar of pickles, green beans, or tomatoes. Since I loved Grandma Benson's pickles, that wasn't a terrible ordeal.

Those shelves are empty now, and last night, when I went down with the deputies, we found nothing unusual. Just that damp, musty smell.

Friends have told me I should tear the place down and build something new and more fuel efficient. I won't. Because, if I did, I would lose something more valuable than money. I would lose the presence of my father.

Now, when I go upstairs to the bedroom he used as a child, I can sit in that room and imagine how he was as a boy. I still remember the time he told me how he tied sheets together and climbed out of his window, just to see if he could do it. He thought it was funny, but he said his mother got very upset. He wasn't sure if she was upset because he could have hurt himself or because he used her clean sheets.

I think my dad always liked a little danger in his life. In his last letter to Mom, he said being assigned to guard an airport was the most boring thing he'd ever done. As it turned out, it was the most dangerous thing he ever did.

I like remembering my father, but I had more pressing matters to attend to. If someone broke into my house last night, it meant he—or she—was after something. And since nothing of mine was taken, I had to assume the desired object was the box taken from John and Julia's place. The box with the genetically altered ladybugs.

So much for hoping those ladybugs were far, far away.

I finished my coffee and grabbed my jacket out of the dryer and slipped it on. I'd already looked around my dining room and kitchen and knew the box wasn't there. Next, I checked the woodshed.

No box there. Not that I really expected to find one. If the man went straight to my back door, how would the box get into my woodshed?

From the woodshed, I went over to my grandparents' old chicken coop. Since the path to the woods went by the coop's broken window, I glanced through that first. Standing on tiptoe, I was careful to avoid the shards of glass, but I didn't see the nail at the edge of the window frame. The rusted metal scraped the back of my hand, and I quickly stepped away. As blood dripped down to my knuckles, I decided to abandon my search, at least for the time being. I needed a Band-aid.

The phone was ringing when I returned to the house, the light on my answering machine blinking. I put pressure on my hand to stem the blood and picked up the receiver. It was Mabel Walters, the octogenarian widow who lives north of Zenith in a house that's been in her family for one hundred and thirty-five years. "Are you all right, my dear?" she asked. "I seen something in the paper about a Jay Benson. Sounded like your place was the one they was talking about. I didn't know you was married."

"I'm not, Mrs. Walters," I said. "You know newspapers. They never get anything right."

"Said someone died in your house."

She wanted details, but I kept it simple. "Someone did."

"Didn't give a name."

"I don't know his name."

She cleared her throat a couple of times, then asked, "You gonna be able to finish my taxes? I can get my niece to do 'em if you can't. She's done 'em before."

And messed them up, according to the story Mabel told me when she first called and asked me to do her taxes. The ad I'd placed in the local paper had brought me several new clients. I didn't want yesterday's event losing them. Quickly, I reassured her. "I can get them done. In fact, I was working on your return this morning. I should have it finished by this afternoon."

"If you're sure." She didn't sound convinced.

I told her I was sure and listened to her repeat the story she'd told me when we met—about how her niece messed up her taxes and she had to pay a fine. Finally, I managed to get her off the phone. I then doctored my hand, played back the messages on my answering machine, called a couple more clients who were worried about their taxes—having also read the article in the paper—and decided I had better work on Mabel's forms.

Hers were simple—the short forms for federal and state and a homestead property exemption. How her niece messed up, I don't know. After I finished Mabel's, I started the forms for Sporbach's Nursery. They're located just south of Kalamazoo and loyally stayed with me when I went into business on my own. I was still working on their taxes when Baraka whined to go out. I needed a break, so I again slipped on my jacket and took him outside.

The sun was shining, but the wind gave a nip to the air.

Baraka did his business, then pulled on his lead, eager for a walk. I wasn't up to repeating yesterday's experience, and the way he was jerking my arm, I knew what he needed was work on his obedience training.

An adult male Rhodesian Ridgeback can weigh a hundred pounds or more, and can reach a height of twenty-seven to thirty inches at the shoulders. Allowed to do what they like, they can be a nuisance at best and possibly a danger.

"Baraka, sit," I ordered and gave a light jerk on his choke chain. He shot me a questioning look with those big brown eyes of his and pulled even harder.

Ridgebacks have won obedience and tracking awards at top shows across the country, but they are hounds, and if a Ridgeback doesn't want to work, it doesn't matter what you say or do. I tried another command.

"Baraka, heel."

After five minutes of walking back and forth in front of my house, Baraka usually ahead or behind me, never exactly at my left side, I gave up. Once again, I tried the sit command. I motioned with an upward sweep of my right hand and said "Sit."

To my pleasure and surprise, Baraka sat.

I then held my hand in front of his nose, palm open, and said, "Stay."

Slowly I backed away from him, always facing him as I fed out the twelve-foot lead so there was no pull on his choke chain. Baraka watched me, his head slightly cocked to the side, then he smiled, his lips curving upward, rose to his feet and trotted toward me, tail wagging.

Quickly I made a sweeping motion toward my body and said, "Come." Maybe I could trick him into thinking he was obeying.

Or maybe he was training me.

We were on our fifth attempt when a tan Jeep Cherokee

pulled into my driveway. Though I still hadn't gotten Baraka to sit and stay for more than fifteen seconds, I knew it was time to stop. All puppies get bored easily, and a visitor was obviously more interesting to Baraka than me standing in front of him with the palm of my hand held in the air.

At first, I didn't recognize the car. Then the driver got out. "Detective Kingsley," I said, reining in Baraka's lead so he couldn't jump on the man. "What a surprise."

"We decided to take a drive in the country." He glanced into the back of his car and motioned with his hand for someone to get out.

Only then did I realize there was a child in the back seat. The car door opened and blocked my view, but just below the door I could see a pair of cowboy boots, miniatures of Detective Kingsley's. The boots moved to the edge of the door, and about four feet up from the ground, the top of a boy's head peeked around the side. Mostly, I saw a mop of brown hair, freckles, and big, blue eyes. "Will he bite?" the boy asked, staring at Baraka.

"No, he doesn't bite," I assured the child. Except Baraka kept pulling on his lead, in spite of the choke chain, and I decided he must have gained five pounds since the last time the vet weighed him.

"My dad says your dog's different from other dogs." The boy stepped out from behind the door, allowing me my first full view of him.

I guessed his age around six or seven. Even if he hadn't been dressed in jeans, cowboy boots, and a denim jacket, just like Detective Kingsley, I would have known the boy was his son. The eyes were the same . . . as well as the long, lush eyelashes.

So much for using the lack of a wedding ring as proof of a man's availability.

Detective Kingsley held out a hand for the boy. "Jason, come here. This is Ms. Benson. And her dog's name is . . . ?"

I could tell he'd forgotten, so I spoke up. "Baraka. It means blessing."

"My dad says I'm a blessing." Jason moved closer to his dad. "My mother says I'm a curse 'cause I look so much like him."

I looked at Detective Kingsley, surprised by the statement. He explained. "His mother and I are divorced, and we're not on the best of terms."

"Ah." I understood. A number of my friends come from split families. I know all about bickering parents.

"This is my dad's weekend," Jason explained. "He said you wouldn't mind if we came and saw your dog."

I didn't mind, but I gave Kingsley a lift of my eyebrows to let him know he'd been presumptuous. Then I smiled at the boy. "Do you want to pet Baraka?"

"You're sure he won't bite?"

"I'm sure. He nibbles sometimes. That's because he's a puppy and doesn't know better. And he might knock you down or his tail might give you a swat, but that's just because he's so happy to see you." I reined Baraka in a little more, bringing him closer to my side so I could control his enthusiasm.

Baraka, bless him, stayed relatively calm, allowing the boy to pet his head and stroke his ridge.

"Can I play with him?" Jason asked.

"I don't know. He's pretty rough. He likes to play a game of growly when I first let him off his lead."

"What's growly?" The boy continued petting Baraka.

"He runs at you, growling. Sometimes he'll even bump into you and grab your jacket and pull on it with his teeth. He's not really going to hurt you. He just likes to pretend he's strong and fierce, like boys sometimes do when they're playing."

"I am strong and fierce." Jason flexed his right arm. If he had a muscle, I couldn't see it beneath his jacket.

"I think we'd better let Ms. Benson keep the dog on its leash,"

Detective Kingsley said.

"But I want to play with the doggy." Jason gave his father a sad-eyed look. "You said I could."

Kingsley looked at me, and I knew the boy had learned the pleading look from his father. I gave in. "We could give it a try. But you've got to help me teach him not to play growly."

"I can do that," Jason said.

We went over to the field on the west side of my house. It's far enough off the road that the boy and dog would be safe, and the trees and bushes that line its edges create a boundary. It's also open enough for the two to play and for Detective Kingsley and me to watch them.

At first I loosened my hold on the leash, giving it a snap when Baraka got too rough with the boy. Then I let go of the leash, but left it on Baraka so I could grab it if necessary. Which I did a few times. Finally, I felt Baraka had calmed down enough to chance letting the two actually play.

"He likes to chase a ball," I said. "I know there's one somewhere out here. See if you can find it."

Jason and Baraka set off looking for the ball. Baraka ran ahead, then came back toward Jason at a full run, growling the entire distance. I yelled at him, and Baraka swerved to the side. The next time he tried it, Jason yelled at the dog, and to my surprise, Baraka stopped running and began trotting just slightly ahead of the boy, nose to the ground.

I knew then that all would be fine.

"He's great," I told Detective Kingsley. "Does he have a dog?"

"No, I'm afraid not. My ex doesn't like animals. She feels they're too messy . . . too much of a bother."

"That's a shame. Well, you can bring your son out here any time you want."

"Thanks. I appreciate this."

We stood beneath an apple tree that was just beginning to

blossom and watched boy and dog play. For a few minutes, Kingsley said nothing more, then he spoke in a hushed tone. "We know the name of the man who died in your house."

EIGHT

I looked up at Kingsley. "Who was he?"

"A Carroll McDaniels. Ring any bells?"

"Carol? That's a man's name?"

"Spelled with two *r*s and two *l*s it is." Kingsley pulled out his notebook. "He went by a nickname."

He started flipping pages in the notebook, but I knew the name. "Punk?"

Kingsley stopped his search and looked at me. "Yes. I thought you said you didn't know him."

"I didn't. My neighbors, John and Julia, came over last night. They wondered if it might have been a guy named Punk. In fact, maybe John's the one who identified him."

Kingsley shook his head. "The body was identified by one of the volunteer firefighters who was here yesterday. And then the Battle Creek police found McDaniels's truck in the Meijer's parking lot off Helmer. The keys he had in his pocket fit, and his wallet was in the change holder. The guy probably pulled it out of his back pocket while driving and set it there. Those things can get uncomfortable."

"Any idea yet who shot him?"

"We're working on it. What can you tell me about McDaniels?"

Too much, I thought, but said, "Not much. Julia recommended him for some work I wanted done on my house, but I'd already hired someone else."

"Speaking of your place . . ." Detective Kingsley's gaze drifted toward my house. "I understand Deputies O'Brien and Chambers came out here last night. Something about an intruder?"

"Not 'something.'" I emphasized the word. "Last night someone was in my house while Julia and I were in Battle Creek. There were footprints all over my dining room floor."

"The report said the footprints probably belonged to your neighbor, John Westman."

"That was their conclusion. I disagree. That floor was clean when Julia and I left. When I came back, there were footprints."

"By any chance are you related to Flora Benson?"

I saw the lift of his eyebrows and knew why he'd asked. Reluctantly, I answered, "Yes. She's my mother."

"You didn't mention that before."

"I didn't feel I needed to. I am not crazy, Detective Kingsley." He had to believe that. "Someone was in my house last night while I was gone."

"But nothing was taken."

"No. Nothing was taken. At least, not as far as I can tell."

"And you say your doors and windows were locked."

"Yes."

"Were these muddy footprints?"

"No, not muddy. Just faint impressions."

"And you're sure you or your neighbors didn't make them?"

"Positive. Look, I may not be a great housekeeper, but I know a clean floor when I see it. That floor was mopped and waxed before Julia and I went to dinner. The surface was smooth as glass. When I returned, I could see footprints on it."

For a moment, he said nothing. Then he nodded. "Okay, let's assume someone was in your house. Any idea what that person was looking for?"

"A box," I said before I thought of my promise to Julia.

"A box?"

"Well, maybe a box. Didn't John and Julia tell you a box was missing from their pole barn?"

"No. What sort of a box?"

That Kingsley didn't know about it bothered me, but I felt it was John's responsibility to tell him. "Just a box." I indicated the size and shape with my hands.

"And you think this box is in your house?"

"Actually, no." And that was the truth. "I didn't see a box yesterday." I looked at Kingsley. "Did you or any of your people find one?"

He shook his head, and I went on. "Well, whether it was a box or not, I think the person who broke into my house last night believes Punk left something in there."

"How did this person know you were going out last night?"

"I don't know. John and Julia came over after the yellow tape was taken down, but John only stayed a while, then left to see if he could find . . . Find, ah . . . a friend."

I'd almost said Punk. Nothing like blabbing too much. I continued at a slower pace. "Julia stayed and helped me clean the floor. Then we drove into Battle Creek for a hamburger. It was a last minute decision."

"Could John have come back after you two left, entered your house, and left those prints?"

I shook my head. "He doesn't have a key to my house, so he couldn't have gotten in after I left."

"Locks can be picked. The ones on your doors are old. Or someone may have had a key. Another neighbor, perhaps?"

"I haven't given anyone a key."

"You said you recently moved in, that you inherited the place from your grandfather. People often give keys to neighbors, ask them to watch the place while they're away, bring in the mail, or feed the animals. Did you change the locks when you moved in?"

"No." But the idea sounded good now. "So you do believe someone broke into my house last night?"

"At this point in the investigation, I'm open to all possibilities." He frowned, looking toward the back of my house.

I also looked in that direction and saw his son and Baraka heading toward the old chicken coop.

"I'd keep him away from there," I said and showed Kingsley the Band-aid on the back of my hand. "It's a mess inside and this morning I scraped myself on a nail near the window."

"Don't go in there," Kingsley yelled at his son.

Jason looked our way, then back at the chicken coop.

I could almost read his mind. That chicken coop is just the right size for a playhouse or fort. I remember the allure it had when I was a child visiting Grandma and Grandpa Benson. But I wasn't allowed inside. Grandma worried about the chicken manure and disease. Grandpa didn't want me messing with his old bottles. "Collector's items," he called them. "Junk," according to Grandma.

"Jason," Kingsley repeated, his gaze never leaving his son's face.

Baraka nosed an old tire by the side of the coop, and a chipmunk popped out. Baraka jumped back, and the chipmunk made a dash for a pile of rocks by the edge of the field.

The chase was on, Baraka lumbering after the chipmunk and Jason following.

I heard Kingsley sigh in relief, and I gave a sigh of my own. "I really do need to clean this place up," I said. "I have to keep the door closed so Baraka can't get in there. One day he came out with an old sweater that smelled like chicken poop, and another time he pulled a box of magazines out and proceeded to shred them into dozens of tiny pieces. I swear my grandfather was the biggest packrat alive."

"A few of the deputies were commenting on the mess they found in the woods."

"Once this weather warms up and tax season is over, I'm getting a Dumpster. It may take me a year, but I am going to get this place cleaned up so your son and my dog can roam around without us worrying about their safety."

Kingsley kept watching his son. "Thanks for letting Jason play with your dog. In the summer I have the boat I can take him out on, but this time of year I don't always know what to do with him when it's my weekend."

"Your son's good for Baraka. He'll tire him out. But is it a good idea to bring your son along on an investigation?"

He smiled. "Believe it or not, this is a social visit." I raised my eyebrows, and he chuckled. "Okay, so now you know one of the reasons why I'm divorced. I couldn't leave the job at the office."

"Have you been divorced long?"

"Three years." He looked back at his son. "He's the one who's suffered."

"Kids always end up in the middle."

"Speaking from experience?"

I shook my head. "My parents didn't divorce. My father died in the service of his country."

Kingsley's attention switched back to me. "I know about your mother. One of the other officers brought her file to my attention. With all of those misdemeanors she's been charged with, I'm sure life hasn't been easy for you. How long has she been diagnosed with schizophrenia?"

Over the years, I've grown accustomed to questions about my mother's mental health. Even when I was a ten-year-old, when they came to tell us about my father's death, I had to explain my mother's odd behavior. My answer was simple. "All of my life."

"It must have been difficult, living with someone in that condition."

"Yeah." I wondered what he was leading up to. In a moment, I knew.

"The deputies who came out here last night," he said, "think you either called because you were having an anxiety attack or liked the attention you received yesterday afternoon."

"Then they're the ones who are crazy." People who make assumptions—any kind not based on fact—make me angry.

"Tell me about your mother."

"What do you want to know? How many times she's been institutionalized? Or how bad the mental health system is in Michigan?"

"Whatever you want to tell me."

I didn't want to tell him anything, but knew I'd have to. I'd moved twenty-five miles from my mother, but the shadow of her illness still hung over me. With a sigh, I proceeded. "Well, like many schizophrenics, my mother had a normal childhood. At least, as normal as you can have when your parents name you Flora Gardenia."

"The name did stop me when I first saw it."

"Gardenia is a family name. I guess my grandfather came up with the Flora bit. He had a rather sick sense of humor. Poor Mom went through school being called Flower Garden. She prefers Flo."

"And you prefer P.J."

I nodded. I figured if he'd read my mother's file, he knew my birth name. "At least I didn't get the Gardenia bit," I said. "Or Petunia."

"Priscilla Jayne's not a bad name."

I gave him a slight lift of my eyebrows, and I'm sure he was trying not to smile when he said, "Go on about your mother."

"Well, her name didn't stop her from being valedictorian of her class or popular with the boys. In fact, from what I've been told, up until she got pregnant with me, she was perfectly normal. She started college, met a handsome Marine, fell in love, and got married. And then her world turned upside down."

Detective Kingsley leaned back against the tree. "It happened that quickly?"

"Yes, though my grandmother says they didn't realize what was happening at first. It wasn't until Mom had a screaming episode that Dad took her to see a doctor. Even then, from what Grandma says, they didn't want to believe the diagnosis."

"What are the chances you might be schizophrenic?"

So that's what he's leading up to. I decided to get it all out in the open. "The chances are high. One percent of the world's population suffers from schizophrenia. That's one out of every one hundred people. But if you have a parent who has the disease, the ratio goes up to one out of ten."

"Any way to tell if you'll become schizophrenic?"

"You mean, can I be tested?" I shook my head. "No. Brain scans are helping indicate differences in the brains of schizophrenics from normal people, but there's no true indicator of who might get it and who won't. It usually comes on between the ages of fifteen and thirty, but with women it may take longer for the symptoms to show. I'm twenty-eight. I might have it and not know it until I'm in my mid-thirties."

"That's got to keep you on edge."

I shrugged. "Hey, mental disease runs in my family. My grandfather had dementia. My father was considered a kook."

Kingsley's frown deepened. "A 'kook'?"

"People thought he was a crazy for re-enlisting in the Marines."

"Some people would call that patriotic."

"Patriotic." I laughed at the word. "Do you consider demonstrating against a pharmaceutical company patriotic? That's what my father did. He didn't trust big business or the government, said corporate greed was polluting the environment and lawyers were taking away our freedoms." Not that I'd understood any of that when I was a child, but over the years I'd read the letters of protest he'd written. I'd found them in the archives of our local paper as well as national publications.

"Seems strange that a man opposed to the government would re-enlist."

"I think he had to." It was the only explanation I'd come up with. "He'd been laid off from his job, Mom was getting worse, and he needed medical insurance. Besides, my dad liked playing soldier. Probably like you like being a detective."

Kingsley didn't respond, but his gaze switched to his son. Jason and Baraka were still investigating the pile of rocks. I wondered what Kingsley was thinking as we watched his son and my dog. I wasn't prepared for his next question.

"Is there something going on between you and this John guy?"

"John Westman?" I laughed at the idea. "Heck no. Whatever gave you that idea?"

"He was here last night."

"Because I called Julia right after I dialed nine-one-one. John came up to check out my house. That's all. Trust me. John wouldn't leave Julia for me. She's beautiful."

"And you're not?" Kingsley looked me up and down, then smiled. "Don't underestimate yourself, Ms. Benson. If I weren't involved with this case, I might ask you out."

" 'Might' being the key word, right?" I wasn't about to be duped by a little flattery. "I saw how that Marge Bailey looked at you. I think you're involved with more than just this case."

He shook his head. "Marge and I went out once. And I think

she'd like me to ask her out again, but she's not my type."

"Oh, and I am?" Call me a cynic, but I've heard too many come-ons to get excited over a line like that.

"Maybe."

I almost scoffed, then stopped myself. Maybe he was serious. The look in his eyes certainly tempted me to believe what he'd said.

For a second I considered the possibility, then reality kicked in. "And, if you asked me out, I'd have to turn you down."

He quirked an eyebrow. "Why? Because of Marge Bailey?"

"No. If you say there's nothing between you, I believe you."

"Because you prefer women?"

Oh great, now I had two people thinking that. "No. Men are definitely my type. And, to be honest, I find you quite attractive, Detective Kingsley. The reason I'd turn you down is you don't believe me. You either think I'm crazy or lying."

"Have you lied to me?"

I stared into his eyes—those gorgeous blue eyes—and felt guilty as hell.

"I haven't lied," I said. I just hadn't told him everything I knew. "But I am curious. When those people went through my house yesterday, they picked up a lot of things. Bits of cloth. Dog hairs. Did they find a bunch of ladybugs?"

"Yeah." He gave me a strange look. "You had quite a few."

"What did they do with them?"

"I don't know. Why? Do you want them back?"

"No. Well, yes. Maybe." If I got them back, John could tell if they were "his" ladybugs.

Kingsley raised his eyebrows, then shrugged. "That's about the oddest request I've ever had, but I'll see what I can do."

I decided I'd have to be satisfied with that. I also knew I needed to get away from Kingsley before I said too much. I glanced at my watch and grimaced. "I've got to get back to work. The fifteenth of April is approaching all too quickly."

Kingsley didn't argue. He called his son, and Jason and Baraka left the rock pile. Once Baraka was close enough, I slipped the choke chain over his head. Then the four of us walked toward the Jeep, Jason enthusiastically showing his father an arrowhead he'd found under one of the rocks. At least, it could have been an arrowhead. Or just a triangular rock.

A blue Ford, heading west, neared my house. I recognized both the car and the old man driving. "Howard Lowe," I said and raised my hand in greeting. "He's my neighbor to the east."

The car went by, Howard Lowe making no gesture of greeting. Kingsley noticed. "He's not very friendly."

"He's mad." As soon as I said it, I realized Kingsley might take that statement the wrong way, especially considering the conversation we'd had about my mother.

"By mad, I mean angry," I explained. "I won't let him hunt in my woods. Since I posted my land, he's been in huff."

"A big enough huff to break into your house?"

I hadn't thought of that possibility.

NINE

Detective Kingsley's Jeep had just left the yard when I heard my telephone. With Baraka by my side, I ran to the house and answered on the fourth ring, breathless. Julia immediately started talking.

"It's Punk," she said, sounding sick with the news. "He's the one who was killed, the one who died in your house. I'm at the bank, and I just talked to Tom Anderson. He was one of the volunteer firemen at your place yesterday. He said none of the guys who went inside knew Punk, but later, when they were talking, Tom realized it had to be Punk. I guess he called the sheriff's department and told them who he thought it was. I called John, to let him know, but he's not home."

Julia took a breath, giving me a chance to respond. "Detective Kingsley just left my place. He told me, though when he first said the dead man was Carroll McDaniels, I didn't recognize the name."

"Not surprising. No one called him that, not even his mother. Oh dear." Julia sighed. "I think she's still in Florida. I wonder if she knows."

"I'm sure the sheriff's department will contact her. Now that we know it's Punk, do you have any idea who shot him?"

"None whatsoever. Oh jeez, this is all my fault. I'm the one who suggested hiring Punk. If only . . ."

Julia's voice trailed off. She sounded shaky, and I hated seeing her blame herself when it wasn't entirely her fault. "Who else knew John was working with those ladybugs at your place?"

"The ladybugs?" Julia repeated. "No one. John couldn't tell anyone or the Feds would have stepped in."

"Well, just remember, if he hadn't brought a dangerous project home, none of this would have happened."

"I know. I know." Julia sighed again. "Look, I've got to get back to my window, but I wanted to let you know about Punk. If you see John before I do, tell him."

I promised I would.

After hanging up the phone, I fed Baraka a treat, poured myself another cup of coffee, and went back to work on Sporbach's taxes. Julia called again at three o'clock. She was home now. John had been in, knew about Punk, but was now at a department head meeting at B.C. BioTech. Julia suggested we go out to dinner before heading for the euchre party. "It would give us a chance to talk," she said. "Besides, I don't want to cook."

I don't think Julia ever wants to cook, but I'll admit I wanted to hear what John had to say after his department head meeting. I also wanted to make John and Julia understand that Kingsley needed to know about the box and the ladybugs.

So I agreed to dinner, and at five thirty I left my computer, headed for my bedroom, and pawed through my closet.

Julia had said no one dressed up for these monthly euchre parties, but having both Kingsley and Nora questioning my sexual preferences, I realized how rarely I did wear anything but jeans or sweats. Even when I worked at Quick Sums, pantsuits were my usual attire. I own three dresses. That's all. One I bought for my graduation six years ago, one I had to buy for a wedding I was in, and one I wore to my Grandfather Carter's funeral. That one is really old.

I wanted to show my neighbors a more feminine side of me, but I knew the bridesmaid dress wouldn't work, and I wasn't sure I could get into the dress I'd bought for Grandpa Carter's funeral. That left my graduation dress. Which wasn't a bad choice. The blue wool was lightweight and subtly feminine. Just what was needed. I would even wear pantyhose.

I took a long, hot shower, letting the steamy water pelt my back and shoulders and ease some of the tension of the last two days. Tax season is always rough. Long hours. Meticulous concentration. Add a man dying in my dining room, the invasion of the Zenith volunteer fire department and the Kalamazoo County sheriff's department and stress took on new meaning.

I was toweling myself off, feeling totally relaxed, when I heard a noise. Nothing loud. Just a click. Like the sound of a door shutting.

I sucked in a breath and didn't move. Water trickled down the sides of my face from my wet hair.

The way this house is designed, the back door opens into the kitchen, which is the width of the house. From there you enter a huge dining room, also the width of the house. My front door opens into that room. Off the dining room, the house is divided into two parts. The front side is a long, narrow living room, the end of which will become my office next month. The back side is divided into three rooms: the bathroom, which is right off the dining room; a small laundry area, and my bedroom. A stairway goes up the middle of the house, leading to two more bedrooms and a huge storage room on the second level. I rarely go upstairs, and usually keep the stairway door closed. Under that stairway and between the bathroom and living room sections is the cellar door.

It's an old house, and I often hear noises. A clunk in the cellar. A creak upstairs. To be honest, I not only bought Baraka so I could show him, but also for protection and peace of mind. If he doesn't react to the sound, I don't worry about it.

But Baraka wasn't in the bathroom with me. He'd been asleep when I decided to take my shower. Exhausted from his romp with Kingsley's boy, Baraka didn't even stir when I checked to make sure both the back and front doors were locked.

So if my outside doors were locked, what did I hear?

I shivered, though steam still covered the mirror over the vanity. I quickly grabbed my underwear, slipped on the bra and bikini pants I'd brought in with me, and wrapped the towel back around me.

Minimally decent, I moved closer to the door leading to the dining room and again held my breath and listened.

I heard nothing.

No, I was wrong. I did hear something. A slight whine. Maybe a scraping sound.

"Baraka?" I whispered.

Heart pounding in my chest, I glanced at the door on the other side of the bathroom. I could go through there, into my bedroom, put on some clothes and climb out a window.

Again, I heard a scraping sound. "Baraka, is that you?"

He whined.

My dog was on the other side of the door. But was he alone?

I looked around the bathroom. I wanted to let my dog in, but I needed a weapon, something I could use to defend myself if necessary.

The only viable possibilities I saw were a plunger next to the toilet and a plastic bottle of mouthwash, half-full. I picked up the plunger, holding it so I could wield the wooden handle like a club.

Slowly, I turned the doorknob, trying not to make a sound. Plunger ready, I opened the door a crack.

Baraka pushed against the door, ready to come in. I held it steady, blocking his entrance, so I could look around first. I didn't want any surprises.

I looked toward my front door. Closed. Just as I had left it. I glanced down at the linoleum. No footprints, though footprints wouldn't have been as evident this evening as they were yesterday. Three trips outside with Baraka had tracked in a fair amount of dirt. As soon as the weather warms up, I'm putting in sidewalks. I may not be a great housekeeper, but there is a limit to how much mud even I can stand in a house.

I opened the door wider and Baraka came trotting into the bathroom, tail wagging. He hadn't barked, I realized. Didn't give any sign that someone else was in the house. Carefully I stepped out of the bathroom and looked around.

No one in my dining area. A few steps more and I could see into my living room. No one there. A trip to the kitchen doorway produced the same results. Still, I wasn't convinced. So, Baraka by my side, I checked the upstairs and down in the cellar. Although he sniffed under the bed upstairs and around the shelves in the cellar, not once did he give any indication that we weren't alone.

Shivering, I stepped back into the warmth of the bathroom, Baraka following me in this time. "You." I pointed my finger at him, then kneeled and gave him a hug. "You scared me."

He licked my face, his tail thumping against the side of the toilet, and I knew if he could talk he'd tell me I'd scared myself. "If I tell people I'm hearing things, they're really going to think I'm crazy." I sighed, stood, and put the plunger back beside the toilet. "What next, Baraka? Will I be seeing little green men? Ghosts?"

I swear he smiled, his tail wagging. I closed the bathroom door, and he trotted over and began licking water from the floor of the shower. I considered telling him no, then decided shower water was better than toilet water. Ever since I'd caught him drinking out of the toilet bowl, I'd tried to remember to keep the seat down. I put it down now.

By the time John and Julia arrived, I'd dried my hair and donned my dress, pantyhose, and low-heeled pumps. Baraka was fed. I expected him to balk at being put in his crate another night, but he went in willingly, and only gave a slight whine when he saw me slip on my coat and pick up my purse. "Watch the place," I ordered and left a light on in the living room.

I made sure I locked the front and back doors, then climbed into the truck next to Julia. "Sorry," I apologized. "I had to make sure everything was secure."

"I don't blame you," Julia said. "Not after last night."

"I'm glad you believe me. The sheriff's department certainly doesn't."

John chuckled as he backed out of my yard and onto the road. "I got that feeling last night when they were questioning you about those footprints. Is that why one of them stopped by your place today?"

"That and to tell me it was Punk who died in my house." I saw no need to mention Kingsley's son wanting to see my dog. "You should have told me Punk's real name. I didn't realize who Kingsley was talking about at first."

"Don't blame me," John said. "I didn't know his name was Carroll. I've always heard him called Punk."

"It's like you, P.J.," Julia added. "If someone called you by your birth name, I wouldn't know who they were talking about. What surprised me was none of the paramedics knew him."

John chuckled. "I guess they don't spend their evenings in the bar. Did the detective say anything else, P.J.?"

"He said he didn't know anything about a missing box."

"You told him about the box?" John and Julia spoke almost in unison.

Their attitude upset me. "I thought you had. How can Detective Kingsley help if he doesn't know what he's looking for?"

"P.J., we don't want him looking for that box," Julia said.

"Why not?"

"Because . . ." She looked at John. "Because he might accidentally let the ladybugs out."

I didn't buy that. "If he knows what's in it, he'll be careful, and you'll have your beetles back in no time."

"No!" John slammed on the brakes, throwing Julia and me forward. I braced myself with a hand against the dash.

Julia yelled at him. "Hey! Cool it. She doesn't understand, so don't take this out on her."

"Then she needs to understand." He looked directly at me. "P.J., the fact that someone broke into your place last night tells me that the person who shot Punk doesn't have the box. Which means it's probably somewhere on our property or yours. If that detective or any of his men find that box before we do, Julia and I will be in big trouble. Big, big trouble."

Julia was right. I didn't understand. "Isn't it more important to find those ladybugs? What did your other department heads say?"

"They didn't say anything." John sighed and looked away. The road was deserted, his headlights outlining the two lanes. "Because they don't know anything about the ladybugs. I wasn't supposed to have them. If they find out, I'll lose my job. We'll have to sell our house and land."

Maybe I should have felt sorry for him, but I didn't. His experiment was messing up my life, and I wanted him to understand that. "Look, you may be worried about your future. Well, so am I. First off, there may be a box of dangerous ladybugs somewhere around my place. And second, Detective Kingsley thinks I'm connected to Punk's murder. How do I prove I'm not if he doesn't understand why Punk was murdered?"

"Just give us some time," Julia pleaded. "A week. Give us a chance to find the box. If we do, I'm sure we'll figure out who shot Punk."

"Do you realize what you're asking?" I did. "You're asking me to withhold evidence from a law enforcement officer. I could get in big trouble."

"Can't you pretend we didn't tell you anything?" John asked. "In a week . . ."

He didn't finish, just kept looking out at the road. I wanted more. "In a week, what?"

He shrugged. "I don't know. In a week, we'll figure out what to do next."

As if that answered everything, he took his foot off the brake and eased the truck back on the road.

TEN

Everyone was at Rose and Nora's by the time we arrived, and everyone knew we'd been out to dinner. The local grapevine amazes me.

Rose took our coats. She gushed that she was glad I'd come and said she wanted to hear all about my adventure the day before. The moment I saw Nora, I knew she didn't share Rose's enthusiasm. Although she wasn't outright hostile, I could sense the animosity. She called Rose away before I could say a thing.

"She'll get over it," Julia said. John merely shrugged and gave me one of those who-understands-women looks.

We headed into the dining room, and Julia made the introductions. I'd met a few of the people before. In our mile by half-mile section, Jim and Ione Fuller live diagonally opposite from me. The southwest corner of their land butts up against the northeast corner of mine. They could have been the original Jack Sprat and his wife. Ione probably tipped the scales at three hundred pounds and Jim's bib overalls hung on his lanky frame.

He'd stopped by a month after I moved in to see if the arrangement he'd had with my grandfather to farm the tillable land would be agreeable to me. I took a day to look over the lease agreement and told him yes. I wasn't about to start farming, and it seemed ridiculous to let thirty acres of land sit fallow. Also, what I'd be paid for the use of the land would cover part of my property taxes. Not a bad deal in my mind.

Bill and Sondra Sommers live farther east, on the same road

as Nora and Rose and Jim and Ione. I hadn't met Bill and Sondra before, but I'd smelled them. They have a dairy farm, and sometimes, when the wind blows from the east, I get a good whiff of cow manure. Country air is not all they make it out to be.

The fourth couple, Ray and Tina Mason, live closer to Zenith but evidently have been playing cards with the others for years. Ray, with his shock of white hair, long white beard, and bushy white eyebrows made me think of Santa Claus, and Julia said Ray usually does play Santa for the grammar school's Christmas assembly. His wife, Tina, however, reminded me more of the wicked witch in *The Wizard of Oz* than of Mrs. Claus.

The only other single guest was Carl Dremmer. Julia had talked a lot about him during dinner, and I had a feeling she was playing matchmaker. She'd told me that Carl lost his wife two years ago to cancer, that he was thirty-five, had no children, and did all sorts of odd jobs from laying brick to tree trimming.

I can't say I was overly impressed by his looks. Maybe it was the long, stringy blonde hair, pulled back in a ponytail. Or maybe it was the torn jeans and faded flannel shirt. On the other hand, he had nice eyes. They were a mossy green that made me think of a quiet meadow. And I liked his handshake. Firm, but not overbearing. He towered over me, but most men do, carried no excess weight, and didn't have a beer belly. That was a point in his favor. I've dated guys who had much less appeal, and decided to keep an open mind about Carl.

Rose bustled around, making sure there were bowls of nuts and popcorn on each of the three card tables and that everyone had a drink, be it coffee or soda pop. Nora kept a close eye on Rose, especially whenever Rose was near me. Now that I knew they weren't sisters, I understood why they didn't resemble each other.

Rose is in her early forties, quite slender and attractive. She wears her hair long and if it's not naturally blonde, it's a good dye job. Tonight she had on a pale pink dress that accentuated her fair skin and brought out the blue of her eyes. The way she was seeing to everyone's needs, I had the feeling she loved playing hostess.

Her partner, however, isn't the congenial hostess type. If Nora were taller and didn't have the broad hips of a woman, she could easily pass for a man. Watching her, I thought of the saying, "Your mother wears combat boots." And I guess Nora did wear combat boots at one time. Julia said Nora served in the army when she was younger. Julia also said Nora was as good with a gun as any man. That didn't reassure me.

Especially the way she kept glaring at me.

I didn't have to be told that Nora didn't issue the invitation for me to join the party tonight. I wanted to go over and tell her not to worry, but the opportunity never presented itself. And Rose didn't help the situation. Maybe she was just being friendly when she put a hand on my shoulder, gave a squeeze, and again said she was glad I'd come, but Nora saw the interchange and if looks could kill, I'd be dead. I wished I had a big pin or something that said, "I date men, not women."

Since Carl and I were to be partners, I decided I'd better get to know him. I also figured asking him questions about himself would solve two problems: I would avoid the possibility of saying too much about what had happened at my house and would show Rose and Nora that I did prefer men.

I think the idea was a good one. The problem was, Carl Dremmer wasn't much of a talker. I'd ask a question. He'd give me a one-syllable answer. I'd try again. Same results.

I don't think even Jay Leno or David Letterman could get this man gabbing. After a while, I gave up and concentrated on playing cards.

We won a few hands and lost a few. Keeping track of what

was trump and what had already been played was hard work, and by eleven o'clock, I was exhausted. The moment Rose announced it was time for refreshments, I slapped down my cards and called it quits.

Up until then, talk at the tables had centered around kids, school, and farming. Safe topics. But as we put away the cards and moved around the room, Sondra looked up at the ceiling, then said with disgust, "Ladybugs."

Without thinking, I glanced in John's direction. He was stacking the decks of cards on a desk in the corner, but I could tell he was listening.

I looked back at Sondra. "What about ladybugs?"

"What about them?" She pointed at the light fixture above her head. You could see the bodies of the dead insects inside the glass. "Every time we have a sunny day," she said. "I'm plagued by them. I swear they come out of the woodwork. I vacuum them up and twenty minutes later they're back. They're everywhere. Aren't you being bothered by them?"

In more ways than one, I thought. "Yeah." I nodded, again glancing John's way.

Bill chuckled at his wife. "The most beneficial predatory insect introduced for biological control, and you aren't happy."

"They're out of control," Sondra said. "These Korean ladybugs were supposed to stay in the south and take care of the aphids destroying the pecan trees. Now they're up here, driving out our native species. And they bite."

"One bit her the other day," Bill explained. "And she's been fuming ever since."

"One bit you?" I remembered what John had said about the coworker who died. "When?"

Sondra shrugged. "I don't know. Wednesday afternoon. Thursday morning. Why?"

That would have been before John's ladybugs were stolen.

And since I didn't want to explain why, I said, "Just curious."

"Yeah, well, they're driving me nuts." Sondra turned back to her husband. "When they start clogging up your tractors and combines, don't come complaining to me."

If John's missing ladybugs got loose, I doubted Bill and Jim would be complaining about their tractors. Plant-eating ladybugs wouldn't leave them anything to combine.

"Sondra," John said, finally speaking up, "Korean ladybugs don't really bite. It's more like a pinch."

"Felt like a bite," she argued. "And of course you're going to defend introducing them to the environment. You and your biotechnology. But I've been reading about it. It's not all great. How about the killer bees that were introduced in South America? Or those snails in Hawaii? They not only wiped out whatever they were brought in to wipe out, they wiped out a bunch of other snails."

"Those incidents didn't involve qualified biocontrol workers," John argued. "Testing has improved."

"Are you going to tell me genetic mutations don't happen?" Sondra shook her head. "I saw *Jurassic Park*."

Julia came to her husband's defense. "Sondra, that was a movie."

"Yeah." Bill laughed. "I can just see it now. *Attack of the Ladybugs.*"

I hoped he wouldn't see it. I could understand why Julia didn't want anything about the missing ladybugs told to the media. People like Sondra would panic.

"Ladybugs don't attack people," Jim said. "People attack people." He looked at me. "So, did you really shoot Punk?"

"No." That someone thought I might amazed me. "I didn't even know the guy."

"Any idea who did shoot him?" Jim asked.

I don't know why, perhaps because of what John had said

yesterday, but I glanced across the room at Nora. Immediately she frowned. "Don't you go accusing me. I didn't shoot nobody. I was in town yesterday, with Rose."

"I wasn't accusing you."

"Then why did those sheriff's deputies come snooping around asking us all sorts of questions?" Nora glared at me. "What me and Rose does is our business. And you'd better stay out of it."

"I didn't—" I started, but my explanation fell short as Nora marched into the kitchen.

"Oh dear," Rose muttered, and followed after her.

I looked at the others. "I didn't accuse her," I said. "And I'm not a lesbian."

For a moment, no one said a word, simply stood around looking uncomfortable. Then Ray Mason spoke up. "Seems strange, Punk getting killed like he did. I saw him at the Pour House just a few nights ago. He'd had a few too many beers, as usual. Kept talking about screwing up, that he should have kept his big mouth shut, 'cause now he was in big trouble. Was almost like he knew he was going to be shot and killed."

The Pour House is the local bar and grill. In a town like Zenith, it's about the only place to go if you want a drink or a quick hamburger. It's also a good place to catch up on gossip. It dawned on me that Ray might know who shot Punk. So I asked. "Did he say who was going to shoot and kill him?"

Ray shook his head. "Naw. I figured it was just beer talk. Punk's always had a habit of drinking too much. I don't like to speak ill of the dead, but Punk was one strange guy. I mean, living with his mother the way he did. Never holding a full-time job."

"He was a damned good handyman," Jim said in Punk's defense. "I think we all used him, one time or another."

"He helped me build a pole barn," Bill agreed. "And added a

bedroom to our place when Sondra got pregnant with our fourth child."

"He helped me on a job more than once," Carl added.

Ray raised his hands, stopping the testimonies. "I never said he weren't a good worker . . . just a bit odd. And that night I saw him, he was real depressed. He kept saying he'd never learn to keep a secret, and it were gonna to be the death of him."

"And now he's dead," Bill said.

The four men nodded, then John spoke up. "Did Punk say what this secret was that he told?"

Again, Ray shook his head. "Just kept drinking and mumbling about his big mouth."

Rose came back into the room, Nora sullenly following behind her. The two carried an array of snacks, ranging from barbequed chicken wings to a bread made with Michigan dried cherries. With food in front of us, Carroll McDaniels, otherwise known as Punk, was momentarily forgotten.

I stuffed myself in spite of the large meal I'd had only a few hours earlier. Everything tasted so good, I had to tell Rose, so when she went in to check on the coffee, I followed her into the kitchen.

"Delicious," I said. "Everything, but especially those chicken wings. I'll have to get your recipe."

"I'm glad you liked them." Rose came over to my side. "They're really quite easy to fix. Here—" She pointed at a recipe she had taped to her wall.

"Oh great, I turn my back for a minute, and I find you two in here."

Nora blurted out the words, and both Rose and I turned toward her, surprised by the outburst. It didn't help that when we turned we ended up shoulder to shoulder and Rose started blushing. Her cheeks turned a brighter pink than her dress. "I'm just . . . That is . . . We . . ."

Rose kept stammering, never finishing a sentence. I simply stared at Nora, stunned by the amount of anger and hatred in the woman's eyes. I've never been accused by another woman of trying to steal her date. That the date was another woman made me want to laugh, but Nora's look kept me silent.

"Well?" Nora said.

"Well what?" I could see Bill and Jim in the doorway behind Nora, watching and listening. I hoped one of them would step in and tell Nora she was being a fool.

Neither did, and I realized I'd have to handle this myself. "Rose was showing me a recipe," I explained. "For the barbeque chicken wings."

Nora's gaze switched to Rose. "Now I know why you wanted to invite her. It's not enough that you two sneak around behind my back. Now you're doing it in front of me."

"Oh, get off it," Rose shot back, showing more backbone than I'd seen her display all evening. "If you had your way, you would lock me in a closet and throw away the key. I'm being a good neighbor. That's all."

I hate arguments. I heard enough when I was a child. "Look," I began. "I don't want to—"

"Stay out of this," Nora ordered, and I decided I would.

"Fine," I said. "In fact, I think it best if I leave." They could solve their domestic spat without me.

I scooted past Nora, hoping she wouldn't decide to take this argument to a physical level, squeezed between Bill and Jim and found Julia and John in the next room.

"Well, that went off nicely," I said, once we were in the truck. "Let's see. One neighbor thinks I shot Punk, and another is accusing me of hopping into bed with her partner."

"Why did you ask Sondra when she was bit by that ladybug?" John asked, no humor in his voice.

I glanced his way. "Well, if they were loose and one bit her, wouldn't you want to know?"

"They are not loose." He revved up the engine and took off from Nora's. "We never should have told you about that experiment."

"Well, you did, and last I'd heard you hadn't found them."

Julia put a hand on my arm. "It was a good question, P.J. John's just a little tense."

"So am I." I leaned back against the seat. "I think a week's too long to wait."

John pulled into my yard, the truck's headlights reflecting off the first floor windows of the farm house. "P.J., I promise," he said, his voice calmer than before, "nothing is going to happen to you or any of our neighbors. We're the ones who have the problem."

"But—?"

"It will be fine," Julia repeated, patting my arm. "We're working on it."

I stared at my front door. It wasn't just the missing box that worried me. Someone had entered my house last night. Violated my sanctity. I shuddered at the thought.

"Are you okay?" Julia asked.

"Just a little spooky."

She gave my arm a squeeze. "I'll walk with you to the door."

"I, ah—" I hated acting like scared rabbit, but I'd had enough surprises. "Okay," I said. "If you don't mind."

"No problem." Julia scooted out after me.

With Julia by my side, and the truck's headlights giving us plenty of light, the walk to my front door was easy. I did keep shivering, but that was more from the cold than fear. I doubt the temperature was above forty degrees.

Cautiously, I opened my front door and snapped on the light. I gave a quick glance around the dining room and into the living room, then looked at Baraka. He was standing in his crate, wagging his tail and whining a greeting. Or maybe it was a plea to go outside. Next, I looked at the floor. No new footprints. Everything looked exactly as I'd left it. "Looks good," I told Julia, and gave a silent sigh of relief.

"Do you want me to go through each room with you?" She was looking around, just as I was.

"No. It's late. Besides, why would someone break into my house two nights in a row?"

"If you're sure?" Julia waited until I nodded, then stepped off my porch. "You call if you need anything," she said, and headed back to the truck.

By the time I had Baraka out of his crate and outside, John's truck was on their road. I watched them make the short journey to their house, reassured by the glow of their lights. They were less than a quarter of a mile away. Ready to help, if I needed help. I wasn't alone.

Still I shivered and pulled my coat closer. Baraka seemed to be taking forever finding the spot he wanted. Finally he squatted and seemed to give a doggy sigh.

Back inside, I took off my coat and turned up the heat. It was then that I noticed the stacks of folders on my dining room table didn't look the same as when I'd left. To others, my work area may appear messy, but I know exactly where everything is . . . and the Sporbach's folder wasn't where it should have been. It wasn't on top of Mabel Walter's folder. Not only that, on the floor I found one of the Sporbach's 1099-Int forms.

Maybe it was just my imagination, but my computer didn't seem to be in the same position, either. And the rubber cow I received as a gift when I bought the computer wasn't in its usual position on top of the tower. It was on its side on the table. I put it back on the tower.

That's when I remembered I'd snapped the light on in the

living room before leaving with John and Julia. With the headlights from the truck shining into the house, I hadn't noticed it wasn't on when we arrived.

I walked over and tried it. The light came on. No burned out bulb. No blown fuse. Someone had turned off the light.

A knot tightened in my stomach, and I called Baraka to my side. He came, wagging his tail and nuzzling my pocket, looking for a treat. I patted his head for reassurance. My first impulse was to call nine-one-one, but I didn't want to be classified as a nut. I needed proof that someone had been in the house. More proof than a light being out, a toy cow laying on the table, and rearranged folders.

But what if someone was still in the house? I looked down at Baraka. Certainly, if someone was still in the house, he'd let me know. Wag his tail. Go to him.

All he was interested in was finding food.

Keeping Baraka by my side, I checked the other rooms on the main floor. For the most part, things looked the same as when I'd left . . . my usual mess. But some things were different. Crazy as it sounds, I would swear someone swept my dining room floor. It was just too clean. And the top drawer of my buffet was closed. I remembered opening it, but I didn't remember closing it.

In the living room, the cushions of my sofa had been switched. I might not have noticed except one cushion has a small stain, and I always keep that one on the end that Baraka uses. It was now in the middle.

The same was true of the books on my shelves and the magazines on the coffee table. At first glance, everything was fine. Only if you knew how you'd left them would you know they'd been moved.

I knew how I'd left them.

I grew tenser with each discovery and watched Baraka for

any sign that we weren't alone. My stomach churned, and I wished I hadn't eaten so many of Rose's chicken wings. Stomach acid and barbeque sauce don't make a good combination.

Baraka sniffed each area I investigated and wagged his tail, but he never gave any indication that we might not be alone. "Who was here?" I demanded, looking down at his wrinkled head.

If only he could talk.

In my bedroom I checked the closet, then looked under the bed. I found lots of dust bunnies, but no bogeyman. Baraka crouched beside me and made a cat-like swipe of his paw, pulling out the rubber pull toy I'd placed there after getting tired of playing with him. Pull toy in his mouth, he trotted out of my bedroom and back to the living room.

I followed him and headed for the kitchen. I needed a drink of water and some antacids. Or maybe a shot of bourbon. This was enough to drive a woman to drink.

I didn't get any bourbon. The moment I stepped into the kitchen, I noticed the back door wasn't locked. It wasn't even completely closed.

That made up my mind. Maybe I did leave Mabel Walter's tax forms on top of Sporbach's, and maybe I did close that buffet drawer, but I knew I didn't leave that door open. I called the number on the card Detective Wade Kingsley had left.

ELEVEN

Sunday morning I loaded Baraka into my car and headed for Kalamazoo. I needed to talk to someone who would understand what I was going through. My grandmother was that person.

I brought Baraka into the living room with me, and made him lie down by the couch. A couple of doggy biscuits and a chew toy would keep him busy. Grandma had already made coffee, the fresh-brewed aroma almost countering the smell of stale cigarette smoke. Mom was upstairs getting dressed, and I didn't waste any time pouring out my story to Grandma, detailing all of the events of the last few days.

I know she could tell I was frustrated, especially when I came to what had happened last night.

"I don't know why I bothered calling the sheriff's department," I grumbled as I held out my mug for a refill of coffee. "First of all, that detective who left his card wasn't even home. All I got was his answering machine and a message to contact the sheriff's department if I needed help. I could have done that in the first place.

"Then I got the same two deputies who were at my house Friday night. I tried to make them understand this was serious. I even broke my promise and told them about the ladybugs that had been stolen from John's lab."

"So what did they say?" Grandma straightened, coffeepot in hand, and waited for my answer.

"They started asking me questions like, 'What do these ladybugs look like?' Well, I didn't know. John never told me. Then they asked if I'd been bitten by one. I told them no. And it went on and on. Stupid questions I couldn't answer. Finally, they did go through the house. Checked every room, including the cellar. When they found nothing, and I said nothing of mine had been taken, they blew me off."

"Treated you like they do your mother. Right?" Grandma started back for the kitchen with the pot.

"Exactly." I took a sip of the warmup—Grandma makes great coffee—and leaned back against the sofa. "That's when I decided to call John," I said, talking a little louder so she could hear. "I asked him to tell the deputies that I wasn't lying about the ladybugs. But, of course, he didn't."

Grandma poked her head out from the kitchen. "What do you mean, 'he didn't'?"

"He didn't verify my story." I sighed. "I imagine those deputies laughed all the way back to Kalamazoo."

"Doesn't matter. Not as long as you know the truth."

Grandma came back into the living room and sat down next to me. For a woman in her seventies, she's amazing. She's short, like me, wiry, in great health—in spite of smoking since she was in her teens—and is always busy, either cooking, sewing, or gardening. When she gave my knee a pat, I voiced my real concern. "Grandma, how do you know what's the truth? I mean, the real truth. Mom thinks she knows the truth. She thinks the people she sees and talks to are real."

"That's different. We know her brain is sending false messages. But you . . . you're still in touch with reality."

I didn't like her using the word "still." It implied that I might not be one of these days.

"Did they dust for fingerprints?" Grandma asked.

"No. When I said nothing had been taken as far as I could tell, they said there wasn't much sense in looking for fingerprints. I'm sure, by then, they'd decided I was completely off my rocker. They didn't understand at all when I told them it looked like someone had swept my floors. I tried to explain that the broom had been moved and the dirt I'd tracked in earlier that day was gone." Two days of clean floors. For my house, that was truly unique. "They did say if I found anything missing, to call the station."

"The brush-off, in other words."

"Yep." I drank more coffee. I needed the caffeine. I hadn't gotten to bed until nearly two a.m. and then I couldn't sleep. "Suddenly I don't feel safe out there," I said. "First a man dies in my dining room, then I find footprints, and now things are moved and my back door is left open."

"Death, the ultimate escape."

The words echoed down the stairway, and Grandma and I looked that direction. My mother came into view, a vacant gaze in her eyes. A lush, green velour lounging robe covered her from her neck to her wrists and ankles, while furry pink bunny slippers graced her feet. She had her hair up in curlers, a dyed blonde hair poking out here and there, and her face was a chalky white.

"Sometimes I see dead people," she said with no emotion, and walked into the living room.

Baraka rose to his feet and watched as my mother approached the sofa and coffee table. He didn't growl, but he wasn't wagging his tail.

My mother bothers him. Maybe it's the involuntary movements she makes. Or maybe he senses she's not quite right. This time I had a feeling it was the way she looked.

"What is that you have on your face?" I asked.

"A cleansing mask." She gently tapped a fingertip against the shell of white. "I must cleanse my soul." Leaning forward, she reached for a cigarette from the pack on the coffee table. Baraka backed up.

"Your cleansing mask is cracking near your mouth," Grandma said. "Are you supposed to smoke when you have that on, Flo?"

"Your mask is scaring Baraka," I said. He pressed himself against my leg, always watching her.

Mom looked down at Baraka. "Are you scared, little doggy?" She growled at him, and he barked.

"Mother!"

Mom lit her cigarette and walked over to the window. "I thought of you yesterday." She blew out a cloud of smoke, then touched a finger to her forehead where the clay mask met her curlers. "I could picture you standing beside a pool of blood."

A pool of blood? Sometimes it's eerie how right my mother can be. I mentioned it to her doctor once. He said everyone has premonitions, or what we think are premonitions. Most of the time they don't come true, and we just forget them. It's the ones that do come true that we remember. The doctor figured, with Mom, we just didn't hear about the ones that didn't come true.

Mom looked at me, and I said, "The man who died in my house Friday was lying in a pool of blood."

She came back and sat on the edge of the chair nearest me. Leaning forward, she flicked a cigarette ash in the leaf-shaped ashtray I'd made when I was in the fourth grade. "I know," she said. "It said so in the paper."

So much for premonitions.

"But he's not dead," she asserted. "He will return. Just like the others have. Like your father did." Mom glanced left and right, as if checking if someone was listening, then she leaned closer and whispered, "Did I ever tell you your father came to see me after he died?"

"A few times." Actually she's told me the story many, many

times. The first time I believed her. At eleven, it's easy to believe in miracles. Dad had been gone a year then, and I missed him. When Mom said he was still alive, I was ready to believe her, especially when she told me he'd said he loved me and would always watch over me.

Only as I grew older did I realize Mom never did see or talk to Dad, that it was simply one of her delusions. Visual hallucinations are not uncommon when a wife loses her husband. In Mom's case, anything else would have been uncommon.

"Dead people come back because they want something," Mom said.

Grandma leaned my way. "We watched *The Sixth Sense* with Bruce Willis the other night. Now she's sure the people she sees are dead people with messages."

"They are," my mother insisted. "And they have picked me to relay those messages. You listen to me, Priscilla Jayne, not your grandmother."

"P.J., Mother. P.J." Most of the time she respects my wish to be called P.J., but whenever she gets excited or upset, she forgets and goes back to my birth name.

"You just want to be called that because Paul called you that. You always liked him better than me."

"Mom, it has nothing to do with Dad calling me P.J." I tried to remain calm and mature. We'd been through this before. "I changed my name because I was always being teased in school. You know how it was, how cruel kids can be. You didn't like being called Flower Garden. Well, I didn't like being called Prissy."

"Prissy, Prissy, Prissy." She began rocking back and forth in her chair, chanting. "Missy Prissy. Prissy Missy. Prissy Missy is having a hissy."

I glanced at Grandma and rolled my eyes toward the ceiling. Grandma knows what I went through as a child. Prissy rhymes with too many words, some not as nice as the ones my mother was using. It's a get-beat-up-on-the-playground name, and as soon as I was out of high school and able to sign the necessary paperwork, Priscilla Jayne became a bad memory.

"I'm P.J. now, Mom. Everyone calls me that. It's on my checks. Even on my driver's license. And, as far as I'm concerned, I don't want to see any more dead men. One was enough."

"Maybe you don't want to see more, but you will. He'll be back."

"Who will?"

My mother cocked her head to the side, as if listening to someone, then she stubbed out her cigarette and stared intently at me. "Did I tell you I saw your dad after he died?" She didn't wait for an answer. "He didn't look the same. You change when you die. Does something to you, I guess."

"I guess." We were back to my father.

"Nevertheless," Mom said, "I knew who it was the moment he spoke. I recognized his voice. And there was the way he shrugged his shoulders. You remember how your dad used to shrug his shoulders when he didn't know what to say?"

"Yeah." I did remember that. Eighteen years have gone by since I last saw Dad, but I remember a lot of things about him. Mostly, the deep, hardy sound of his laughter and the feel of his hands, so strong yet gentle. I remember him calling me his princess and twirling me around the room. He was my Prince Charming. My knight in shining armor.

Mom and he sometimes argued, and Grandma and he used to get in terrible arguments with each other, but Dad was always nice to me. When he re-enlisted, I couldn't understand why he had to go away. I wanted him to take me with him, but he said he couldn't. He said I'd be fine as long as Grandma was around, and if I ever truly needed him, he'd come back.

"I saw your grandfather, too," Mom said, pulling me out of

the past. "Saw him just the other day." My mother started rocking back and forth on the edge of the chair again. "We were shopping in Meijer's, and there he was in the sporting section."

"The man did look like your grandfather," Grandma said. "But, of course, it wasn't."

Mom leaned toward me. "That's what she thinks, but I know better. As I said, they change when they come back, but I know it's them."

I haven't seen my mother this bad in some time, and it worried me. "Mom?" I asked. "Are you taking your medication?"

She looked at me—empty eyes surrounded by cracking white clay—then reached for another cigarette. "It makes me feel funny. I think they're putting something in it. Poison. They want to stop me from relaying the messages."

"Your mother has a doctor's appointment Tuesday," Grandma said.

"I can't go to the doctor's Tuesday," Mom told her, more matter-of-fact than angry. "I'll be busy Tuesday. You forgot. I'll be working at my new job."

I looked at Grandma. She hadn't said anything about Mom getting a new job.

Grandma sighed and explained. "Seems your mother was fired from Brown's a couple of weeks ago. She's been leaving the house at the same time and simply going to the coffee shop and drinking coffee and smoking cigarettes all day."

"But now I have a new job," my mother said proudly. "Now I can stay home and work. Now I'll have enough money to buy my own cigarettes."

"Paying someone so you can address envelopes for them is not a job," Grandma grumbled. "It's a ripoff."

Mom ignored her. "You, too, can make thousands of dollars right in your own home. It's easy. It's fun. Just call five-five-five-one-two-one-two."

I'd seen the ads in the newspaper and on telephone poles. Come ons that promise quick wealth and end up costing the unsuspecting sucker money. From the sounds of it, they'd found another sucker.

Grandma confirmed it. "Your mother gave them my credit card number. Yesterday a box arrived filled with envelopes to be addressed. Thousands of envelopes."

"Make money at home." Mother kept repeating the litany, her voice expressionless. "It's easy. It's fun. You can do it in your spare time."

I shook my head. "Mom, I thought you promised not to use Grandma's credit card again."

My mother began rocking back and forth on her chair, puffing on her cigarette and repeating the slogan. "It's easy. It's fun." Without warning, she stood and made a face, the white clay around her lips cracking even more. "You just don't want me to have any money. You don't want me to have anything."

With that, she turned and walked away. At the bottom of the steps, she paused, looked back at Grandma and me, blew out a puff of smoke, and, without another word, marched up the stairs. Her slippers made flopping noises and one of her curlers nearly fell out of her hair, but it was a regal exit.

Abrupt departures are common events when Mom gets this way. I looked at Grandma for an explanation.

She shrugged. "Until the other day, I didn't realize she'd stopped taking her medication. Oh, there were a few signs, but she's been so good about taking her pills that I didn't take those signs seriously. And the doctors keep saying it's best to let her take responsibility for her health. I didn't want to harp. But as soon as those envelopes arrived, I confronted her. Once she told me she'd stopped taking her pills, I called the doctor. Tuesday's the earliest I could get her in."

"Will you need help?"

"No," Grandma said. "You know your mother. She may say she's not going, but she will. She's not that hard to handle."

"I don't want to get like that, Grandma." The threat continually hung over me.

"I don't want you to get like that, either." She leaned close and patted my arm. "Sure, I know there's a chance, but you've made it this long. You'll be fine."

I didn't feel all that confident. "Don't forget, besides a schizoid mother, I had a grandfather who didn't know me by the time he died. What chance do I have?"

"Your grandfather may have had Alzheimer's, but he was seventy before he started showing signs of it."

"What about Dad?"

"What about your father?"

"I remember Grandpa Benson saying he was crazy."

Grandma nodded and lit a cigarette for herself. "There's crazy, honey, and then there's crazy. Right from the start, your Grandpa Benson thought your father was crazy for marrying your mother. And he thought your dad was crazy to re-enlist. He figured one stint in the Marines should be enough. But considering all that junk you showed me around your grandfather's place, I don't see where he got off criticizing his son. If we're talking about crazy, I think he was."

I wasn't surprised by her vitriolic accusation. Grandma Carter and Grandpa Benson never did get along. But she wasn't making me feel any better. I had enough crazy relatives without adding another to the list.

"I vaguely remembered my grandfather yelling at Dad before he went overseas, telling him he was crazy to go. And I remember Dad yelling back something like, 'Well then you pay the bills. You live with that woman.' "

Grandma nodded and flicked an ash off her cigarette. "That's probably what he said, all right. I think your dad was looking for a respite from your mother. Marriage hadn't quite turned out as he'd expected. Not that he didn't love you, but your mother simply wasn't the woman he'd married."

I suppose Grandma's right. The woman my father married was smart and witty according to stories I've heard. A champion for equal rights for women, minorities, and gays. "I still sometimes tell people that my father met my mother at a gay rights rally. That usually raises a few eyebrows."

"I'll bet." Grandma put out her cigarette, then took a sip of her coffee. Immediately, she made a face. "Cold."

The mug of cold coffee went back on the table, and Grandma Carter leaned back on the couch. "So what do they say when you tell them that story?"

"I usually don't give them a chance to say anything. Once the initial shock has occurred, I explained that my parents were both there to support research for AIDS and legal rights for same-sex couples, not because they were gay."

Grandma's smile returned. "Your grandfather and I probably shouldn't have taken your mother to those peace rallies when she was young."

I've seen photos taken of my grandmother and mother during the late sixties. Mom was around fourteen then; Grandma in her late thirties. The pictures showed the two of them marching with other long-haired "hippy"-type people. "You sowed the seeds," I said.

"In a flower garden." Grandma sighed. "I never thought people would transform Flora Gardenia into flower garden. Just like I never thought marrying a man fifteen years my senior would turn out as it did. Maybe I'm a little crazy, too."

"I don't think so, Grandma. You're the sanest person I know."

"That's not saying much around here, P.J. Some days, I . . ." Grandma didn't finish.

She closed her eyes, and I knew the tears were there. I

wondered how it would feel, to be a parent and watch your child change from a bright, beautiful woman to a shell of a person tormented by voices and visions. I'd read the books. Parents of children with mental diseases go through stages of anger, guilt, and depression. They need the same support as someone who's experienced the death of a child. Except, in some ways, it's worse. The child is always there.

For a moment, neither of us said anything, then Grandma gave my hand a squeeze. "I'm so glad you were born, P.J. I don't know what I would do if I didn't have you around. I couldn't talk to your dad. It bothered him, seeing how Flo was and not being able to do anything about it. He was a man of action, a man who had to be in control. He couldn't take it."

"And they say men are the stronger sex."

Grandma grinned. "We know better don't we? But that man did love you. It tore him apart to leave you. If he could have, he would have come back."

Twelve

Monday I woke with the crazy idea that life would get back to normal, I'd somehow get everyone's taxes filed before the fifteenth of April, and I could forget everything that had happened in the last three days. At ten o'clock a Jeep pulled into my yard, and I knew that wasn't going to happen.

Detective Kingsley was back, and he didn't have his son with him this time. The way he strode to my front door, I knew this wasn't a social call.

"What's up?" I asked, trying to keep my voice level and Baraka calmed down at the same time.

"May I come in?" Detective Kingsley asked, glancing down at Baraka, who wagged his tail and wiggled with enthusiasm.

I probably should have said no. Kingsley's tone had an edge that warned of trouble, and a guy I once dated said you never willingly invite the law into your home. But I'm the trusting sort, and I had nothing to hide. At least, I didn't think I did.

I held the door open, and Kingsley stepped inside, looking around before focusing his attention on me. No smile today. No flirting.

I closed the door behind him, then released my hold on Baraka, who began sniffing Kingsley's pant legs. "Coffee?" I asked, and pointed at the coffee maker on my buffet.

"No thank you." He ignored Baraka, pulled out his notebook and flipped it open. "I understand you called my number

Saturday night. That you had two of our men come out here again."

I didn't like the way he said that. He made it sound as if I'd wasted their time. "Saturday night, someone was in my house while I was at a card party."

"According to the report I read, there were no signs of forced entry and nothing was taken."

"My back door was left open and things were moved. I think the intruder was looking for something specific."

"Ladybugs?"

"Yes." To be honest, I was surprised the deputies had included that in their report. "A box of ladybugs."

"Ladybugs that came from your neighbor's house."

"Yes."

"That your neighbor denies ever existed."

"I don't care what John told those deputies. Friday night he was up here, worrying about some ladybugs he was experimenting on. He said they'd been stolen, along with a box. He figured they were taken by Punk McDaniels since Punk knew they were dangerous and might be valuable to terrorists."

"And when did you start finding these lethal ladybugs in your house?"

He was looking past me, and I knew there were ladybugs on my window. Probably some crawling on the walls and floor. Definitely some in my light fixtures. "I'm not talking about those ladybugs," I said. "I'm talking about—"

"Special ladybugs," he finished for me.

I ignored the sarcasm in his voice. If he needed it spelled out, I would spell it out. "Yes, special ladybugs. A type of ladybug that eats plants as well as aphids. Ladybugs that bite and cause infections."

A slight frown and a narrowing of those blue eyes of his indicated he didn't like my condescending attitude. And it didn't change his tone. "So if these aren't the ones"—he indicated the multitude on my windows—"where are you keeping these special ladybugs?"

"I'm not keeping them anywhere." As if I would want to. "But someone evidently thinks they're in my house. Probably the man who shot Punk."

"By Punk, you mean Mr. Carroll McDaniels?"

I said yes, and Kingsley gave me a long, piercing stare, then looked back at his notebook. "According to your report, your neighbor has been experimenting with these ladybugs in a lab he has in his pole barn. Is that right?"

"That's what he told me."

I repeated what Julia and John had said. When I finished, Kingsley closed his notebook and put it back in his pocket. "P.J., do you know how crazy that sounds?"

"I am not crazy." That he thought I was angered me. "Go down and look in John's pole barn. You'll see the lab. You'll see the security area."

Kingsley shook his head. "Sunday the deputies did go there. They found the lab all right and a container of ladybugs. Mr. Westman let them handle the ladybugs and assured them that he's never been involved in any secret experiments. The deputies also looked in a supply room the Westmans said Mr. McDaniels built for them. There was a lock on the door, but all they found inside were some engraving supplies. Nothing secretive."

"You're kidding." I stared at him, unable to fully comprehend what he'd said. "But John said . . . Julia said . . ."

My legs took that moment to turn to rubber. Since they weren't going to hold me up, I reached for the edge of the table. Kingsley must have realized I was about to collapse at his feet. He stepped forward, pulled a chair out, and helped me sit.

Then he walked over to the coffeepot and poured me a mug of coffee.

"I don't believe it." My thoughts were a confused jumble. "Friday night John and Julia came up here all worried about what would happen if the ladybugs got loose."

Kingsley handed me the mug of coffee. "They told Deputy O'Brien that one of your neighbors was complaining about ladybugs at the party you were at Saturday night and that you must have jumped to some crazy conclusions."

"Me?" I set the mug down. I didn't want coffee. I wanted the truth. "They're lying. They're the ones who told me John was working with dangerous ladybugs."

Kingsley pulled out a chair and sat in front of me. "There are no predatory ladybugs, P.J."

"Because they were stolen," I insisted.

Kingsley sighed. "P.J., have you seen a doctor lately?"

"I am not crazy." I closed my eyes and took in a deep breath. Declaring my sanity wouldn't help. I knew that from being around my mother. She could say what she wanted. We knew better.

Or did we?

Kingsley gave me a second to recover, then went on. "You're sure you closed your back door before you went out Saturday night?"

I opened my eyes. "Yes, I'm sure. Closed it and locked it."

"The deputies said there were no signs of forced entry."

"Maybe not, but I also turned a light on before I left, and it was off when I got home. Someone turned it off."

"Still you went into the house."

"Because I didn't realize the light was off. I rode with John and Julia. When they dropped me off, John's truck lights were shining into the house. It wasn't until after they left that I remembered I'd left the light on and it wasn't."

Kingsley looked down at Baraka, who had stretched out on the floor. "Was he loose at the time?"

"No. I'd put him in his crate."

"Do you always put him in his crate when you leave?"

"Yes. Dogs like crates. A crate is like a den for the dog. And it's safer than letting him run free. No chewed slippers. No accidents. It also prepares them for when they're at dog shows."

"Too bad he can't talk."

I agreed. "If he could, he'd tell you I'm not crazy, that someone was in my house, both Friday and Saturday nights."

Kingsley nodded and reached down to scratch Baraka behind his ears. "I want you to see this from our point of view, P.J. You've got some expensive machinery here. A fancy computer. A fax machine. TV and VCR/DVD in the other room. You've even said your dog's quite valuable. In the case of a robbery, these are the things that are taken."

I was willing to see things from his point of view if he'd see them from mine. "If this was simply a case of robbery, I'd agree with you. But I don't think it is. I think this guy, whoever he is, is looking for those ladybugs."

"That your neighbor says don't exist."

I wanted to scream that they did exist. Instead, I tried another approach. "At the party Saturday night, one of the other guests said he saw Punk at the bar in Zenith last week. He said Punk was acting scared, that Punk said something about saying too much, making a big mistake."

"So you think Punk told someone about deadly ladybugs and this person killed him?"

"It's a possibility." As good as I could come up with at the moment.

"Okay. Let's assume you're right and this unknown person is looking for ladybugs. You believe he's come into your house twice. Has he contacted you? In person, by phone or mail?"

"No."

"Doesn't that seem strange? Wouldn't you expect him to?"

"I suppose." I could see what he was getting at, but it didn't matter. "Is it my fault he hasn't?"

"I suppose not. But you would let me know if he did contact you, wouldn't you?"

"Of course."

Kingsley nodded and stood. "Good. Now, what was the name of the person who talked to McDaniels last week?"

I tried to remember. Names have never been my strong point. Faces, yes, but not names. "Ray," I said and rose to my feet. "Ray . . . Ray . . . ?" It was on the tip of my tongue. Mentally I began going through the alphabet. And then it came. "Ray Mason."

Kingsley pulled out his notebook again. "Ray Mason," he said and wrote down the name. "Do you have an address for him? Phone number?"

I stepped over to my phone book and turned to the M section of the residential listings. In a second I had both an address and phone number. That's one more advantage of living in a small community. Not that many people, and even if you can't find the person you're looking for, you probably know someone who does and can give you all the information you need.

Kingsley added Ray's address and phone number to his notebook, and then he was gone. I stood at the door and watched his Jeep pull out of my yard. For a minute I simply followed its progress down the road, not really seeing anything—no vehicle, no trees, no clouds in the sky or birds. My mind was on John and Julia. Either they'd lied to Detective Kingsley or to me.

I went to my phone and punched in John and Julia's number. By the time their answering machine clicked on, my anger had reached a peak. I couldn't say what I wanted to say. Couldn't find the words. All I managed was "Damn you!"

That said, I slammed down the phone and picked up the phone book. I knew there was no sense in trying to call John at B.C. BioTech. The company does not allow direct calls to employees. Their policy is to take a message and have the employee return the call. I wasn't about to give a secretary the message I wanted delivered. So I called the bank.

As luck would have it, Julia answered the phone. "Why?" I asked, not even identifying myself. "Why did you tell those deputies I was crazy? How can you and John not tell them about those ladybugs?"

"P.J.?" Julia's response was cautious. "Are you all right?"

"No, I'm not all right. Detective Kingsley just left my house. You not only denied the existence of those ladybugs, you made it sound like I'm off my rocker. Here I thought you were my friend, instead you . . . you . . ."

"I'm sorry, I can't help you right now," Julia said in her most professional voice. "I'll have to talk to you later."

"Fine." I'd gotten my message across. There was nothing more to say.

I slammed down the phone, and sank into the nearest chair. Baraka came over and laid his head on my knees, his liquid brown eyes full of sympathy.

"I am *not* crazy," I told him.

He licked my hand.

THIRTEEN

After I'd recovered from Detective Kingsley's visit, I started calling locksmiths. I finally found one who would come to my house, redo my locks, and put on deadbolts. Problem was, he couldn't do it until Wednesday.

Since I had no choice, I told him Wednesday would be fine. That taken care of, I sat down at the computer, ready to get back to work. And that's when my computer decided to go bonkers.

I first noticed trouble when I went to print out a form. The tax program closed. A box with the message "Illegal operation" came up on my screen and that was it. I had to start over.

The second time it happened, I decided to go on the Internet and contact the program manufacturer. Five times I tried making a connection. Five times I received the same message. My modem was not connecting. Finally, I gave up.

I cursed and telephoned the computer company, punched number after number in response to the prerecorded message and after listening to movie themes regularly interrupted by a soothing male voice telling me that my call was important and they would be with me as soon as possible, I discovered one more road block. The company had no record of my purchase. "Sorry," Customer Representative Clare said, but she couldn't help me.

I wanted to scream that she'd better help me or my business was going down the tubes. Instead, I decided to take a break.

Maybe if I ignored the problem, it would go away.

I was on my front lawn, playing tug-of-war with Baraka, an old wool sock of Grandpa Benson's acting as our rope, when I saw Howard Lowe's blue Ford coming down the road heading for his place. Instead of driving by, he pulled over to my side of the road and lowered his window.

Baraka went bounding up the grassy bank toward the car, immediately jumping up and putting his front paws on Lowe's car door. Lowe cuffed him, and Baraka gave a yelp and backed off. "Don't hit my dog," I yelled, and hurried up the bank to grab Baraka by the scuff of his neck.

"Then keep him off my car." Lowe leaned out, looking at his door as if my dog's nails could do more damage to the already scratched and battered car.

"What do you want?" I asked, too irritated to care if Baraka had done any damage.

"You ready to move back to the city yet?"

"No."

"Heard your house keeps gettin' broken into."

"Did you happen to hear who's been doing the breaking in?"

He gave me a steady look. "Weren't me."

"I didn't say it was." Though I will admit, I'd wondered.

"Been in that house once, and only once. Back when your grandfather was alive."

I moved closer to the car, holding onto Baraka so he couldn't jump up on the side again. I could see empty Styrofoam coffee cups littering the floor on the passenger's side, and an array of tools, clothes, and old newspapers on the back seat. Poking out from under a heavy, tan jacket was an open box of shotgun shells.

"Seen enough?" Lowe growled, snapping my attention back to his face.

I hoped he'd think the flush now warming my skin was caused

by the cool weather and not embarrassment. "You didn't answer my question," I said. "Do you have any idea who's been getting into my house?"

"Maybe. Maybe not." He smiled, showing a chipped front tooth and lots of dental work. "How does it feel to have a crazy mother?"

"My mother has nothing to do with this." That much I knew for sure.

"She drove your father underground."

Nice way of putting things. The man had no tact. And he was avoiding my question. "So you have no idea what's going on?"

"Might. Might not. You ever heard of the crows?"

"The singing group?"

"Not no singers. One of them acronyms." Lowe looked at the trees across the road, and pointed at the largest maple. "See them crows?"

I checked out the maple and saw three crows on one branch. Not an unusual sight. We have a lot of crows in lower Michigan. Had even more before the West Nile virus hit the area.

"Yeah, I see them," I said, not sure what he was trying to tell me.

"You know what a flock of crows is called?" Lowe answered before I had a chance. "A murder. That's what they're called."

I looked back at him. One murder was enough. I didn't need a flock.

"Carl Dremmer . . . You know Carl?" he asked, and I nodded. "He likes to write poetry. He told me that."

Lowe spit out the window, the liquid from his mouth flying past me and landing on my lawn. I jerked back, but if he noticed my distress, he didn't show it. He simply went on speaking.

"I guess the word fits. Some people see crows as murderers. Me, I see them as beneficial. Crows clean up the environment, get rid of waste. They'll warn you of danger."

I remembered how the crows started cawing right before the shooting Friday. Nevertheless, I didn't understand what Lowe was trying to say. "So?"

"If you hear from the crows, listen. Don't be like your grandfather." Lowe shook his head. "He was an ornery cuss."

I wouldn't disagree with him about that. Not that Lowe gave me a chance to. Without another word, he raised his window and drove away, leaving me there by the edge of the road.

I released my hold on Baraka. He sniffed the spot where Lowe had spit, then trotted back down the bank toward the house. Before I followed him, I looked back at the maple tree, its new leaves barely visible. The three crows were still watching me. "So say something," I yelled.

They flew away.

Back in the house, I tried printing a form again and got the same message. My break hadn't helped. So I started calling numbers listed in the telephone book for computer repair. It took three tries before I connected with a living, breathing person named Ken, who sounded as if he had peach fuzz on his chin. He listened carefully as I explained my problem. To my relief, he said he thought he could help me. Not only that, he could do so over the telephone.

For the next half hour, Ken talked me through a series of changes in my computer set-up. When we were finished, the tax program worked. From initial opening to the final printing of the forms, everything functioned beautifully. My Internet server, however, was another matter.

Ken worked on that for another half hour, then called my Internet provider. In one way, his message was helpful. In another way, it wasn't. "Problem's on their end," he said. "They're overhauling their system. Improving it. Be a day or two before everything's up and working. You got one of those free AOL discs? You could load that and get onto the Internet that way."

Changing providers would mean changing my system again. Since Ken had helped me get my tax program working, I could wait. "How much do I owe you?" I asked.

"Nothing," he said. "Always willing to help a damsel in distress."

"You're not going to make much money that way." I figured I'd taken up at least an hour of his time.

"So maybe we could meet for a beer some time."

Ha. The guy was coming on to me.

I told him I was much too busy and would be until after tax time, but to give me a call after that. Who knows. He might be older than he sounded. Might actually be someone fun to go out with.

With the tax program working, I zipped through two more clients' forms, inputting numbers on the correct lines and allowing the computer to do the necessary calculations. I might cuss my computer on a regular basis, but I'll take it over paper and pencil any day. And e-filing is easy as pie . . . at least it is when your Internet provider is working.

I'd just finished one tax form when an old, green Chevy coupe pulled into my yard. I went to my front door. I'd seen the car in town, but I didn't realize it belonged to Nora Wright until she got out. The way she'd acted Saturday night, I certainly didn't expect her to stop by and pay a visit. I watched from inside the house, and rather than coming toward me, she reached into the back seat.

Nora might have been a trim, good-looking woman in her prime, but she'd let the pounds slip on and her rear view wasn't the most flattering. When she straightened, she was holding a blue and white ceramic pot. She used a hip to push the car door shut, then started for my front door.

I figured if she had her hands occupied carrying a ceramic

pot, she wasn't here to start a fight, so I pulled the door open and stepped out on my porch. Baraka came bounding out with me and ran straight for Nora. I yelled at him, praying he wouldn't jump on her and knock her down. To my relief, he simply sniffed her pant legs . . . then stretched his neck toward the ceramic pot, his tail wagging with excitement. He practically turned himself inside out trying to get her attention, but Nora didn't even acknowledge Baraka's presence with a glance. The entire distance from her car to my porch, her gaze stayed on me. I wouldn't call it a friendly look.

"Brought you something." she said, coming up the steps. "You can call it humble pie. I've come to eat crow."

I looked into the pot. I'll admit, I half expected to see a crow's head. Instead, I saw chunks of meat, carrots, and potatoes.

"It's a stew. Beef stew," Nora said. "Rose made it. She makes great stews, and we got talking about how I acted Saturday night." Nora stared down at the pot of stew. "Rose said I owed you an apology and that you might appreciate having someone bring you dinner since you're so busy right now with taxes and all."

"I do appreciate this." If Rose's stew was as good as her cooking Saturday night, it would be delicious. And since I hadn't even thought about dinner and didn't have anything out of the freezer—or even in the refrigerator—an already prepared meal was a Godsend.

Nora held out the ceramic pot. "So enjoy."

It sounded like an order, and I didn't feel I'd received a humble apology, but I decided I'd take what Nora was offering. I thanked her, adding that I really enjoyed playing cards at her house Saturday night. Nora grunted a response, then stepped back. "We tried to buy this place, you know," she said, looking at the side of the house. "Offered your grandfather a decent price, I think, considering how old and run down the house is and all the junk lying around. Old goat wouldn't sell to us, but he said he'd put a clause in his will so I'd get the woods after he died."

"The lawyer never said anything about a clause." But it did help explain some of Nora's animosity.

"I know. I checked." She looked back at me, her eyes narrowed with hatred. "He lied. Pulled a good one. Gotta say, I never thought he'd give the place to you. He always said his daughter-in-law was loony tunes, and he figured you were too. Said anyone who became an accountant must be crazy."

"This time of the year, I agree with him."

"So what about the woods?"

I knew what she meant, but feigned ignorance. "What about them?"

"You interested in selling?"

"No." I didn't see any reason to beat around the bush. Those woods might be a mess right now with all the junk my grandfather dumped back there, but I've been told they hold some valuable timber, and I like being able to step out my back door and take a walk in the woods. Once I get the junk out, I'm going to develop some well-defined walking trails. Make the area a wildlife sanctuary.

Nora said nothing for a moment, then shrugged. "Maybe you're more like your grandfather than he realized."

That said, she turned and walked down the steps and back to her car. Less than five minutes after she arrived, she was gone. I took the stew into the house, put it into the oven, and turned the temperature on to warm. Later, I would kick up the heat so it would be nice and hot for dinner.

I didn't think about eating until almost eight o'clock. I get that way when I'm working with numbers. Most people dread doing their taxes. For me, any form of accounting is like a puzzle. A mystery to be unraveled. I'm probably the only one who jumps up and down with joy when I get packages from the IRS.

Which maybe proves I'm a little crazy.

When my stomach started growling, I remembered the stew. I'd kept the pot in the oven for so long, the meat and vegetables near the surface were dried out and much of the liquid had evaporated. I skimmed some of the surface goodies into a pan for Baraka, did a quick zap in the microwave on a bowl for myself, then buttered a slice of bread and poured myself a glass of milk. I placed my dinner at one end of the table—the only space not covered with tax papers—and sat down to relax and enjoy my meal.

Except, to my surprise, I didn't like it. I can't say exactly what was wrong with the stew. It looked good and smelled great. It just didn't taste right. Maybe it was from leaving it in the oven for so long and evaporating out most of the liquid. Whatever, it had a bitter flavor. I managed to consume about a third of the bowl and gave up.

Baraka, however, didn't show any hesitation in gobbling up the portion I'd dished out for him, and I considered letting him have the rest of mine, then decided against the idea. His breeder had warned me not to feed table scraps. She said a dog doesn't get a well-balanced diet when you feed from the table.

I scraped the leftovers into the wastebasket under my sink. In the morning I'd empty it into the garbage can out back. I then washed my bowl and the blue and white ceramic pot and put them on the counter to dry before going back to work on the tax forms.

I couldn't have spent more than a half hour on the forms when I suddenly realized I could barely keep my eyes open. And Baraka wasn't doing much better. Sprawled out next to my chair, he was snoring away, giving a whimper every so often and moving his legs, as if chasing after something.

I leaned down and patted his side, and he managed to open one eye for a moment before dozing off again. I chuckled and decided he had the right idea. When tired, one should sleep. Even though it was just after nine o'clock, I decided to head for bed. Obviously, the excitement of the weekend had caught up with me.

Crows lined a tree branch, a mass of black silhouettes against a blue sky. As one they cawed their warning, the sound grating on my nerves. I wanted to escape the cry, but my body refused to move.

Again came the sound, loud and piercing.

"Listen to the crows," a voice murmured deep inside my conscious. "Listen to the crows."

I didn't want to listen to them. I wanted them to go away, to stop their incessant noise.

They cried out again, only this time I realized it wasn't crows. It wasn't birds of any kind. Slowly my mind struggled to separate dream from reality. I was in bed. Asleep. Except, I wasn't asleep now. Something had awakened me.

The telephone.

Again, it rang, and I managed to sit up, my head fuzzy.

Several seconds went by. Nothing. No phone ringing. No crows cawing. I was about to lie back, when it started again.

I stumbled out of bed, through the laundry room and bathroom to the dining room. Blurry eyed, I found the phone on the table. I picked it up just as it finished ringing.

"Yeah," I said, dopey with sleep.

"What took you so long?" the voice on the other end asked.

"I was asleep." And I wanted to go back to sleep.

"Look, Princess, I didn't want to involve you, but I need your help."

I leaned against the wall, then sank to a sitting position. My muscles had no strength and my mind was in a turmoil. "Who is this?"

"Someone you haven't heard from for a long, long time."

"Dad?" My father always called me Princess, and the voice did sound like his. At least, the caller sounded the way I remember my father sounding.

"Before he died, did he say anything? Did McDaniels tell you anything?"

"No. Nothing." My eyes wouldn't focus and my head kept spinning. "Dad, is this really you?"

"Are you crazy, Princess? Dead people don't come back to life."

Maybe so, but the caller sure sounded like my father. "Mom says they do. She says she's talked to you."

"Your mother is crazy." Again, that deep chuckle. "You sure you don't know where that box is?"

"Don't open the box if you find it," I said, remembering Julia's orders.

"Right," the voice said.

The laugh was all I remember.

FOURTEEN

"The crows woke me," I said, then realized that wasn't right. "I mean the phone . . . the telephone." A stupefying fog still enveloped my mind, and I knew I wasn't making any sense.

I was sitting on an examination table in the emergency room, still in my nightgown, though someone had thought to put shoes on my feet and my jacket over my shoulders. Detective Kingsley stood nearby. He'd arrived soon after the ambulance brought me to the hospital, but had waited to question me until the doctor finished his examination.

Doctor Mayer now stood in a corner of the room, making notes on a sheet of paper. By his side, his nurse labeled the blood samples she'd taken from my arm. The doctor had grilled me as he took my blood pressure and temperature and checked my heart. He'd wanted to know what medicine I'd taken, over the counter or prescribed. I'd told him I hadn't taken anything.

Kingsley wanted to know what had happened.

"The phone woke you," he repeated. "Then what?"

"I answered it." I remembered that much.

"Then what?"

"A man said he needed my help."

"Do you know who this man was?"

"It was . . ." I couldn't tell him it sounded like my father. My father was dead. I knew that. Kingsley knew that. If I said the man was my father, Kingsley would be sure I was crazy.

Still, in addition to the voice sounding like my father's, the man had called me P.J. Called me Princess.

"Who was it?" Kingsley prodded.

"I don't know." That was the truth. "But he wants the box." I was sure about that. "He asked me if I knew where it was, if McDaniels had told me anything."

"And what did you say?"

Kingsley had his pen poised, ready to write my response in his notebook. I wondered how many notebooks he went through in a year. I bet plenty. The man was so serious. "You know, you need to smile more," I said. "You're really cute when you smile. Makes you look sexy."

He frowned. "P.J., what did you say?"

"I said that you're cute." I laughed and looked away, biting my lower lip. I could feel my cheeks getting warm.

My God, I was flirting with the man. Whatever was wrong with me had loosened my tongue. I had no idea why I'd said that. I mean, it was true, but I don't usually go around telling homicide detectives that they turn me on.

He cleared his throat and repeated his question. "What did you tell the caller?"

"The caller . . . . The caller." I tried to focus on his question.

"Yes, the caller." Kingsley sounded irritated.

"I'm trying." I forced my thoughts back to the phone call. "I don't think I told him anything. I mean, what could I tell him? I don't know anything. Before McDaniels died, all he did was swear. He didn't tell me any great secret."

"Okay, did your caller say anything else?"

"He said my mother was crazy. And he laughed at me." I must have passed out while he was laughing. "I'm pretty sure he's the one who's been breaking into my house."

"Did he say that?"

"No. But I got the feeling he's been looking for them and hasn't found them."

" 'Them' being the ladybugs you say were stolen?"

"Yes. And I don't think the crows found them, either."

"The crows?" Kingsley's frown was becoming perpetual.

"The ones flying around my dining room. First there was one. Then another. Except . . ." I knew I did sound crazy. It was so confusing. I closed my eyes. Last night something black—shadowy—was moving around in my house. Crows? People? A dream?

I looked at Kingsley again. "Crows wouldn't be in my house, would they?"

"It's doubtful, and the paramedics didn't report seeing anything out of the usual when they found you on the floor."

I looked over at the doctor. "Why do I feel so lightheaded? So confused and groggy? Why can't I wake up?"

The doctor came back to stand by my side. "You're sure you didn't take a sleeping pill last night? Maybe two or three?"

"Positive. I've been trying to stay awake late so I can get more work done, not go to sleep early."

"How about a cold capsule?" The doctor again took my pulse.

"I don't even have a cold pill in the house."

"Doral. Halcion. Something like that?" Using a light, he looked into my eyes.

I squinted at the brightness. "No. I keep telling you, I didn't take anything, not even an aspirin."

Kingsley spoke up, looking at the doctor, not me. "According to the firemen who responded to her call, her house was checked for carbon monoxide. None was detected."

"That's good." The doctor snapped off the light and stepped back. "Hopefully, the blood sample will tell us something. Otherwise, her vitals are good. And, as far as those birds, hallucinations are a common side effect of sleeping pills. So is confusion, a feeling of lightheadedness, and expressing a more aggressive, outgoing behavior. If she took an overdose of sleeping pills, she didn't get enough to seriously harm her, but she could be experiencing all of those symptoms."

"I didn't take any sleeping pills. Not one, not an overdose." I hate being talked about as if I'm not there.

Kingsley kept looking at the doctor. "What about the phone call. Could it be a hallucination?"

"It was not a hallucination. I received that phone call," I said firmly. I knew that for sure.

He looked back at me. "When? At what time?"

"Sometime after I went to bed."

"Which was—?"

"Nine o'clock or so."

"Nine o'clock or so. Not very specific. How long were you asleep before you got the call?"

"I don't know." His attitude irritated me. "I don't remember looking at a clock. I barely remember stumbling into the dining room to answer the phone."

"All right then, how long between when you received the call and when you called nine-one-one?"

"I . . . I don't know. I don't even remember calling nine-one-one."

"Dispatch says the call originated from your house. You didn't say anything, but you groaned, so they sent someone out."

"Then I guess I made the call."

"What exactly do you remember?" Kingsley asked.

"That the caller sounded like. . . ." I couldn't say it.

"Sounded like who?"

Okay, he asked. "Like my father."

Kingsley looked at the doctor. "Her mother's schizophrenic. Do you think . . . ?"

"I am not crazy," I snapped before the doctor had a chance to respond. "I said the caller sounded like my father. I didn't say it was my father. I realize it couldn't have been my father."

Kingsley rubbed the back of his neck, took in a deep breath, and changed his tone. "Okay, tell me this. Do you ever feed your dog pills?"

His question about Baraka confused me. "No. I mean, he will get heartworm pills, but I haven't started them, yet."

"Are you aware that your dog barely raised his head when the paramedics arrived?"

"Baraka?" No, I hadn't been aware of that. When the paramedics pounded on my door, I was barely able to let them in. I couldn't form a coherent sentence. Couldn't concentrate. Couldn't function. Even now, I barely remembered the ride in the back of the ambulance. "Is he all right?"

"Seems to be. I talked to the deputy we left at your place. He said your dog's still snoring away."

"But that's not normal for him. No more than me being unable to keep my eyes open. Yesterday afternoon Baraka was full of energy, and I felt so good I worked right through dinner. It was eight o'clock before I even thought about eating."

The doctor stopped writing and Kingsley raised his eyebrows. "What did you eat?" they both asked.

What did I eat? It took me a minute to remember, then I swore. "Damn her."

"Damn who?" Kingsley asked.

"Nora." I felt as if I'd been slapped up beside the head. "She brought me a pot of stew yesterday. She said it was an apology, that she was eating crow."

"That might explain your preoccupation with the crow image," the doctor said.

"Nora?" Kingsley repeated.

"Nora Wright. My neighbor. She's the one who lives with Rose. Their place is on the street north of mine . . . almost directly north of mine."

"And why would this Nora need to eat crow?"

"Because that card party I was at Saturday night was at their place, and after we stopped playing, Nora accused me of flirting with Rose and got all upset."

"Flirting?" Again, the two men spoke in unison.

"They're lesbians."

Kingsley's eyebrows rose. "And were you flirting?"

"No." It upset me that he had to ask. "At least, not with Rose. I did try flirting with Carl. Mostly to let Nora know I preferred men to women."

"So you think this Nora was so upset that she put something in the stew to make you sleepy?" Kingsley looked doubtful.

"Maybe." The timing was right. "When I took a break at eight, I decided to have some. Except, it didn't taste good, so I didn't finish it."

"And your dog ate some, too?" the doctor asked.

I nodded.

Kingsley was writing in his notebook. "What did you do with the rest of this stew, the portion you didn't eat?"

"I scraped it into the wastebasket under my sink."

He looked at the doctor. "I'll have one of my men get it. Our labs can test for drugs."

I watched Kingsley leave the room, then began questioning the doctor about the types of drugs that would make me so sleepy. He went into detail about hypnotics, listing several. I think he still thought I'd taken one or more to get to sleep.

For me, simply knowing why I felt so rummy improved my outlook. I wasn't crazy. I'd been drugged. That's why I'd had those weird dreams. There were no black forms flitting around my house. No crows. And the voice on the phone had merely sounded like my father's.

The moment Kingsley returned, my euphoria disappeared. His frown said everything. "The wastebasket under your sink is empty."

"It can't be." But then I realized it could be, that someone could have emptied it. "What about a blue and white ceramic pot? That's what Nora brought the stew in. It should be on the counter by the sink. And a bowl should be there, too. I washed them, but maybe I didn't get them completely clean. I've been known to miss spots."

He shook his head. "When I called, I asked the deputy about cooking pans and bowls. He said he didn't see anything."

"But the pot . . . ? It was right by the sink. I know it was. A blue and white one. Upside down. Draining." I started to slide off the table. "Take me home. I'll show you."

The doctor stopped me from getting down, and Kingsley's head shake said I wasn't going anywhere. I closed my eyes again. Maybe I *was* going crazy. "They were there last night," I said, barely above a whisper. "Both the ceramic pot and my bowl. I know they were."

I didn't get back to my house until after one in the afternoon. Kingsley drove me there. We didn't say much during the ride, but I could feel his disappointment. Baraka greeted me with a wag of his tail, but he lacked his usual energy and enthusiasm.

The deputy who'd stayed at the house while I was at the hospital informed Detective Kingsley that the phone had rung twice, both calls from people who identified themselves as clients of mine, that he'd taken the dog out twice, and that everything seemed normal. Kingsley looked around my kitchen himself, with me at his elbow, but there was nothing to corroborate my story. No ceramic pot. No bowl. And just an empty wastebasket.

He then told me to make an appointment with a doctor.

I knew what kind of doctor he meant.

Both men left a few minutes later, and the moment the two cars drove out of my yard, I went into my bedroom, stripped off my nightgown, and put on some clean underwear, my blue jeans, an old Western Michigan University sweatshirt, and my boots. Anger helped wipe away my exhaustion. I grabbed my keys, Baraka went into his crate, I locked up the house, and I got into my car.

The drive to the opposite side of the section took only a minute. I passed John and Julia's house, surprised to see a black truck parked back by their pole barn. Then I remembered it was Tuesday, and Julia had the day off. She'd probably hired someone to repair the damage done to the pole barn last Friday. Maybe Detective Kingsley didn't believe ladybugs had been destroyed in that barn, but I did.

At Nora and Rose's place, no vehicles were visible, still I pulled into the yard and went straight to the front door. Rose answered my knock. She was wearing a dress, heels, and makeup and looked the image of a fifties-era housewife. She also looked disturbed. "P.J.," she said. "What are you doing here?"

"Where's Nora?" I demanded.

"She's not here. Are you all right? You look pale."

"That's probably because Nora tried to kill me last night." The evidence might be gone, but I knew the truth.

"Kill you?" Rose's delicate features contorted into a frown. "What are you talking about?"

"I'm talking about that stew you made. Nora brought some over yesterday. She said you'd told her to apologize for Saturday night. But that's not why she brought it. She put something in that stew. Sleeping pills or something."

"I didn't make any stew," Rose said. "I haven't made any stew for a week or more. And I wasn't here yesterday. Sunday, I went to Lansing to visit my mother. I spent two nights there and didn't get back here until an hour ago."

"But Nora said . . ." I didn't finish. It didn't matter what Nora said. In fact, it made more sense if Rose didn't make the stew. It might explain the bad taste.

"Do you have a blue and white ceramic cooking pot?" I asked. "About so big." I used my hands to give an indication of the pot's size.

"Yes." Rose glanced toward her kitchen.

"Could I see it?" I didn't know how that would help, but I needed confirmation that the pot did exist.

"I suppose."

Rose didn't invite me in, but closed the door and left me standing on the porch while she went into her kitchen. I thought that unusual, but decided she might be worried about Nora coming home and finding us together. The way Nora flared up Saturday night, I could understand Rose's caution.

I flexed my shoulders to ease some of the tension and glanced through the window nearest the door. I could see just a portion of the living room and suddenly I understood why Rose hadn't invited me in. It wasn't because of Nora. Caution be damned. Rose had company.

I could see the back of an upholstered chair, the back of someone's head, a bit of that person's right shoulder and arm, and a portion of a right leg. My guess was male. Not that I was certain, but the shape of the head, the cropped haircut, and the clothing looked masculine. He, if it was a he, was dressed in black.

I kept watching, hoping he would move so I could see his face. He didn't, and moments later, Rose returned to the front door, holding the ceramic pot I'd washed just the night before.

She held it up, and I studied it. It had to be the same pot.

It had to be.

"She tried to kill me," I said, then wished I hadn't. Rose's expression stated her thoughts loud and clear.

"I'm not crazy," I argued. "She brought me stew yesterday afternoon. In that pot." I pointed at the one in her hands. "I ate some and gave some to my dog. It put us to sleep. She must have come and gotten the pot back while I was asleep. And she emptied my wastebasket. She didn't want any evidence left."

The more I said, the more Rose's expression relayed her doubts of my sanity. "P.J.," she said. "I'm, ah . . . I've, ah . . ." She stepped back, holding the pot like a wedge between us. "I need to get back to work."

She started to close the door, but I stopped her. "Who's with you? Who's in the living room?"

Rose glanced that way, then back at me, panic in her gaze. "No one. There's no one here but me."

"I can see—" I moved to the side, so I could see through the window. The chair was still there, but no one was seated in it. "He was—"

Rose shut the door, and I was left on the porch. Alone. I gave one more glance into Rose's living room, saw the chair was still empty and gave up. It was time to go home.

FIFTEEN

I returned to my place more confused than before, automatically let Baraka out of his crate, and went outside with him. As he investigated the yard, I sat on the porch steps, a slew of unanswered questions plaguing my mind.

I could remember Nora's arrival yesterday, what she said and the ceramic pot. I'd held that pot in my hands, dished stew out of it, and washed it. All of that was clear. It was after I went to bed that everything became a blur.

I was sifting through my memories when Baraka came around the corner carrying something in his mouth. He plopped down on the lawn, put a paw on the object, and began tearing at it. "Now what do you have?" I grumbled and reluctantly got up to check.

As I neared him, I could see it was a sheet of newspaper. That Baraka didn't try to stop me from taking the shredded strips told me he was suffering as much from the aftereffects of whatever Nora put in that stew as I was. He didn't even object when I wadded up the dog-slimed mess and headed for the garbage can at the back of the house.

I wasn't sure where he'd gotten the paper until I rounded the corner. The door to the chicken coop was open.

It had been closed when I took Baraka out Monday morning. Which meant someone had opened it between that time and now. But who? The sheriff's deputy who'd stayed with Baraka while I was in the emergency room? Or my late-night caller?

I decided it was time for me to personally investigate the chicken coop, and, although there was no light bulb in the socket, plenty of daylight came through the broken window and open door. I used my body to block Baraka's access to the coop and looked around.

The first thing I noticed was the smell of dust and mold. Not exactly good stuff to breathe in. Holding my breath, I glanced at the wall across from me.

Square boxes, three levels high and eight across, covered the wall. When chickens inhabited the coop, these were their nesting boxes. I'd helped Grandma Benson gather eggs from there when I was very little.

I couldn't remember when Grandma stopped raising chickens and the coop became one more storage area for my grandfather. Now the nests, along with the cardboard and wooden boxes he'd piled on every inch of the cement floor, were filled with old magazines, newspapers, and empty bottles. A vast network of cobwebs hung from the ceiling, and a fine veil of dust covered everything.

I could see water stains on several of the boxes near the broken window, and some of the boxes on the floor had been tipped over. I figured Baraka—along with opossums and raccoons—had been in here more than once.

There was no easy access to the area near the broken window, but if I was going to see what lay beneath the window, I was going to have to make my way over to that spot. Cautiously, I stepped onto the nearest stack of magazines. They didn't fall, but Baraka now had space to scramble past me. The moment he did, magazines and newspapers went everywhere, along with a box of Mason jars. One jar hit an open patch of cement and shattered. I grabbed Baraka and pulled him back. I did not need him cutting a paw.

Keeping a tight hold on my dog, I backed out of the coop

and closed the door. Only when I heard the door click shut did I release Baraka and go around to the side of the coop to look through the broken window.

This time I watched where I put my hands . . . and my head. The height of the window, along with the shards of glass still clinging to the frame, made maneuvering to see inside difficult, but I checked out as much as I could. If Punk tossed a box in there, it was out of my viewing area. The only way I would know for certain was to clean out the entire chicken coop.

I was trying to decide if that's what I should do when I spotted Julia's car coming down the road. Since I didn't want to talk to her, not after the lies she'd told those sheriff's deputies, I started for my front door.

Julia pulled into my yard before I made it inside, and Baraka headed for her car. I yelled at him, but he ignored me and greeted Julia like a long-lost friend.

"I know you're mad at me," she said, sliding out of her car and letting Baraka sniff her hand. "And I don't blame you. But you've got to understand, we had to lie. John could get in big trouble if word got out about those ladybugs. What else could we do?"

"You could have told the truth." But I could understand her predicament. She was a wife protecting her husband. I would probably do the same thing in her position. I know I've lied to protect my mother.

As much as I wanted to stay angry with Julia, I couldn't. I waited for her to reach the porch.

She stopped at the bottom step. "Will you ever forgive me?"

Forgive, yes. Let her off the hook, no. "The Kalamazoo Sheriff's Department thinks I'm crazy. Someone is breaking into my house, and no one believes me. Nora tried to poison me or something, and—"

"Oh my gosh. Nora?" Julia came up the steps and put a hand

on my arm. "Are you all right? I knew she was jealous of you, but to actually try to harm you. What did she do?"

We went inside, took off our jackets, and I washed my hands. As I made a fresh pot of coffee, I explained all that had happened. Julia listened without interrupting until I told her about the telephone call.

"He asked you where the box was?" Julia clapped her hands together. "Glory be. That means he doesn't have it, that it's still somewhere around here."

Her delight didn't excite me. "Maybe," I said as I took my mug of coffee into the living room.

She hung back. "What do you mean, 'maybe'?"

"I just found the door to the chicken coop open."

Julia still looked confused, but she also came into the living room. "So?"

I sank down on the couch cushion with the stain. "So either the sheriff's deputy who was here this morning opened it or whoever called me last night was in there. And if it was my caller, maybe he found the box."

"Damn." Julia looked as crestfallen as she'd looked delighted moments before. "So how do we find out?"

"I don't know. There's so much junk in there, even if Punk did throw the box through the broken window, I'm not sure anyone could find it."

"So we clean out the chicken coop."

Julia stood, as if the decision had been made. I glanced toward my dining room table. "I need to get those taxes done."

"P.J., finding this box is more important." She put up a hand before I could argue. "Look, I know this mess has put you behind schedule, but once we find the box, there won't be any more interruptions."

I sure hoped not. "This is going to take all day, you know."

"I know." Julia grabbed her jacket. "Do you have any face

masks? Gloves?"

"No. And if my grandfather did, I don't know where he kept them."

"No problem. We have masks, gloves, and garbage bags. Come on, we can drive over to my place and pick up what we need."

The moment Julia said "Come on," Baraka was at the door, ready to go, tail wagging in anticipation. I knew I couldn't let him down. "Baraka and I'll walk over and meet you there."

She looked at Baraka, then shrugged and smiled. "What the heck. I can use the exercise. Let's all walk."

We were almost through the woods when I asked Julia, "Who was working in your barn earlier today?"

Julia stopped walking and looked at me. "What do you mean, 'working in' our barn? Who was working in our barn?"

"I don't know. When I drove over to see Nora, I saw a truck back by your pole barn. I just assumed—"

"Oh my gosh."

Before I finished, Julia started running toward her pole barn. I hurried to follow. The black truck was gone; nevertheless, Julia opened the barn's side door slowly and looked around before stepping in. She flipped a series of switches, and the overhead lights came on.

Everything appeared the same as the first time Julia and John showed me their two work areas. John's side contained his mini-lab. Six months ago, when I first saw his ongoing experiments and he talked about creating new species, I teased him about playing God. Now I knew I'd been closer to the truth than I'd realized.

Julia's side had a large table that was almost completely covered with the tools of her trade. She'd shown me the copper, steel, and zinc plates she used for her etchings, along with the bottles of acid that would eat away at the metals, revealing the designs she created. In a cupboard on the outside wall, she stored her inks and paints, along with a variety of papers.

She'd framed a few of her prints, and some hung on a wire strung across her end of the barn. Her subject matter ranged from portraits to landscapes, and in my opinion, her prints were as good as any I've seen in a museum or art gallery.

A small room divided the two work areas. It wasn't there on my first visit, and I could see a combination lock on the door. "Is that what Punk built?" I asked.

"Yes." Julia walked over and punched in a series of numbers, opened the door, and stepped inside.

I followed her. I could see a few empty glass cages on the floor and a dozen or so bottles marked with chemical symbols on a shelf. There was also a metal file cabinet, its lock obviously broken and the top drawer open.

"He got the paper," Julia said, her voice hollow.

"What paper?" I asked.

She looked at me, as if just realizing I was there, shook her head and walked by me and out of the room. "What paper?" I repeated, trailing her back into the main part of the barn.

"Paper . . . Papers . . ." Julia kept shaking her head.

"What was on these papers?" She seemed in a stupor. "Did they have anything to do with the ladybugs?"

"No," she said, then looked at me. "I mean, in a way, yes. It's paper we shouldn't have had."

"Papers about the experiment?" I still didn't understand.

Julia hesitated, then nodded. "Yes. Oh, P.J., if he took the paper, he must have the box."

Which meant we didn't need to look for it. "Then I'm going back to my house, Julia. I have work to do."

I called Baraka to my side and walked out of the pole barn. Maybe I sounded cold and callous, but I didn't see anything I could do to help.

Baraka trotted head of me, crossing John's and Julia's field toward the trail in my woods. He had his nose to the ground, following a scent totally indiscernible to me. Perhaps his own since we'd come that way.

With his head down, he didn't see the man on the far side of the field, standing by the gnarled live oak with the broken branch. In truth, I only caught a glimpse of the guy. Just a long enough glimpse to know he'd been watching Julia's barn.

I turned back toward the barn and saw Julia standing in the doorway. "Did you see him?" I yelled.

"See who?" She took a few steps my way.

"The man. He was standing by the oak tree." I pointed that direction. "Watching us."

Sixteen

I led the way to the oak tree, Baraka bounding by my side, and Julia following. The oak tree stands right at the point where Nora's and Rose's woods jut up to mine. Julia and I checked around the base of the tree, then fanned out a few feet, but neither of us found any footprints. The dead leaves on the ground covered all of our tracks.

"He was watching us," I insisted.

"I believe you," Julia said. "But which way did he go? Toward your place or Nora's and Rose's?"

"I don't know." As far as I knew, he could be just beyond our sight, somewhere in the shadows, watching us. That idea gave me a creepy feeling.

I heard a thunk, the sound coming from the direction of my house. Then another thunk, like something hard and solid hitting something else hard and solid. I looked at Julia.

"I don't know?" she said, answering my unasked question.

The sounds continued, some thunks more hollow sounding than others, the rhythm irregular. Baraka heard them, too. He cocked his head to the side. "What is it, boy?" I asked.

He trotted into the woods, then stopped and looked back at me, as if asking why I wasn't coming. I glanced at Julia, then followed my dog. Those sounds had to be coming from my house.

The closer we got, the louder the thunking became. Not a mechanical thunking, but systematic. And then I heard a man swear and the thunking stopped.

Julia and I hurried past the old chicken coop and around the corner of the woodshed. I stopped first, and Julia ran into me, knocking me forward a step before I regained my balance. Dumbfounded, I stared at a rusted, black truck.

Not the same black truck I'd seen at Julia's earlier. That truck had been newer. Shinier. This truck had seen a lot of miles and a lot of abuse. In addition to rust, there were dents and scratches and a few parts held together with wire.

The truck was backed up to the doorway of my woodshed, the tailgate lowered. And standing on the bed, now sucking his index finger, was Carl Dremmer.

He wore faded blue bib overalls, a red-and-black checked flannel shirt—slightly frayed at the elbows—and heavy brown work boots. A stubble of beard covered his chin, and his long, dirty-blonde hair was pulled back in a ponytail at the nape of his neck. With a wool stocking hat covering most of his head, he looked like a man straight out of the Kentucky hills.

The truck was half full of firewood, irregular chunks that looked about the right size for my wood burner. A couple of the logs lay on the ground just below the truck's tailgate. I was pretty sure, if I could see into my woodshed, I'd find a pile of them there. The thunking sound had been explained. Wood hitting wood.

Why Carl was delivering firewood was another thing.

"Howdy, ladies," he said, after pulling his finger from his mouth. A big smile accentuated the laugh lines near the edge of his lips.

"What are you doing?" I asked.

"Bringing you some wood. The other night, while we were playing cards, you mentioned you were almost out. I had a tree go down last storm, so I decided to cut it up today and bring you a load."

"Without asking?"

"I didn't think you'd mind."

Maybe I shouldn't have. It was a nice gesture. Neighborly. But the way people had been sneaking around my house and woods, I didn't like not being told. "I just wish you'd asked first."

"I'll remember that. I had a chunk fall on my finger. Hope you didn't hear what I had to say."

"The air was blue," Julia said. "Did you see anyone come out of these woods, Carl? A man?" She looked at me. "How was he dressed, P.J.?"

"I'm not sure." He'd been in the shadows. "Dark clothing. Maybe black."

"A man dressed in black?" Carl shook his head. "Of course, I've been busy here. I suppose someone could have snuck by. Why, you see somebody?"

Julia answered before I had a chance to. "She thinks she did," she said.

Maybe I'm getting sensitive, but it sounded as if Julia was implying it was a delusion. Well, it wasn't. "I know I did," I said firmly.

"Maybe it was Howard," Carl said. "I saw his dog go by a bit ago, a squirrel in its mouth. I know Howard used to hunt squirrel in these woods."

"They're posted." I didn't think I needed to say that. I had signs every fifty feet around the perimeter.

"Maybe his dog slipped its chain again. Old Jake's been known to do that. Damn good hunting dog. Howard could have just been looking for him."

"I don't think this was Lowe. The man I saw was leaner. Taller."

"Can't help you, then." Carl leaned over and picked up three chunks of wood. "Think one load will get you through until next fall?"

We were back to the wood he was unloading. Wood I hadn't asked him to bring. "How much is this going to cost me?"

"Nothing." He smiled again, and tossed the chunks into the shed. "My way of saying welcome to the neighborhood."

I hoped his welcome wasn't like Nora's humble pie.

I considered telling him I didn't want any wood—not what he'd already tossed into my shed and not what he had in his truck—but I did need some. Although it's spring, my house gets cold in the morning, and with the price of oil constantly going up, a wood fire helps keep the cost down while giving the house a warm, cozy feel.

"Well, thank you," I finally said.

Carl nodded and gathered up another armload of wood. "I used to bring firewood to your grandfather. After I delivered a load, he'd invite me inside, and we'd sit at that dining room table of his and drink coffee. He'd ask me to recite some of my poetry."

"Carl's quite a poet," Julia said before I had a chance to question his comment. "He's had some of his poems published. Haven't you, Carl?"

"Just a couple." He chuckled. "About all I've ever made off my poetry is free coffee."

That was his second reference to coffee. I had a feeling he was hinting that he'd like some coffee when he was finished. No big deal. I could handle that. "So you and my grandfather drank coffee and recited poetry." That was a new side of my grandfather, one I hadn't imagined.

"I recited the poetry. Your grandfather just drank his coffee and listened. He used to say he'd probably die sitting at that table, a coffee cup in hand. Wonder if he was disappointed that he died in his sleep."

"My grandfather died in his sleep?" I stared up at Carl. If Herman Green, my grandfather's lawyer, told me that, I'd forgotten. All I remembered was he said my grandfather had a heart attack. But had he?

"I thought you knew," Julia said, wandering over to Carl's truck. She looked up at him. "Were you at my place earlier today?"

"It was a different truck," I said, even as Carl shook his head. And I didn't want to talk about Carl's truck. I wanted to know more about my grandfather's death. "Did they do an autopsy?"

"An autopsy?" Carl asked.

"On my grandfather."

"I don't think so," Julia said. "I remember talking to one of the paramedics after your grandfather died. He mentioned your grandfather had a history of heart problems. Isn't that what they put on his death certificate?"

"Yes." But did he die of a heart attack? I hadn't even known he had a bad heart. But then, there were eighteen years of not knowing the man. His choice.

I'd always considered dying in your sleep the way to go. But considering my experience the night before, I wondered if my grandfather did die of natural causes. "Did my grandfather ever get Nora Wright upset with him?"

Carl chuckled and looked down at Julia. "Most all the time. Wouldn't you say?"

Julia nodded, then glanced my way. "Your grandfather and Nora never got on very well."

"That's strange. She told me that my grandfather had promised her the woods, should he die. Did he ever say anything about that?"

Carl laughed. "Sounds like something he'd do. Tell her that, I mean. Those woods used to belong to an uncle of hers, way back in the twenties. Your grandfather's father bought the land during the depression. For years now, Nora's been trying to buy it back. Your grandfather probably figured telling her he would give it to her when he died would get her off his back."

I wondered if telling her that had put him on his back, six feet under. "Did she ever bring him food?"

"Nora?" Julia shook her head. "I don't think so. I mean, I don't know. Not for sure. I guess you'd have to ask her."

I could ask. I didn't think she'd tell me.

Carl went back to work, tossing the wood into my shed, and Julia glanced at her watch. "Speaking of food, I guess I'd better get home and get dinner started." She looked at me. "I'll talk to John and see if he thinks we should tackle your chicken coop."

I wanted to say, "You mean look for those ladybugs you and your husband deny existed?" But I stayed quiet. If I did say something in front of Carl, Julia would probably come up with a logical explanation, and I'd end up sounding crazy.

Okay, so I am getting paranoid.

Julia went to her car, and I started for my back door. Baraka was already on the cement landing, waiting to go inside. The temperature had dropped, and he's not a cold weather dog. He appreciates the wood stove as much as I do.

"Knock on my door when you're finished," I yelled at Carl between thunks. "Let me pay you for this."

He nodded.

Carl didn't knock, and he didn't let me know when he finished unloading his truck. I was working at the computer, completing another tax form, when I heard his truck start up. By the time I stood and went to the window, he was turning his old black truck onto the road, heading back toward his place.

The entire situation seemed bizarre, and I merely shook my head and went back to the computer. The next time I stood, it was late. Quite late. But I'd finished the federal and state forms for two clients.

I decided to call them and let them know their taxes were finished, and was on my second call when the first of three Kalamazoo County Sheriff's Department patrol cars, followed by one all-too-familiar Jeep, pulled into my yard.

I quickly ended the phone call and went to my front door. I could see six uniformed sheriff's deputies. They'd gotten out of their cars but hadn't moved away from them. Detective Kingsley was walking toward the house.

Something was up, I just didn't know what.

I opened the door and stepped out on my porch. "Why Detective Kingsley, how nice to see you again." I gave him an exaggerated smile.

"Ms. Benson, we've received a tip that evidence involved with the Carroll McDaniels's case may be on your property. I have a search warrant."

He waved a piece of paper that looked official. I took it from his hand, scanned the words, which also looked official, then looked back at him. "I don't understand. This says you want to search my woodshed. Why? Your deputies went through my outbuildings last Friday. Whatever there was to be found, you should have found."

"So we thought, but we've received more specific information." No smile. No signs of any familiarity. He did nod at the deputies, and they took off for the back of my house.

"Who gave you this information?" I asked.

"A contact."

That told me nothing. "What did your 'contact' say? What are you looking for?"

"It says on the warrant."

I looked at the paper again, finally finding my answer. "A gun?"

"Yes ma'am."

"I told you I don't have a gun."

"Then I'm sure we won't find one."

He stood on the front porch with me, unsmiling and immovable. Not truly looking at me, keeping a distance between us.

He'd shaved since dropping me off this morning. He wore the same leather jacket he'd had on then, but tan chinos, a black turtleneck, and a tan sweater replaced the jeans and flannel shirt. I hated to admit he looked good. But, dammit all, he did.

Finally, he asked how I felt. The question wasn't posed as a friend would ask, but in a clinical manner. I told him I'd live. I didn't say anything more. I could feel a wall between us.

A cold wall, I realized as goose bumps rose on my arms. The temperature was dropping as quickly as the sun was setting, and I thought about inviting Kingsley inside.

Before I had a chance to voice the invitation, one of the deputies came around the corner of my house, holding a paper bag. "Found it," he said. "Right where the caller said it would be."

Kingsley nodded. "Take it in."

"Let me see it," I said, but the deputy had already turned away and was walking toward one of the patrol cars. Kingsley turned to me, and I shook my head. "I don't own a gun."

"Well, there was one in your woodshed. And it just happens to be a Smith and Wesson thirty-eight. Same type of gun as the one that shot Carroll McDaniels, the man who died in your house last Friday."

"No way." It couldn't be. "I—"

He held up a hand, stopping me. "You have the right to remain silent. You have the right . . ."

SEVENTEEN

Kingsley proceeded to recite the Miranda warning, but I didn't hear a word. He was wrong. This was ridiculous. I didn't own a gun. Never had.

I started protesting before he finished. "I don't know how that gun got there, but it isn't mine. Someone must have planted it. The person who called you, that's who must have planted it." And I had a feeling I knew who that person was. "Carl planted it. He hid it in my woodshed, then called you."

"Carl?" Kingsley repeated.

"Carl Dremmer. He brought me a load of wood this afternoon. I didn't ask him to. He just showed up. And now I know why."

"Why?" Kingsley asked calmly.

"To plant that gun."

"And why would he do that?" Kingsley motioned for one of the deputies to come over.

"I don't know." I just knew it had to be Carl.

Personally knowing something, however, isn't good enough for the sheriff's department. I was handcuffed and led away from my house, protesting and proclaiming my innocence every step of the way. Just before I was shoved into one of the patrol cars, I begged Kingsley to take care of my dog. "Call Julia," I yelled. "My neighbor. Her number's taped to the table, next to the phone. She'll take care of Baraka."

I might not be happy with the situation she'd put me in, but

I trusted her when it came to my dog.

At the station, I was frisked, my photo and fingerprints were taken, my jewelry—a gold chain, gold stud earrings, and Timex watch—were placed in a bag. I was taken to a small room with a table and two chairs and left there. Alone.

The room was small and cold, both physically and psychologically, with nothing hanging on dull gray walls, no windows to see out, and a door that I was sure was guarded on the outside. I couldn't see a two-way mirror, still I had a feeling I was being watched. I was too numb and confused to think straight. Too shocked to do anything but sit in one of the chairs, shiver, and cry.

With my watch gone, I had no idea how many hours I'd been at the station or how long I sat there before the door opened. I glanced up and saw Kingsley and a woman. She wore a sheriff's deputy uniform and looked to be in her mid-thirties. She might have been pretty if she'd smiled, but her expression was stern, and I sensed she'd be a strong adversary. The kind of woman who worked out regularly, who probably knew martial arts and how to defend herself.

Not that I was considering taking her on physically.

She positioned herself by the door as Kingsley came toward me. I blinked and wiped away the tears running down my cheeks, snuffed to clear my nose, and licked my lips. Kingsley sat in the chair opposite me. He said nothing, just sat there staring at me.

I stared back, anger beginning to replace shock. His mouth was a straight line, his lips tight, and his eyes held no emotion. Certainly none of the concern he'd shown that morning when he was with me in the emergency room. Finally, he spoke. "Anything you want to say?"

"The gun's not mine." If he didn't believe that, then there

was no sense in saying anything else.

"Was he a boyfriend? Did you two have an argument?"

"Carl a boyfriend?" That was a laugh, but I didn't laugh. "I hardly know him. I met him just last Saturday night."

"No, I'm talking about Mr. McDaniels. Did you have an argument with him? Is that why you shot him?"

Kingsley hadn't listened to a word I'd said last Friday and Saturday. Damn him. I took in a deep breath and tried to keep my voice level. "Punk McDaniels was not my boyfriend. I didn't have an argument with him because I didn't know him." I looked at the officer by the door. Maybe she would listen. "I didn't shoot anyone."

If I'd hoped to gain her as an ally, I'd wasted my energy. She made no response . . . showed no emotion. I looked back at Kingsley. "Have you asked yourself why no one found that gun last Friday when your deputies searched that woodshed?"

"You could have hidden the gun there after we searched the area. Even if it was there Friday, according to Deputy Powell, who found the gun, it was wedged between a wall stud and a board used to hold tools. Not exactly in plain view."

"Doesn't it seem strange that you suddenly got a call telling you where to look?"

"We often receive tips days after the crime has been committed. The caller today said he saw the gun when he went to hang up a tool he'd borrowed from your grandfather some time ago."

"Saw it?" I wanted to scream. "Don't you mean planted it?"

"We always consider that possibility." He sat back in his chair. "Now, would you like to go over your previous testimony, see if there is anything you'd like to change or add?"

"There is nothing to change." But I started repeating everything that had happened since Friday afternoon. I was up to Monday night when there was a knock on the door. The woman officer answered it, then came over to Kingsley and whispered something in his ear. He looked toward the door, then said, "Just a minute."

He went out of the room, leaving me with the woman officer. She smiled tentatively, but said nothing. Which was fine with me. I wasn't in the mood for idle chitchat.

Kingsley returned a short time later, said something to the woman, and she left. Then he came back to the table. "Looks like you're off the hook," he said. "The preliminary analysis shows the fingerprints on the gun don't match yours and ballistics says it's not the same gun as the one used to shoot Mr. McDaniels. In fact, the gun is registered to your grandfather."

"Who probably put it in the woodshed." I stood. "So, am I free to go?"

"Yes."

I walked past him and opened the door. Drained of emotion, I didn't have the energy to vent my anger. All I wanted to do was go home, get something to eat, and go to sleep.

Then I remembered one important point.

I looked back at Kingsley. "How do I get home?"

"I'll take you."

"I'd prefer someone else."

"We'll get your things and discuss it."

Except there was no discussion. Once I had my watch and jewelry back, Kingsley guided me out the door to his Jeep. I considered arguing with him, then decided against it. At least with Kingsley, I wouldn't have to give directions.

"I'm going to know this route by heart," he said as he drove his Jeep along the narrow, tree-lined paved road heading toward my house.

I didn't say anything. I'd vowed not to speak to him, and I was determined to keep that vow.

His headlights cut a triangular path through the darkness,

and I kept my eyes focused on the edges of the road ahead of us. I could feel Kingsley's gaze on me, sense the tension between us.

The Jeep's left front tire hit a pothole, jarring the vehicle and bringing my attention back to the road. A long winter of snow, freezing rain, and ice always gives Michigan an abundant supply of potholes. Road crews begin patching the worst as soon as weather permits, but back roads, such as the one I live on, are always the last to receive any attention. That is, unless a politician or tax payer with clout lives on the road. Sadly, we have no such person living on my road.

I almost said something about another big pothole I knew was up ahead, then stopped myself. If Kingsley ruined the Jeep, so be it. He wouldn't be on this road if he hadn't arrested me.

As we neared Julia and John's road, I could see the yard light from their house. I wondered if Baraka was there. Kingsley anticipated my question. "She came up and got him right after I called her. Do you want me to take you there first, so you can get him?"

I considered the idea, then immediately discarded it. "I'll get him later."

All I wanted was to be home and for Kingsley to disappear. Once he was gone, I could pick up Baraka. Pick up my life.

We traveled on to my house. Only five days ago, I had considered inheriting that house a blessing. Now I wondered if it was a curse.

Blessings. Curses. I was starting to think like my mother.

That scared me.

Detective Kingsley pulled his Jeep into my yard and parked beside my car. I was out and had started for my back door before he turned off the engine. He rolled down his window, and calmly asked, "Do you have your house key?"

House key. I hadn't thought about that. I stopped walking

and looked back at him, a sinking feeling hitting my stomach. "You didn't give me a chance to get my keys. Remember? You dragged me off in handcuffs."

He didn't react to my snide tone, just got out of his Jeep, stretched, and snapped on a flashlight. "I'm afraid I forgot about keys, too," he said. "After your neighbor picked up the dog, I locked the two doors and left. What about a spare key? Everyone hides a spare."

"Well, I'm not everyone." When I wasn't locking my doors, it didn't seem necessary to have a spare. And with the locks about to be changed, why bother? "So how do you propose we get inside?"

"How has your house invader been getting inside?"

"Don't ask me. You're the detective."

"There are ways that work, especially on old locks like yours." He came up beside me.

"Does that mean you break into houses often?"

"Only when necessary."

I walked beside him to the back of my house. The storm door was still missing. It had been taken as evidence. No one had told me when it might be returned.

The beam of Kingsley's flashlight lit up the door, and I knew it wouldn't be necessary to break into my house.

Eighteen

I definitely needed new locks. And a new doorknob. The one that had been on my back door was hanging at an odd angle, the door partially open. Kingsley stopped, swung the beam of his flashlight over the back of the house, across the walkway between the woodshed and the house and into the opening of the woodshed.

All I saw was a mouse scoot under a chunk of wood.

"You go back to the car," Kingsley ordered. "If anything happens, there's a cell phone on the dash. Call nine-one-one."

He drew his gun, and I did take a step back, but I didn't go to the Jeep. Heart lodged in my throat, I watched Kingsley go up the steps and slowly push open my back door. He took a moment to scan my kitchen with his flashlight, then entered my house. Next the light came on in the kitchen, then I lost sight of him.

Curious, I went up the steps and stood near the doorway, listening. For voices? A gunshot? I wasn't sure.

Kingsley was gone longer than I expected, and I was just beginning to worry when he returned to the kitchen. He frowned when he saw me. "Didn't I tell you to go to my car?"

"I wanted to know what was going on."

"What if there'd been someone in here? If shots were fired?"

"I would have run to the car and called for help. Here, at least, I could hear if you were in trouble . . . hear if you called for help."

150

"Are you always this stubborn?"

"According to my grandmother, yes."

He looked as if he was going to say something else, then shrugged. "I'm going to check the upstairs, now," he said. "I don't suppose it would do me any good to tell you to go to the car."

I shook my head.

"Then, at least stay here, where you are."

He walked back into the dining room and out of sight. I thought about staying where I was, then decided I really needed to be closer, in case he did need help. I stopped at the doorway to the dining room. I might be stubborn, but I'm not stupid. If there was any shooting, I wanted an easy exit.

I heard Kingsley start up the stairs to the second floor, heard each of the old stairs creak under his weight, then his footsteps on the floorboards overhead. Barely breathing, I listened to his journey from room to room. Five minutes passed, and he finally came back downstairs. "Nothing," he said when he saw me in the doorway.

He pointed a finger at me, and I thought he might say something about where I was, then he shook his head and turned his attention to the door to my cellar. "I'm going down here, next."

I nodded. "Light switch is on your right."

He opened the door, snapped on the light, and started down, gun ready. Again, I waited . . . listened. Only when he reappeared did I sigh in relief. His gun went back in its holster, and he came toward me. "I've looked everywhere. There's no one in here, and it doesn't look like anything was taken. You stay here, and I'll check your outbuildings."

"I think I should go with you. Just in case you need a backup."

"No. And this time, I mean it." He pointed toward my phone. "If you hear anything unusual, call for help. Meanwhile, look around. See if you think anything is out of place or missing."

As he'd requested, I looked around, starting with my dining room. The drawers of my buffet were closed, and nothing on top had been moved or taken. TV, VCR, fax machine, and telephone were all in place. Computer monitor, tower, and printer were just as I'd left them. And this time, the tax folders on my dining room table hadn't been disturbed.

Everything was fine, except—

I may be a messy housekeeper, but when it comes to my paperwork, I don't throw it on the floor. I either file papers in their appropriate folders or I shred them. So there was no reason for a crumpled sheet of paper to be on my floor. But there it was, just under the end of my table.

I walked over and picked it up. Carefully, I straightened out the page. It was a wide-lined piece of paper—not the kind I use—with several lines of words scribbled on it, no one line taking the entire width of the page.

I decided it was a poem. Not the rhyming type my mother used to read to me when I was a child. More like the kind I've read in the *New Yorker.* And it appeared to be a rough draft, since some of the words had been crossed out and the paper itself was dirty and looked like it had been stepped on. The handwriting was almost illegible, and it took me a while to decipher the words.

The Messengers

The CROWS know more
than vision foretells,
perched upon a pedestal,
surveying.
Only the CROWS care,
not by chance,

always aware.
Mankind destroys.
The CROWS clean up.
The wounded die,
the guilty flee.
Call in the CROWS,
before it's too late.
The seed of insanity
must be destroyed.

I stopped there and stared at the paper, a sickening knot forming in my stomach.

The seed of insanity.

Once, when I was thirteen, a social worker called me the seed of insanity. She wanted me to see a psychiatrist. I've always thought she was the crazy one, but the term hurt and I've never forgotten it. Seeing it again didn't lessen the hurt.

"No one outside," Kingsley said, coming through the kitchen to the dining room.

I looked at him, but I didn't know what to say.

My expression must have relayed my emotions. He stopped in the doorway. "What's wrong?"

"This," I said, holding the paper so he could see, my hand shaking. "It's . . . It's a poem. I, ah . . . I think it was left for me to find."

Kingsley walked toward me, and I gave him the paper. It took him a second to read the words, then he looked back at me. "I don't get it. What's it mean?"

"I think it's a threat. See that—" I pointed to the line that said "The seed of insanity." "I'm the seed of insanity, the child of a schizophrenic. This was left for me."

"Who left it?" Kingsley frowned. "And why?"

"Carl did." It made sense. "He's a poet. When he brought me that load of wood today, we talked about him reading poetry to my grandfather. Carl had to have been the one who called you and reported that gun in the woodshed. He probably saw me carted off in that patrol car. Probably knew when you left. Then he came here, broke in, and left that poem."

"Okay, let's say it was your friend Carl. I still don't understand what the point is in leaving this."

"He's not my friend, but he is friends with Howard Lowe, and Lowe hates me. And . . . And he thinks I'm crazy, too."

A tear slid down my cheek, then another. I didn't want to cry. I'd cried enough as a child when the kids teased me about my crazy mother. I cried when my father left to go to Beirut. Cried when they said he was dead and that I'd never see him again. Cried every time they took my mother away. I even cried when my grandfather refused to acknowledge me.

I thought I'd used up all of my tears, but they came, and once they started, I couldn't stop crying. My body shook, and I stood there, in front of Detective Kingsley, bawling like a baby.

He put his arms around me and drew me close, the gesture awkward and tentative. I suppose his initial intention was simply to console me. I'm sure it wouldn't have gone any further if I hadn't wrapped my arms around his waist. He just felt so good, so solid and sturdy.

I hugged him, pressing my body against his. With my cheek touching his jacket, I could smell the aroma of the leather and the musky odor of male sweat. A manly smell. Sexy and arousing.

His breath blew into my hair, and the beat of his heart carried to my ear. A strong heartbeat. Rapid.

Maybe too rapid.

He took in a deep breath, and beneath my fingertips, I could feel his muscles tensing. I looked up and saw the awareness in his eyes. I wasn't the only one being aroused.

Where our emotions might have taken us, I don't know. The telephone rang, its clamor shattering the mood. Kingsley jerked back like a kid caught with his hand in the cookie jar. I gave a gasp.

Again the phone rang.

"Are you expecting a call?" he asked, his voice huskier than before.

I stared at him, stunned by the need he'd awakened in me. The phone rang again.

"P.J.?"

I shook my head. "No. Not this late."

"Want me to answer it?"

I nodded.

Kingsley walked over to the phone, and I followed him. Too much had happened in the last few hours. I touched the sleeve of his jacket, needing the contact. He glanced at my hand, then at me. His smile was slow and warm, and he touched my lips with a fingertip before he lifted the phone to his ear. "Benson residence," he said, the huskiness still in his voice.

I kept my hand on his sleeve, and held my breath, waiting to hear his next words. "She's home," he said. "Yes, this is Detective Kingsley. No, it wasn't the gun." He looked at me. "I don't think so. She's not going to be staying here tonight. If you can keep the dog until tomorrow, I'm sure she'll pick it up then."

"Julia," I said, realizing who was on the other end of the line. She'd probably seen the lights go on in my house.

Kingsley nodded and continued listening to whatever Julia was saying, then said, "Just a minute." He looked at me. "She'll keep your dog there tonight. Anything you want to tell her?"

"No." I was afraid if talked to her, I'd say something I'd regret. "Just tell her to take good care of him."

Kingsley relayed my message, then hung up. He stared at me, and I shook my head. "Don't look at me like that. I don't know what's going on."

"Neither do I. Sit down." He pointed at a chair, and I obediently went and sat. Once again he looked at the piece of paper in his hand. "There's a remote chance we might be able to get some fingerprints off this. But it will take time. Weeks. Still, it's worth a try. I'll write down a copy of the poem, then I'll get this sheet to the lab. Meanwhile, I don't want you staying here. Not with that lock broken. Do you have somewhere you can go? Somewhere safe?"

Safe? Once family services had worried about my safety. They'd threatened to put me in foster care. My grandmother convinced my caseworker that I would have a good home with her. Grandma said I was always welcome.

"I suppose I could spend the night at my grandmother's. But I really hate to. Both my grandmother and mother smoke and it gets to me."

"I understand," he said. "I had a roommate, before I got married, who smoked." He shook his head. "Never again."

"I suppose I could get a motel room."

"Definitely a possibility, but I'd like to suggest another possibility. You can say no if you'd like. I don't want you to feel you're under any pressure, and I don't want you to think I'm suggesting anything immoral."

That caught my interest. "Immoral?"

He didn't smile. "I'd like to take you to my sister's place. She lives in Galesburg, only twenty minutes away, has a spare bedroom and loves riddles. I'd like her to take a look at this poem."

"And how is your sister going to feel about this idea?"

"Why don't we ask her?"

NINETEEN

Kingsley's sister, it turned out, thought it a wonderful idea. Ginger, or Ginny as she said she preferred to be called, greeted us at the door with a hug for her brother and a handshake for me. Like her brother, she was tall—probably five-eight or -nine—and she had one of those willowy figures that would look equally good in sweats or a slinky designer's dress. At the moment she wore sweats, the teal blue color a perfect match to her eyes. She had long blonde hair, probably not natural, that hung past her shoulders, and she brushed it back from her face frequently. She smiled easily, and spoke with a Marilyn Monroe voice, the kind that makes you want to stand close so you won't miss a word.

"Come on in," she said in a near whisper, and turned and walked back into her house.

I followed her, Kingsley behind me, carrying the overnight bag I'd packed before leaving my house. On the drive to his sister's house, he'd told me she was an interior decorator. When we pulled up in front of the house, I was surprised to see a simple L-shaped ranch. The evergreens and stonework surrounding it were nice, but nothing remarkable.

The inside, however, was a different story.

The only places I've seen house interiors like this are magazines like *Home and Gardens* and *Architectural Design*. I guess I must have made some sound of appreciation because Ginny glanced back at me and grinned. "You like it?"

"It's gorgeous."

No one thing made the house beautiful. It was a combination of color, texture, furnishings, and unique art pieces. A huge woven tapestry hung on one wall, the design modernistic, while a variegated blue-green metal sculpture, geometric in shape, graced a glass-topped coffee table. Throw pillows ranging in color from magenta to ultramarine covered the sofa. Those same colors were repeated in the placemats on the circular oak dining table in the dining area. Ginny led us there.

"Coffee?" she asked. "Tea? Hot cocoa?"

"Coffee," Kingsley said. "I have a feeling it's going to be a long night."

"What about you?" Ginny asked me.

"I really don't—"

"Fix her some hot chocolate," Kingsley said and sat down.

"Coffee," I said, more because I didn't want him deciding for me than because I wanted any.

"Two coffees coming up." With that, his sister headed for the kitchen.

"Where are Spike and the boys?" Kingsley called after her.

"In my office. I wasn't sure how your girlfriend felt about animals."

"I am not his girlfriend," I said quickly. I hoped I hadn't given her that impression. "I barely know your brother."

He glanced up at me, the dining room light catching the sparkle in his blue eyes. I wondered if he was remembering our embrace in my dining room, the way I'd wrapped my arms around his waist. I didn't want to be aroused by this man, yet there was something in the way he looked at me that set my pulse racing.

Quickly, I turned toward the kitchen. "I like all animals . . . even your brother."

I heard Ginny laugh and the click of coffee mugs. Kingsley

patted the chair on his right. "Sit down and relax," he said.

I stood where I was. "Relax? Detective Kingsley, whether you believe me or not, my neighbor tried to kill me yesterday, someone has been breaking into my house on a regular basis, and now I'm getting threatening poems."

"If it is a threatening poem."

"And what else would you call it?"

He pulled the copy he'd made out of his jacket pocket, and carefully unfolded the paper. As he silently read through the poem, I did sit, scooting my chair near him. He pointed at the first line. "The word 'crows' was all caps. Does that mean anything to you?"

Kingsley's printing was easier to read than the original handwriting. I'd suggested making a copy with my fax machine, but he didn't want to handle the page any more than necessary.

When I first read the poem, I'd focused on the last three lines. Now I looked at the beginning.

> The CROWS know more
> than vision foretells,
> perched upon a pedestal,
> surveying.
> Only the CROWS care.

"My neighbor, Howard Lowe, told me to listen to the crows. I thought he meant the birds."

"When was that?"

"Monday morning. He stopped when he was driving by, told me if I heard from the crows, I should listen . . . that my grand-father didn't."

"Sounds like I need to talk to this Mr. Lowe again."

"Two coffees, one hot chocolate," Ginny said, coming out of the kitchen carrying a tray with three steaming mugs and a plate of cookies. The mugs went in front of each of us, the plate of cookies in the middle of the table. "I hope you like chocolate chip, P.J. They're Wade's favorites. He would cry if I didn't have some around."

They were my favorites, too, but I decided not to say anything. I wasn't quite sure how I felt about Kingsley, and that bothered me. I didn't want him thinking I had the hots for him. That really would be crazy. Still, that sleepy look he was giving me was downright sexy.

"So tell me about your animals," I said, deciding I had to get my mind off the man seated next to me.

"Spike and the boys." Ginny grinned. "If it's all right, I will let them out."

"Fine with me."

Ginny walked down the hallway, and I heard a door open, a bit of commotion, then swearing. Next thing I knew, Spike came bounding into the dining area, followed by "the boys," which turned out to be two male Siamese cats. The cats were haughty and beautiful, but it was Spike who surprised me.

"Spike is a poodle? A miniature poodle?"

Ginny followed the trio into the room, a wad of tissue in one hand. "He has one of those long, fancy names on his pedigree, but I felt he needed a strong identity if he was going to cope with the boys." She carried the tissue into the kitchen. "He also has a tendency to forget his potty training when he gets excited."

"Ah. I know what you mean. I just went through potty training with a puppy."

"Puppies are cute," Ginny said, water running in the background. "But also a pain in the butt. Spike chewed everything."

"I give Baraka lots of chew toys and keep him in a crate when I'm gone."

"He's in a crate now?" Ginny came out, drying her hands. "Wade, you should have had her bring him with her."

"The dog's at a neighbor's house tonight. I thought it best to leave him there."

Wade's pager went off. He glanced at the number, then went into Ginny's kitchen. A second later, I heard him talking on the phone. When he came back into the dining room, he was frowning. "That was one of my deputies. P.J., did you know you had an underground room off your cellar?"

"No way. A room off the cellar? Where?" I'd never seen a doorway.

"Behind the shelving unit. I'm going to go back and check it out."

"I'll go with you."

I stood, but Kingsley shook his head and grabbed his leather coat from the back of his chair. "Considering your house was broken into tonight, we need to treat this as a crime scene again. After we've gathered any evidence, you can take a look."

I might have argued, but after all that had happened, I was willing to let him go to my place alone. I did ask, "What about the poem?"

He turned to his sister. "Think you can help her with that while I'm gone?"

Ginny pulled the paper that had been in front of Kingsley's chair over to her side of the table. She glanced at the poem, then looked back up at him. "We can give it a try. You do your thing. We'll do ours."

Two minutes later, he was gone, and I was left with his sister. She sipped at her hot chocolate and re-read the poem. Finally she looked at me. "He likes you," she said.

Ginny's comment caught me off guard. "He?"

"My brother. He wouldn't have brought you here if he didn't. And he looks at you in a way that says he knows he shouldn't be involved with you, but he wants to be."

"I barely know him." But I believed her. I'd sensed the desire.

He held it in check, but there were times when he looked at me that I knew he wanted to touch me. Wanted more.

"I guess the question is, how do you feel about him?"

It was a question I didn't want to answer, not truthfully. "I, ah . . . I guess I really haven't thought about it." Liar. I avoided looking at Ginny.

"You know he's divorced."

I nodded. "I met his son, Jason. He brought him by my place Saturday . . . to see my dog."

"You met Jason?" Ginny gave a lift of her eyebrows and grinned. "That cinches it. He likes you."

I didn't want her jumping to conclusions, right or wrong. "He stopped by to tell me they'd discovered the identity of the man who died in my house."

"He could have called, couldn't he?"

"I suppose."

"I rest my case." Still smiling, she looked back at the paper. "This is a copy, I take it. In the original, was the word 'crows' capitalized?"

"Yes." I told her what Lowe had said Monday morning and about my dream—or hallucination—Monday night. "I don't know if the two were connected, but it sure seems like this word keeps coming up."

"Interesting. And what does the word 'crows' mean to you?"

"Black birds. There are a lot of them around my place."

" 'Nevermore,' " Ginny quoted. "Of course, that was a raven. But ravens are cousins to the crow, and both are known for giving warnings."

"Lowe said a flock of crows is called a murder."

"I hadn't heard that." Ginny got up and went into the kitchen. She came back with a standard-size notebook. "I want to write these things down. The word 'murder,' in your circumstance, is appropriate. Same with warning. It fits what's written in this poem. I think we can rule out Counting Crows, the singing group. No mention of singing or counting here."

"And they don't spell it in all caps." I liked what we were doing. For the first time all day, I began to feel in control.

"Since the only word that's written in capital letters is 'crows,' it must be significant." She glanced toward the back of her house. "Have you gone on the Internet?"

"No. My server's been down lately."

"Want to use my computer?"

We went to the spare bedroom she used as an office. I pulled up a chair as she connected to the Internet. Once on, she typed "CROWS" into a search engine. A list of possible Web sites matching the word came up. It didn't seem to matter that she'd typed the word in all caps. The list included every combination of the word imaginable. Thirty-four thousand possibilities.

Ginny began to scroll down the selections, skipping those Web sites that didn't look promising. "Wade's ex is a nut case," she said, her comment catching me completely off guard. "Has he told you anything about her?"

"No." I read over her shoulder, skipping all listings about the group Counting Crows and the sites about the genus *Corvidae*.

Ginny kept scrolling . . . and talking. "She's a child in a woman's body. Absolutely drop-dead gorgeous, but as self-centered as a five-year-old. She knew Wade was a deputy when she met him. She knew he was conscientious and devoted to his work. But did that stop her from trying to change him? No sir-ree. She wanted a man like her daddy, someone who'd make lots of money, buy her expensive toys, and give in to her every wish. The one I feel sorry for is Jason. What do you think about this one?"

She'd stopped at a listing for a Web site called "OLD CROWS." The description was sketchy. "Give it a try," I said.

We waited for it to load, read two lines, looked at each other, and Ginny clicked off. She continued going through the site listings. She also continued talking about Kingsley's ex-wife.

"Linda used to call me, whining that Wade spent too much time on the job. She'd bother him at work. When he told me she wanted a baby, I warned him it wasn't a good idea. In her case, it's a child raising a child." Ginny shook her head. "She's the one who filed for divorce. She didn't feel fulfilled, she said. Wade didn't spend enough time with her. Pooh, I don't think any man would spend enough time with her. Or would want to."

Ginny clicked on to the next group of listings. We kept bringing up sites about the singing group or the bird and I was beginning to think the entire endeavor was a waste of time. Then one Web site caught my attention.

C.R.O.W.S. A group dedicated to controlling wayward biotechnology.

"Let's take a look at that one," I said, and Ginny clicked on it.

The graphics took a while to load. Slowly, a huge black crow filled the screen, a miniature man in a white lab coat held in its beak. Ginny scrolled down, revealing oversized black letters beneath the bird.

C.R.O.W.S.

Below the acronym was the explanation. "Civilian Resistance Opposing Wayward Science."

Sounded like a radical group, and one sentence below that caught my attention. "CROWS clean up the errors of mankind."

"It's almost the same," I said, looking back at the poem. "Here it says, 'The CROWS clean up.' "

Ginny continued scrolling down. "Says the group has been in existence for twenty-five years. Have you ever heard of it?"

"Never." I read over Ginny's shoulder. "Sounds militant to me. So maybe I was wrong. Maybe Lowe left the poem."

"You think he belongs to this group?"

"I don't know. Keep going. Let's see what it says."

Ginny scrolled on, and I read the group's mission statement. It sounded benign. To oversee scientific research for the good of mankind.

"I wonder if 'for the good of mankind' means shooting people."

"Look, maybe we can find out if your neighbor is a member." Ginny had reached the bottom of the page. To go on, we had a choice of two buttons. One said "Operations," the other "Operatives."

"Like oh oh?" I asked, being funny.

Except, the laugh was on us. When Ginny clicked on the "Operatives" button, we were taken to a screen that asked for ID and password. "Use LOWE," I said. "And HUNTER for a password." It seemed as good as any.

Ginny did, then clicked OK, and for a moment, I thought Lowe's name and password had been accepted. Then the picture of a bomb filled the screen, along with the sound of ticking.

Before Ginny had a chance to get out, the bomb visually blew up, an explosive sound matching the picture. Immediately, Ginny's computer shut down.

"Oh, oh, is right," Ginny said, staring at her darkened screen. "I sure hope that wasn't a virus."

It took her fifteen minutes to reboot her computer, check for viruses, and reconnect with her Internet provider. She didn't go back to that site.

It was nearly midnight when the phone rang. Spike jumped to his feet and barked. Ginny reached behind her and grabbed the phone on the desk. I held my breath.

"Yes," she said, sounding both sexy and sleepy. "I wondered if you'd call." She looked my way and mouthed the word "Wade." "Sounds good." She listened, then responded. "Hmm.

Interesting. I'll tell her. See you in the morning."

She hung up, then explained. "That was Wade. He's exhausted and heading home. He said he'll pick you up in the morning, that they found an answer to your mysterious break-ins and why your door was jimmied this time. He'll tell you in the morning."

"In the morning? That's not fair. Doesn't he know this is going to drive me crazy all night? Did he give a hint?"

"Nope." Ginny turned back to her computer. "I don't know about you, P.J., but I'm beat. Other than that resistance group, I didn't see anything promising here. I'm going to shut down. All right?"

I agreed with her. We'd wasted over an hour, and I knew little more than when we'd started. I didn't even think our explosive CROWS was promising. From what I'd read, that group would destroy the ladybugs. They wouldn't steal them.

TWENTY

I shouldn't have had the coffee the night before. I don't know when I finally went to sleep, but Kingsley arrived at seven o'clock on the dot. I know because when the doorbell rang, Spike began barking. I groaned and peeked at the clock on the dresser by the closet. Then Ginny yelled at the dog to be quiet, and I heard her let her brother in. The two of them kept their voices low, and I decided that was a sign that I could keep on sleeping. I yawned and pulled the covers back over my head.

I obviously misread the signs, because less than a minute later, Detective Wade Kingsley was pounding on my bedroom door. "Rise and shine, sleepyhead," he yelled. "Time for all good men to go to work."

"I'm a woman," I yelled back.

"So I've noticed," he said in a lower voice that sent a tingle through my body and created a tension between my legs.

I wasn't sure how I would respond if he came into the room, so I said, "I'll be right out."

"I'll be waiting."

It sounded like a lover's promise.

I kept telling myself he was a sheriff's deputy, a detective doing his job, nothing more, but I knew I was lying to myself. Something, sometime in the last few days, had clicked between us.

With a sense of anticipation, I pulled on fresh underwear, a clean shirt, jeans, and shoes. Then, with my cosmetic case in hand, I scooted down the hallway to the bathroom, relieved that I didn't run into Kingsley . . . and disappointed. There I used the toilet, then brushed my teeth. I'd forgotten a hair brush, so I ran my fingers through my hair, once again thankful that short, naturally curly hair doesn't take much care. Having done as much as I could to beautify myself, I stepped into the dining area.

Kingsley was seated at the table, a mug of coffee on the teal placemat in front of him. He didn't see me. He was listening to his sister.

I couldn't see Ginny, but I could hear her voice coming from the kitchen. "We checked the Internet," she said. "We didn't find anything."

I wasn't sure about that, so I spoke up. "We did find one listing for CROWS—all caps—that might be relevant. It's an acronym for a 'civilian resistance' group."

Kingsley looked my way, and Ginny's poodle came bounding out of the kitchen, yipping and yapping and jumping up and down. This morning he had a blue bow attached to the puff of hair on top of his head. The bow was cute, but I wondered why Ginny named her dog Spike then sissified him with something like that.

I leaned down and gave the little dog a pat on his head, careful not to disturb the bow. I could just imagine Baraka with a bow on his head.

Actually, I couldn't. First of all, his hair's so short, there would be no way to attach a bow. Second, even if I could attach one, he wouldn't leave it there. My bet was two seconds for removal and another second for ingestion of said bow.

The image of Baraka eating a blue bow made me smile. I was still smiling when I glanced over at Kingsley. He was watching me, and the look in his eyes heated my skin.

"Coffee?" Ginny asked, her voice louder.

I jerked my gaze toward the kitchen. She stood in the doorway, looking at her brother and me. Her smile said more than words, and if I wasn't blushing before, I was now. I could deny my feelings toward Kingsley until I was blue in the face, but his sister could tell I was lying.

"Coffee sounds great," I managed, even my shaky voice giving me away.

"You get any sleep?" Kingsley asked.

I stood again, the poodle having left me to return to his mistress's side. "A little. No thanks to you."

"Me?" He lifted an eyebrow, a satisfied male smile crossing his face.

If he thought I'd stayed awake having erotic thoughts about him, he was mistaken. At least, partially mistaken. "You can't tell a woman you've found the answer to how someone broke into her house and expect her to get any sleep."

The smile remained, but changed slightly. Perhaps a little less satisfied. "It was too late to stop by last night."

I walked over and sat across from him. "So, what did you find?"

"A room and a passageway to your woodshed."

"Well, that explains how someone got in my house, but why didn't I see the doorways? I've been in the cellar. Woodshed."

"They're not that easy to find." Kingsley cradled his coffee mug in his hands. "Deputy Perry discovered the room by accident. He heard a clicking down in your cellar."

"My furnace does that before it comes on."

"As he found out. While he was down there, checking out the clicking sound, he noticed the cement in front of the wooden storage shelf looked cleaner than the cement in front of your furnace. He also noticed a slight scratch on the floor, as if something had been drug across it. He did some investigating, thought the wall sounded hollow behind the shelving unit, and figured out how to swing it open."

Ginny came out of the kitchen with a mug of coffee for me and a plate of blueberry muffins. "Sounds like one of those spooky movies. The kind where you see the eyes in the picture blink and the walls move to reveal hidden passages."

"It's been spooking me." I welcomed the coffee, but I wasn't awake enough for food. Kingsley evidently was. The moment Ginny set down the plate, he grabbed one of the muffins.

"How'd you find the underground tunnel?" I asked.

His mouth full, Kingsley motioned for me to wait until he'd finished chewing. Impatiently I did, and he finally downed the last of the muffin with a gulp of coffee.

"You can see it from the underground room," he said. "Leads to a trapdoor in the woodshed. We didn't see that before because it was covered with wood chips and dirt . . . and because we weren't looking for one."

Once he mentioned it, I knew exactly where the trapdoor was located. "I saw it. About a month ago. I remember because my woodpile looked different. It seemed higher and more to the left. There was a spot near the pile where all of the floor boards ended at exactly the same place, rather than being staggered. It seemed unusual, but I didn't think of a trapdoor."

"That fresh load of wood must have pissed off your intruder. We found chunks tossed all around, and part of the stack had been pulled down. He must have realized it would take too long to move the wood, so he broke in through your back door."

"All because he wanted to leave me a poem?"

"No, probably to pick up a tape recorder and tapes. If you'll give me permission, I'd like to check your house for bugs."

"Bugs? Ladybugs?"

"I think he means listening devices," Ginny said, standing by the kitchen doorway, a half-eaten muffin in one hand.

Kingsley nodded. "We found an empty tape container in the

room. I think this guy's been recording what you've been saying."

Listening in. Entering my house whenever he wanted. A shiver ran through me, and I shook my head.

"No?" Kingsley frowned. "Look, P.J., if—"

I stopped his argument. "You can look. I was just wondering how this guy knew about the room and passageway."

"Someone, probably your grandfather, must have told him about it or shown it to him."

"Which means the shooter knew my grandfather."

"Looks like that. We did do a little checking on your neighbor Howard Lowe. He was in Special Forces in Korea. Was trained in surveillance techniques."

That cinched it. I looked at Kingsley. "You have my permission to check for bugs, but I want to be there when you do."

TWENTY-ONE

"You might as well call me Wade."

I glanced his way, but said nothing. Neither of us had said much since leaving his sister's. I don't know what thoughts he'd been having that triggered his permission for me to use his first name, but my mind had been on a secret room and a passage that ran from my cellar to my woodshed.

My lack of comment must have prompted him to go on. "And I'm sorry," he said, "that I didn't believe you when you first said someone had been in your house."

"Apology accepted, Wade." I love it when a man has to apologize, especially a lawman. "I'll admit, I never thought of a secret room and passage. Another key, yes. Or someone who knew how to pick locks."

"The room might have been one of those underground bomb shelters people were building in the fifties. It's a fairly large space, and there is a cot there and some cans of food and jugs of water near one wall."

"So every time I've walked on that path between the house and the woodshed, I've been walking over this tunnel and bomb shelter?" The idea was disconcerting. "How stable is it?"

"It's in pretty good shape. But a few of the beams are rotting. The use of Wolmanized lumber wasn't as common back in the fifties as it is nowadays. You might want to make a few repairs."

"I might want to fill in the damn thing." I wasn't wild about having a third entrance to my house.

"Your decision, but it might be handy . . . in case of a terrorist attack or a tornado."

I wasn't terribly worried about terrorists coming to Zenith, Michigan, but we do get a few tornadoes each year. Not that my house is in a tornado pathway. The closest one seems to run along the Kalamazoo River basin. During a tornado warning, people are supposed to head for a basement or cellar. I wondered if the entrance in the woodshed was in case you were outside when the tornado sirens went off . . . or if your house collapsed and you needed another way out.

"Is there a way to lock the trapdoor?"

"Probably not, but it's still covered with wood. We didn't see any reason to move the pile. You will need a new lock on your back door."

"I have a locksmith coming." The moment I said that, I remembered what day it was. "He's supposed to come this morning."

"Perfect timing."

Wade smiled my way. He had that look in his eyes that made my heart skip a beat. I tried to ignore the way he stirred my hormones, but dammit all, homicide detectives shouldn't look like Nicolas Cage and Tom Cruise wrapped up in one man.

We were nearing my house, and I glanced at my watch. Eighten. Julia would still be home. She didn't have to be at the bank until eight-thirty, and it was only a five minute drive to Zenith. "Think we could stop by and pick up Baraka before we go to my place?"

Baraka would keep my mind on track.

Julia was wearing stained sweat pants and a tattered sweatshirt when she answered my knock. Although the dress code at the bank is pretty lax, I didn't think it was that casual. Baraka and Mr. Stubs, Julia's Jack Russell terrier, each bounced around my feet, demanding my attention. Finally Julia grabbed Mr. Stubs, holding him in her arms so I could stoop down and hug Baraka.

"Aren't you working today?" I asked as Baraka gave my face a joyful licking.

"I took the day off so I could attend Punk's funeral. It's not until one, but also I'm helping with the meal the church is preparing for the family and friends."

Mr. Stubs tried to free himself from Julia's grasp, but she held tight, ignoring his efforts. Her attention was focused on the Jeep parked in her drive. Wade stood by the front bumper, looking our way. "You're not under arrest, are you?" Julia asked.

"No. I didn't take my car last night, so I needed a ride back from his sister's this morning." I gave Baraka a quick kiss on the top of his head and stood before he could lick me back.

"His sister's? You spent the night at his sister's?" Julia grinned. "Next thing you know, you'll be on a first-name basis with the guy. After that, you'll be sharing a bed. See, this isn't all bad."

I didn't want her to know Wade had just asked me to call him by his first name, and I certainly didn't plan on sharing his bed. That would really be crazy. Just so Julia would remember this wasn't a dating game, I said, "Not bad? One man's dead, and you still don't know if his killer has those ladybugs or not."

Julia kept watching Wade, and even though he couldn't hear her from where he stood, she lowered her voice. "I'm thinking, if the guy's still around, he must not have found the box. Did you look for it again?"

"No." And here I thought I didn't have to worry about the ladybugs any more. "How long will they live in that box anyway?"

"Ah, well . . ." She chewed on her lower lip. "I'm not sure. But if you do find that box, don't peek inside to see if they're alive. Okay?"

"And what should I tell him?" I nodded toward Wade. "What

if he finds the box?"

"If he finds it?" Julia stared at him. "In that case, we're screwed."

Julia sighed, and with her Jack Russell under one arm, placed her other hand on the door. "Now, if you don't mind, I've got to get ready. I'm supposed to be at the church in an hour."

She wanted me gone, and there really wasn't anything else I could say. Julia would protect her husband and his career. I supposed if I loved a man I would do the same. With Baraka in tow, I headed back to the Jeep.

"Everything all right?" Wade asked, holding the back door open so Baraka could jump into the Jeep.

"Yeah, I guess." I slid into the passenger's seat. Baraka tried to come up front, and I ordered him to stay back. He licked my ear, but did as told.

As Wade walked around and got into the car, I thought about Julia. Because of a bunch of ladybugs, I'd lost a friend. I've never had many friends. When you have a mother who talks about aliens and does weird things, people have a tendency to avoid you.

"You sure you're okay?" Wade asked.

"Yeah." I didn't want to talk to him about Julia or ladybugs. "She said Punk McDaniels's funeral is this afternoon."

Wade backed out of the drive. "Where's the funeral being held?"

"I assume at the funeral home in Zenith. Julia said the church is putting on a meal after the funeral. She's helping."

"And what time is this funeral?"

"One o'clock."

"Good. We have time before we go."

"Before 'we' go? Why should I go? I didn't know the man. I only met him that once."

"You were there when he died." Wade slowed to a stop at the

corner, then turned onto my road. "And you live in this area. Fewer people will notice my presence if I go with you. I might overhear something that will help me with this case. The murderer might even be there."

That idea really thrilled me. Not!

Deputy Perry was waiting for us at my house. He had a device he showed Wade that was supposed to detect any and all hidden electronic devices. I watched the two men punch buttons and turn dials while Baraka found his favorite spot on the grass and relieved himself. By the time Baraka finished, the men were still playing with the gadget. I went up on my front porch and called to Wade. "I'm going inside. Okay?"

He looked at me as if he'd just remembered I was there, then yelled, "Wait a minute."

I waited, but before Wade reached my side, the locksmith's van pulled into the yard. It was beginning to look like I was having a party. With the locksmith's arrival, I decided I could wait a few minutes more to see this secret room and passageway, especially since the locksmith appeared a bit hesitant when Baraka went bounding toward the van. "It's all right," I called. "He's just a pup."

The man still looked nervous and wasn't getting out, so I walked over to Baraka. With my dog on a leash, I showed the locksmith my back door.

"Whadya do, use a sledgehammer?" he asked.

"Wasn't me and wasn't a sledgehammer." I showed him the chunk of firewood lying on the ground by the side of my back stairs.

As soon as the locksmith had his instructions, I went inside. I found Wade and Deputy Perry in my dining room. Deputy Perry was holding the gadget in front of him and it was making a weird noise. The noise got louder as he held it toward the framed print Julia had given me. The black and white etching showed two birds on a reed. It was her housewarming gift to me. One of her early prints, she'd said. Lately she'd been experimenting with the intaglio steel plate method.

Wade looked at Deputy Perry, then lifted the print off of the nail I'd used to hang it. I couldn't clearly see what was on the wall behind the print, but I knew that dark spot and hole hadn't been there when I hung the picture. Curious, I moved closer.

Wade looked down at me when I reached his side. "Transmitter," he said.

"So that's a bug."

"A very sophisticated one," Deputy Perry said and carefully removed the device, leaving a hole in the wall. He wore latex gloves and used a pair of needle-nose pliers to remove a small watch type battery. Both "bug" and battery went into a paper bag and were marked with the location, date, and time.

Wade hung the picture back on the nail, covering the hole. "Question is," he said, "how long has this been here?" He looked at me. "Any idea?"

"No." I'm not one of those people who moves couches and chairs when vacuuming. I certainly don't move pictures. I figure if the dirt is out of sight, why bother.

Then I remembered.

"Saturday night," I said, a part of the mystery suddenly cleared up. "I told those deputies someone had swept my floor. They didn't believe me. It had to be then." Digging plaster out of a wall would have left a mess on my floor. I would have noticed if the culprit hadn't swept the floor.

I noticed because he did. I simply didn't know what it meant.

Wade nodded. "So that explains the break-in that night."

"Do you think there are more of these bugs or listening devices around?"

"That's what we're here to find out," Deputy Perry said and

put his "bug finding gadget" back to work.

I followed the two men from room to room, but they didn't find anything else. By the time we made a circle of the downstairs rooms, I was tired of the search. I wanted to see this underground room and secret passage.

"I'm going down," I told Wade, and opened the door to the cellar.

He gave me a nod, then followed Deputy Perry, the two heading for the second floor. I snapped on the light and started down the stairs to the cellar.

A portion of the shelves that had always been flush against the cellar wall now protruded three quarters of the way into the room. What I'd thought was a wall behind the shelves was actually attached to them.

A flashlight sat on one shelf. I assumed it belonged to the sheriff's department. I grabbed it and snapped it on.

At first I simply stood in the opening and looked around. The beam of light from the flashlight illuminated only a portion of the underground room at any one time. I saw the cans of food and jugs of water Wade had mentioned . . . then the cot. He'd forgotten to mention the three folding chairs leaning against one dirt wall or the straw broom propped in a corner.

I wandered over to the cot. A plastic cover surrounded the mattress, and I could understand why. A cool, dampness permeated the area, as well as a musty, moldy smell. I had a feeling the ground beneath my feet was damp.

To test my theory, I leaned down and placed a hand on the dirt floor. As I'd suspected, I felt moisture.

Before I straightened, I saw something crumpled between the plastic mattress cover and the bed frame. I reached out and removed it.

It was a twenty-dollar bill. A fairly new one, the paper still stiff.

"Pretty elaborate, isn't it?" Wade said behind me.

Startled, I jumped, then turned to face him. "Don't do that," I demanded.

He smiled, my flashlight beam transforming his face into a series of shadows and planes, his features taking on a Draconian appearance. A shiver ran down my spine, goose bumps creeping over my skin.

"Velcum to my bedroom," he said, imitating the prince of the dead.

I glanced at the cot, half expecting to see it had changed into a casket. The twenty I'd pulled from beneath the mattress remained in my hand. I thought about giving it to Wade, then decided the heck with it. If my intruder was leaving money, I might as well keep it. I stuffed it into my jacket pocket.

"Go to the other end of the room," Wade said. "And you'll see the passage to the woodshed."

I aimed my flashlight in that direction. The passageway was a dark tunnel less than three feet wide and four feet high. I'm a little claustrophobic—enough that I didn't want to go there. I also didn't want to admit that everything down here spooked me. I feigned disinterest. "I think I've seen enough."

I started to move past Wade, but he stopped me with a hand on my shoulder, his hold gentle but firm. "Scared?"

"Of course not." If he felt my pulse, he'd know that was a lie.

Maybe he could read my mind, because he put his fingertips on the side of my throat and my heartbeat raced even faster.

"Of the room or me?" he asked softly.

Neither, I wanted to say. Both would be more accurate. I said nothing. The flashlight hung by my side, pointed down at our feet. We were in darkness, barely a glow illuminating our forms. Still, I could feel the heat of his gaze.

I knew he wanted to kiss me. Even more, I wanted him to kiss me. I wanted to feel his mouth on mine and his arms around me. Logic had no bearing here, only emotions. Mine were on edge.

Neither of us moved, then I heard him take in a shaky breath. "Let's go back upstairs," he said, a tightness to his voice. "Deputy Perry will be wondering what's keeping us."

I nodded and walked out of the room and up the cellar stairs ahead of Wade. I didn't need the furnace going this morning. My body radiated a simmering heat warmer even than the wood stove. Every nerve ending I possessed yearned to be stroked and caressed. I tried to act cool, calm, and collected, but my thoughts were taking me places they shouldn't go.

I think I actually moaned as I climbed those stairs. I hoped Wade would think I was groaning because of the climb. He'd shown restraint. So should I.

I stepped into the dining room breathless.

"All done," the locksmith said, standing by my front door, both his tool box and Baraka by his side. He then proceeded to name an outrageous price for his work, and I groaned again.

TWENTY-TWO

Deputy Perry found another "bug." His device didn't detect this one, just simple luck. He happened to comment on my computer, and I mentioned it had been working fine until Monday. I hadn't made the connection, but he did. A few minutes later, the cover was off my computer tower, and Deputy Perry was pulling something out of the inside. "This is your problem," he said and showed me a small plastic circle that had been attached to one of the boards in my computer. "With this in place, every message you sent or received could be picked up by another receiver."

"Well, it didn't help the guy who put it there. I haven't been on the Internet for days. Not here, at least. When I tried Monday, I couldn't get on. My server was down. I think, however, that it did mess up my tax program. I had to call a computer repair man to get that going again."

"Hopefully taking it out won't mess you up again."

I shared that feeling. I was far enough behind in my work. I didn't need another glitch.

Once my computer was back together and we determined that everything was working fine, Deputy Perry and Wade left. It was ten o'clock, and Wade said he'd be back at twelve-thirty to pick me up for the funeral. That left me with a new dilemma.

What do you wear to the funeral of a man you've only met moments before his death? Certainly not one of my three dresses. Though the blue wool wouldn't be bad, I'd gotten a stain on it the night of the euchre party. Probably some of the sauce from Rose's delicious chicken wings. And my customary sweats wouldn't be appropriate. I finally decided on a clean pair of black jeans, a white turtleneck pullover, and a blue tweed sweater. Sort of a country preppy look.

I hoped I'd blend in with the background. I forgot I'd be arriving with Wade Kingsley. The man is just too good looking to blend in anywhere. I wasn't the only woman who found him difficult to ignore. I'd say half the females in that funeral home watched us when we entered the room . . . and they weren't looking at me. Not at first. When they did notice my presence, they whispered to each other.

I'm not sure if they were commenting on my attire or relaying the fact that I'd found the body. I'm pretty sure some people blamed me for Punk McDaniels's death. After all, I'm the stranger in town. No one they knew would kill a man like Punk.

As the minister droned on about the deceased's virtues and how his soul was now in a better place, I glanced around the room. I was surprised by how many people were at the funeral. I may not have known Punk McDaniels, but he was a very popular man.

Wade had said Punk's killer might be at the funeral. Since I knew it wasn't me, I scanned faces—some familiar and some not—and tried to guess who might have fired those shots in my woods.

Nora and Rose sat three rows up and to my right. I could only see the backs of their heads, but I'd watched them arrive. If body language was an indicator, they were still having a domestic dispute. Rose practically bristled when Nora whispered something in her ear.

I wondered if their problems had anything to do with Punk. I could imagine Nora shooting him if she thought he was playing handyman to Rose's handywoman.

Julia had arrived late and stood near the doorway. I knew she didn't kill Punk. Working at the bank, she had an ironclad alibi. I wasn't sure about John. For that matter, John wasn't at the funeral.

I'd just noted that fact when Jim Fuller stood and offered Julia his chair. His wife, Ione, said something to Julia, and they both looked my way. I smiled and they smiled back; still I felt something was afoot.

Bill and Sondra Sommers, with two of their four children in tow, sat almost in front of me. I couldn't imagine them as killers. Not that I knew either well enough to make a judgment. They just didn't seem the type.

Carl, however, who was seated next to Bill Sommers, was another matter. He had to be the one who called the sheriff's department about my grandfather's gun. And the poem most likely was his. Question was, did he leave it or did Howard Lowe?

Lowe sat to my left, just off at an angle, his position allowing me almost a full view of his face. He was watching me, not the minister or casket. I smiled; Lowe didn't. Nor did he look away. Stony faced, he kept staring at me until I gave in and lowered my gaze.

To compensate for losing a stare-down, I studied the little folder I'd received when we arrived. Carroll "Punk" McDaniels had lived a mere thirty-eight years. He'd been born in Zenith and had died in Zenith. From the number of people attending his funeral, I'd say his wasn't a futile life . . . just a futile death.

A song was played, then people began leaving the chapel. I thought that would be it, but Wade had other plans. "I want to go to the grave site," he said. "Listen to what's said there."

Outside the funeral home, people were already talking. Behind and around me I could hear conversations. Some were discussing Punk McDaniels's ability with a hammer and saw.

Others were talking about his drinking habits. Evidently he spent a lot of hours at the Pour House. That's the problem when a town has only one bar and grill. Everyone knows how often you've been there, what you drink, and how much. From what I was overhearing, Punk was there often, drank draft beer, and lots of it.

A plain woman in her sixties—big boned, gray haired, and dressed in black—came out of the funeral home. Punk's mother, I assumed. She stood at the top of the steps, looking over the crowd of people. I thought how pleased she must be to see so many people at her son's funeral.

To my surprise, she came rushing down the steps toward me, fist raised. Wade stepped in front of me, providing a barrier, but it wasn't necessary. Mrs. McDaniels went right past us on to the sidewalk by the street. She stopped in front of Julia.

"You!" she screamed. "You killed my son."

From Julia's expression, I knew she didn't understand.

"Get out of my sight," Mrs. McDaniels shouted. "I don't ever want to see you again."

Slack mouthed, Julia stared at her, then turned and walked away, head and shoulders slumped. Mrs. McDaniels watched for a moment, then turned and walked over to the limousine that would follow the hearse to the cemetery.

"Now that was interesting," Wade said as we walked back to his Jeep.

I was still in a state of shock. "Julia couldn't have killed Punk. She was at the bank at the time of the shooting."

"She has a perfect alibi, but there's more than one way to execute a murder."

I looked at Wade, but he didn't elaborate.

He put his Jeep at the rear of the procession to the cemetery, and we parked near the road. I was glad I was wearing boots and not high heels when we tramped across the soggy ground to the grave site. At least it was spring. People inconsiderate enough to die in the winter sometimes have to wait for a thaw to reach their final resting place.

I hadn't worn my jacket. I didn't realize we'd be outside for an extended period of time, and even though it was a beautiful spring day and the sun was shining, the temperature wasn't that high. I shivered as the minister went on about Punk McDaniels's future expectations. Wade put an arm around my shoulders and drew me close to his side.

The gesture caught me completely off-guard, and I sucked in a breath. My body temperature soared from freezing to roasting in the leap of a heartbeat. Snuggled against his body, I could smell his cologne, feel the smooth leather of his jacket, and sense the tension of his muscles. I looked up and he was watching me, his expression guarded.

I wish I could disguise my feelings that well. I'm sure he could tell he'd surprised me. "I just wanted to keep you warm," he said quietly, his voice huskier than normal.

I almost told him he was doing an excellent job, then decided to keep my mouth shut. If he sounded husky, I'd probably squeak. To protect myself, I simply nodded, then looked away.

He still had his arm around me when the minister finished and the crowd began to break up. Rather than walking away, he stood where he was. Watching. Listening.

His patience paid off. The other mourners walked by, but Mrs. McDaniels—her eyes red rimmed and her nose scarlet—came directly toward us. "I understand my son died in your house," she said as she neared. "I was wondering . . ." She stopped in front of us and dabbed at her eyes with a soggy handkerchief. "Did he—?"

"Say anything?" I finished for her. It was what everyone asked. She nodded.

"No." I didn't think swear words qualified as a dying man's confession.

I thought that would be it, but then she sighed and said, "I think this is my fault."

Wade perked up. "Why do you think that?"

She looked at him, and I decided introductions were in order, even though I'd never been formally introduced. "Mrs. McDaniels, this is Detective Wade Kingsley of the homicide department. He's working on your son's murder."

"Ah, Detective Kingsley." Mrs. McDaniels held out a hand and Wade shook it.

"Why do you feel you caused your son to die?" he asked again, releasing his hold on me. He was all business now.

"Because he told me to go visit my brother and not tell anyone. But I did tell someone. Julia asked me why I needed traveler's checks, and I told her."

"Julia Westman?" I asked, though I knew it had to be her.

"Yes. The bank teller," Mrs. McDaniels said. "Punk recently did some work for her husband. Built some sort of secure work area, except Punk said it wasn't all that secure . . . not if someone knew how to get in. And that, I think, was the problem."

"I don't understand," Wade said, but I did. It was those damn ladybugs.

Mrs. McDaniels explained. "Punk came home one night bragging that some guy had offered him an indecent amount of money. He rambled on and on about the fine line between good and evil." She stopped and looked at Wade. "Punk was a good boy, but he did have a habit of drinking too much. He never worked a job drunk. Not Punk. You hired him for a day's work, that's what you got—a day's work. But at night—"

"I understand," Wade said. "You say he rambled on about good and evil. Do you remember what he said?"

186

"It didn't make much sense, just that this guy was willing to pay a lot of money for something. Something Punk could help him get. Next morning, when he sobered up, he told me to forget everything he'd said. He wasn't trading trust for no amount of money."

"So he turned down the offer?"

"I think he tried. But I don't think this guy who made the offer wanted to hear that. I think he kept after Punk until Punk had to do what he wanted."

"How did he manage that?" I asked, curious.

She looked at me. "I think he threatened him. I think he killed Punk's dog, though I didn't realize it at the time. Bo was old. When I went out and found him lying by the coop, I thought he'd just died of old age. But something about Bo's passing scared Punk. I could tell it in his eyes.

"Then one day Punk came home all tense. He told me to pack my bags, tell no one where I was going, and to go visit my brother. I've never seen my boy that upset, so I did. At least I packed my bags and went to visit my brother. I didn't think telling Julia where I'd be was such a big thing. She asked and I just told her. And everything was fine for a few days. Then a car almost hit me. Went right off the street onto the sidewalk. Missed me by inches and scared the dickens out of me. I was still shook up when Punk called that night to see how things was going. When I told Punk about the car, he really got upset. He kept asking who I told I was going down there, and when I finally said Julia, Punk said something really weird."

She stopped and both Wade and I said, "What did she say?"

I looked at him, and he looked at me, then we chuckled and looked back at Mrs. McDaniels. She sighed and went on. "He said, 'I guess they deserve it. Don't worry, Mom. You'll be fine.' Now, ain't that weird?"

For me, what he'd said wasn't weird. It made sense.

"When was that, Mrs. McDaniels?" Wade asked.

"One week ago today. Wednesday." She looked at me. "That was the last time I talked to my boy. The last time I heard my son's voice. All because I told Julia I was going to Florida."

She began to cry. I stepped away from Wade's side and hugged her. I told her it wasn't her fault. Not that I knew, one way or the other, but I was pretty sure her telling Julia was only a side issue. Punk McDaniels wouldn't be in a casket if he hadn't said too much at the local bar.

"Do you remember what night your son came home from the bar saying someone had offered him a lot of money?" Wade asked. "The day and date?"

Mrs. McDaniels sniffed a few times, straightened, and looked at him. "It was a Friday night. I remember that. A Friday night in March. Friday the . . ."

I could tell she was thinking back. Wade waited. Finally she came up with the answer. "Friday the thirteenth."

TWENTY-THREE

"I'm going to take you home, P.J., then visit your local bar," Wade said and started for his Jeep.

"Oh no you don't." I wasn't about to be left out of this. "If you're going to the Pour House, I'm going with you."

He frowned. "This is a matter for law enforcement, not civilians."

"What? You think your killer is sitting at the bar waiting for you?" I shook my head. "This is fact finding, nothing more. And I'm sort of a local, so I might be able to find out more facts than you."

Actually, six months doesn't qualify anyone as a local when it comes to small towns, but I was more of a local than Wade Kingsley.

He hesitated a moment, then nodded. "Okay. Let's go do some fact finding."

The Pour House is located on the southeast corner of the crossroads that makes up the center of Zenith. It's a two-story wood-frame building with living quarters on top and the bar and restaurant on the main level. Built in the early nineteen hundreds, it's seen several owners, each new proprietor changing its look. The place's most recent makeover, from what Julia told me, was to meet handicap requirements. Steps had been replaced with a ramp and the bathrooms enlarged.

If this newest owner hoped to make a fortune here in Zenith, it wouldn't happen today. It was mid-afternoon and the place was practically empty. One old man with a scruffy beard sat at the end of the bar, a bottle of beer in front of him, while in the restaurant section the only customers were two workmen finishing hamburgers. A waitress poked her head out from the kitchen, but stepped back out of sight when she realized we were heading for the bar.

Wade flashed his badge at the bartender and asked, "Who was working the bar Friday, March thirteenth?"

The bartender, who looked like he also could be the bouncer, seemed to ponder the question, then walked over to the cash register. From a shelf under the counter, he pulled out a calendar, flipped it back a month, and began looking at the dates. He glanced up. "Afternoon or night?"

"Night," Wade said.

"Chuck VanderVeen," the bartender returned. "He works most Friday nights." He held up the calendar, though it was too far for me to see. "According to this, he was working that night."

Wade said, "Any idea where this Chuck VanderVeen might be this afternoon?"

"This afternoon? Yeah. He's at Punk McDaniels's funeral."

Wade thanked the man and we left the Pour House. Outside, I cleared my lungs of stale cigarette smoke and liquor smell, then looked at Wade. "Friends and family were to go to the church after the graveyard ceremony. It's just down the block. We could walk from here."

"Then let's do it."

He slid an arm through mine and guided me in the direction I'd indicated. I didn't object. I was starting to like being touched by Wade Kingsley. I liked the smell of his cologne, the muscular feel of his body, and the way he matched his steps to mine.

I wasn't thinking sex. Well, not entirely. I was thinking friendship and male companionship. Feeling protected and just a little bit cherished.

Darn it all. I liked the man.

Some people were leaving the church's rec room when we arrived, and I hoped Chuck VanderVeen hadn't already left. I had no idea what he looked like, but I wasn't hesitant to ask. I recognized Ray Mason—Santa beard and bushy white hair—from the euchre party and went over to him. As soon as I told Ray who we were looking for, he glanced around the room, then pointed at a slender man with a shaved head, stubby brown beard, and a mustache.

Wade identified himself to Chuck VanderVeen, pulled out his trusty notebook, and started right in on the questions. It took Chucky boy a few minutes to remember the night, and when he did, I wasn't sure we'd gained a lot.

"Yeah, I do remember," he said. "Punk and this guy were sitting at the bar. Punk was on his third or fourth beer, talking to me about needing a break now that he'd finished the job for John Westman. The other guy had been sitting a few seats down. The way he sidled up to Punk, I figured he needed some work done. I didn't overhear the entire conversation, but I know the guy asked Punk questions about his last job. He wanted details, except Punk wouldn't tell him much. Even half drunk, Punk had control of himself. Well, pretty good control. There was one point when Punk pulled out some money to pay for his drinks and the other guy grabbed it and told him he was a fool. They argued for a minute. I'm not sure about what. Then the other guy paid for the drinks and they left together. That was about it. The next day, when Punk came in, he told me he had the worst hangover he'd had in years. The other guy didn't look all that great, either."

"So this guy was a regular?" Wade asked.

Chuck the bartender shook his head. "Those two nights were the only nights I've seen him. Of course, I mainly work Fridays and Saturdays. I can't say about other nights."

"What did this guy look like?" Wade asked.

Chuck half-closed his eyes and for a moment said nothing. Finally, he spoke. "Medium height. Dark, almost black, hair. Cropped short. And his eyes—" He hesitated. "His eyes were strange. I remember they were blue. A brilliant blue. But they just didn't look natural."

"Do you think he was wearing colored contacts?" I asked.

Chuck nodded. "Could be."

"Anything else?" Wade asked.

"Yeah. He had a lean, mean look about him. Not an ounce of extra weight, but the man wasn't thin. He made me think of my military days, right after we got out of boot camp. You know, when you're in great shape. Except, if he was military, he must have been an officer. He definitely wasn't a youngster."

"Do you think he was from Fort Custer?"

Chuck shrugged. "Could be. No uniform though, unless you consider a black turtleneck and black jeans a uniform."

Wade wrote everything down. "Anything else."

"Not that I recall." Chuck glanced around the room, then back at Wade. "Do you think the guy had something to do with Punk getting killed?"

"That's what I'm trying to find out."

"Just so you know, I was in the bank the day Punk's mother told Julia where she was going. I heard what she said. Other teller could of, too. So Julia wasn't the only one who knew."

Wade made note of that, asked Chuck a couple more questions, then thanked him for his help. I thought we might leave at that point, but Wade had an eye on the food. "Are you hungry?" he asked.

"Not terribly." I'd grabbed a sandwich for lunch.

"Think they'd mind if I had something to eat? I missed lunch."

"I don't think they'd mind at all." I could see plenty of food on the table. Most of the people around us had eaten while Wade and I were at the Pour House talking to the bartender. "Why don't you fix yourself a plate while I use the ladies' room?"

"You really don't want anything?" He continued eyeing the casseroles and salads the church volunteers and friends of the family had contributed.

My gaze went to another table, this one laden with cakes, cookies, and pies. At least what was left of those desserts. My father always said I had a sweet tooth. "I might nibble on something."

We parted ways, Wade promising to save me a place at a table. I used the facilities, taking time to run a brush though my hair and apply a fresh coat of lipstick. I'd just stepped out of the bathroom and started looking for Wade when I sensed someone behind me.

"Heard someone's been living under your house," a gruff voice said, almost in my right ear.

I took a step to the side and turned to face Howard Lowe. He might be in his sixties, but there's nothing frail about him. He makes me think of a blend of Rambo and Willie Nelson, and he gives me the creeps the way he looks at me.

Unwilling to let him know he bothered me, I came back with, "Do you know who it was?"

"Got my guesses."

"So are you going to share your guesses?" His ambiguity irked me.

"Not yet, but I did contact the CROWS."

We were back to crows. The man was certifiably crazy, but I decided to humor him. "And what did the crows say?"

"That they'll check into it."

"That's nice." I inched away from him, moving toward the main room. Lowe made me think of Grandpa Carter the year before he died. Grandpa Carter talked to cats. Live cats. Dead cats. It didn't matter.

Lowe moved with me. "I'm not part of their organization, but I've monitored their Web site."

I stopped moving. "CROWS. You mean like capital C, capital R, capital . . . ?" I didn't finish spelling the word. His nods answered my question. "So you do belong."

"No, I'm not a member." He dropped his voice to almost a whisper. "I'm what they call a listener. I report rumors. They have us all across the country. Probably ninety-five percent of what we report is worthless, but every so often one of us comes up with something worthwhile. Back last fall, I thought your neighbor's company was messing around with something that should be left alone. So I reported it."

"You knew about the ladybugs?"

"That what it was? Ladybugs? I didn't know. But one day, when I was in the bank, I overheard Julia having an argument on the phone with her husband. When she said, 'Man shouldn't play God with nature,' I knew something was up. Those scientists don't know when to leave well enough alone."

"So you reported what she said?"

"Yeah." He sounded proud of it. "She didn't want him bringing any of his experiments home. But he did, didn't he? Had them right there in his barn, didn't he? That's what this is all about, isn't it?"

It was my turn to be vague. "Maybe."

"Scientists." Howard Lowe scoffed. "Can't leave good enough alone. Scientists and politicians. Both going to ruin the world. That's why we need groups like the CROWS."

"So the CROWS are involved in this? Are they the ones who shot Punk?"

"Not exactly. Least that's what they said. Said they think they've got themselves a rogue. Someone who used to live around here." Lowe glanced down the hallway, toward the main room. "I thought maybe he might show up today, but I ain't seen him. Not that I'd know, that is."

"You need to tell Detective Kingsley what you just told me." I took another step down the hallway and looked for Wade. Finally I saw him at the farthest table, talking to two gray-haired women clearing the table. "There he is," I said and turned back to Lowe.

Except, Lowe was gone. As silently as he'd crept up on me, he'd vanished, leaving me with an uneasy feeling that he hadn't told me everything.

Twenty-Four

The two gray-haired ladies left before I reached Wade's table. He was digging into a mound of potato salad when I pulled out a chair and sat next to him. "Howard Lowe just talked to me," I said, barely above a whisper. "Remember that poem I found? Remember how the word 'crows' was capitalized? Well, I was right about that Web site your sister and I found having something to do with it."

"Which Web site?" Wade put down his fork, giving me his full attention.

"The one that's an acronym for a civilian resistance organization. The initials spell 'crows.' "

"One of those militia groups?"

"I'm not sure, but probably. Ginny and I couldn't get past the home page. Lowe, however, seems able to contact them. He says he's not a part of the organization. Called himself a 'listener.' Said he reports anything suspicious."

"Suspicious like what?"

"Like a comment Julia made to her husband last fall about not tampering with nature. Like what's been going on at my place lately."

"This guy Lowe admitted to being involved in the murder?"

"No." I wasn't explaining this well. "All he said was he'd called the CROWS and reported what was going on, and that they told him one of their members might be involved. Someone who used to live around here."

"What else did he tell you about the group?"

"That they believe scientists and politicians are going to ruin the world. They're the soldiers for the little guys."

Wade scoffed. "The little guys already have soldiers. They're called officers of the law. Law," he repeated. "We operate under the laws of the Constitution."

"And sometimes those laws benefit only a few . . . the ones with the money and power." I surprised myself with that speech. I guess I do have a little of my grandmother's and parents' rebellious nature.

"So you approve of anarchy?" Wade's stiff tone defined his disapproval of my attitude.

I wasn't intimidated. "Anarchy, no. But I do think we sometimes need groups to stand up for the rights of those who don't have the power. I don't know if this CROWS groups is good or bad. Lowe said they're weren't happy with what was going on. I suppose any group can have members who go bad."

"When people take the law into their own hands, they're all bad."

"I can see this discussion is going nowhere."

"You're the one who brought it up."

That deserved a scowl, and he got one. "I was telling you what Lowe said. You're the one who became judge and jury."

I noticed the muscles in Wade's jaw tightened, and he didn't say anything for a full minute. Then his mouth relaxed and actually formed a slight smile. "Okay, so last fall Mr. Lowe reported to this group that one of his neighbors was possibly conducting illegal experiments. The group sends someone to check this out. Except, rather than destroying the experiment, our man in black decides to steal these deadly beetles and sell them to a foreign country . . . or use them to blackmail our country. So how does McDaniels fit in here?"

A sheriff's detective was asking me? I could only guess. "I'd say our guy heard that Punk was doing some work for John. Punk probably told people it was 'secret' work. Our CROW learns that Punk spends a lot of time at the bar, waits until Punk shows up, and then gets Punk drunk and talking. He probably promised Punk money. When that didn't work, he threatened Punk. You heard Mrs. McDaniels. She said Punk acted scared, that his dog died and suddenly he wanted her to go to Florida and to tell no one."

Wade nodded. "And then she's nearly hit by a car and tells her son."

"Exactly. So now he's scared someone is going to get his mother."

Wade turned toward the kitchen area. I followed his gaze and saw one of the two gray-haired ladies he'd been talking to earlier. He nodded toward her. "That would fit. While you were gone, I was talking to Harriet and her friend Ina. Harriet works in the church office. She said she found Mr. McDaniels in the church last week. She's sure it was Thursday. She said he was sitting on one of the pews and it looked like he was praying. She thought it strange since he's not a church regular. In fact, she said she mentioned it to his mother today, and his mother said she didn't remember her son going to church since he was a boy."

"Sounds like he was looking for help. A little divine intervention."

"Except he didn't ask for help," Wade pointed out. "Harriet said she asked him if he needed anything. She said he looked surprised to see her, said no, and immediately left."

"Too bad he didn't tell someone."

"And, of course, this is all conjecture." Wade picked up his fork again. "Your friend Lowe say who this rogue was?"

"No." I absently snatched an olive from Wade's plate and bit into it. "But I'm wondering if Rose might know."

"Rose?"

"Yes. Yesterday, after you brought me back from the hospital, I went over to see Nora, except Nora wasn't home, just Rose. And while I was waiting on the porch for her to get that ceramic pot, I saw someone in her living room. I'm sure it was a man. A man dressed in black."

"You didn't tell me that," Wade said, as if I were holding back information.

"Because the next time I saw you, you arrested me."

Wade looked around the room. "I don't see Nora or Rose here."

I didn't see them, either. "They may have already left."

"So you saw a man with Rose—"

"In her living room. He was sitting in a chair, his back to me."

"Did you get a look at his face?"

"No. And he'd already disappeared when I mentioned to Rose that I'd seen him. But later, when I was over at Julia's, I think I saw him in my woods."

"The same man?"

"I'm not sure."

"Did Julia see this guy?"

"No. And neither did Carl." I figured I'd better tell Wade that before he asked. "He thought it might have been Lowe, since he'd seen Lowe's dog running loose."

I grabbed another olive from Wade's plate. Then a pickle. I was chewing on the pickle when I realized Wade was looking at me. "What?" I asked, my mouth half full.

"If you're that hungry, why don't you fix yourself a plate?"

"I'm not hungry, I had a . . ." I looked down at the food on Wade's plate. That potato salad really looked good. And the baked beans.

Sandwiches only last so long.

I smiled at him and pushed back my chair. "Maybe I will. Do you want anything while I'm up?"

"Coffee," he said. "And more olives."

Wade left me at my house just before four o'clock. I let Baraka out of his crate. Poor dog. You could almost hear him sigh when he squatted on the grass. Once my dog was taken care of, I called my grandmother. I hadn't had a chance yesterday, and I wanted to know what the doctor had said about my mother.

The call confirmed what we both knew. Mom had been off her medication.

"She told the doctor it was making her sick," Grandma said. "I don't remember her being sick. She certainly never said anything to me about feeling sick. And now I find out she's been off the pills for weeks."

That wasn't good. My mother does all sorts of weird things when she's not on her medication. Sees weird things. "So what did the doctor say?"

"Just what we already know, that it's not uncommon for someone with schizophrenia to stop taking medication when she feels well. And he did say some people do get sick on those pills after taking them for a while. He gave her a shot this time. He said that sometimes works with patients who don't remember to take their pills. But he also said he couldn't force your mother to take her medicine. Patient's rights, and all that. He should have to live with her. I'll tell you, I hope she goes in for these shots. I don't like watching her like a hawk."

"Or like a crow?"

"Crow?"

"Sorry." I realized Grandma wouldn't get the connection . . . if there was one. "Sick humor. I get this way after attending a funeral."

"Whose funeral?"

"The man who died in my house. And you haven't heard it all." I quickly repeated everything that had happened since my visit Sunday. Grandma made the appropriate comments, deriding the sheriff's department for even taking me in for questioning. She concurred that Grandpa Benson would be just the type to build a bomb shelter, but she was concerned about someone hiding in it. "It's sealed off, now," I said. "And the locks on my doors have been changed. Cost me a fortune for that."

"And a fortune for that guard dog that doesn't seem to be guarding you very well."

Speaking of guard dogs, I suddenly realized I hadn't seen Baraka for a while. Phone in hand, I went looking for him. I found him in the far corner of the living room, busy chewing one of my shoes. "He's just a puppy," I said and took the shoe from him, much to his displeasure. I found a rawhide bone as a substitute, although the look he gave me said he didn't find the two objects comparable.

"You can come here if you want, you know," Grandma said. "There's always room on the couch."

"I know." But I'm not into lung cancer. When people smoke as much as my mother and grandmother do, even an air filter can't keep up.

After I finished talking to Grandma, I decided to call Julia. I might be upset with her for putting me in this position, but I didn't like what had happened to her after Punk's funeral.

"Are you okay?" I asked when she answered the phone.

"Yeah, I'm fine."

She didn't sound all right. She sounded down and depressed. "Mrs. McDaniels was looking for someone to blame," I said, hoping to cheer her up.

"It doesn't matter." Julia's sigh was audible. "I feel responsible. If we hadn't hired Punk, none of this would have happened."

"And if he didn't drink a lot, none of this would have happened," I reminded her. "You want to come over for a coffee or something?"

"No. But thanks. I started a woodcut I want to work on. It's in memory of Punk McDaniels. I want to give it to his mother."

"That would be nice."

We said our good-byes, and after I hung up, I decided I'd better get back to work. As far as I knew, the IRS still expected taxes to be paid by the fifteenth. They weren't interested in secret rooms, breakins, or funerals.

I'd just started on a 1040 form when a car pulled into my yard. Sondra—the dairy farmer's wife—got out. I went out on the porch and kept Baraka by my side. Sondra stayed on the grass.

"I saw you at the funeral," she said, one hand shading her eyes against the afternoon sun, the other clutching a black shoulder bag. "You were there with a good-looking man. Someone special?"

"No." I wondered why she'd stopped by. She never had before. "That was Detective Kingsley, from the Kalamazoo Sheriff's Department."

"Nora did say she thought you were under arrest."

"Oh, she did, did she?" Nora wasn't just trying to poison me, she was poisoning my neighbors against me. "Well, I'm not. We were looking for a killer."

"Wow, you're helping the sheriff's department?"

I lied a little. "Just incidentally."

"I'm impressed." Sondra stepped closer, keeping an eye on Baraka. "He's just a puppy, isn't he?"

"Just four months old."

"He's going to be big. Look at those paws."

He was also going to be strong. Having been cooped up for most of the afternoon, he wanted off the porch. I struggled to hold him back. "Was there something else?"

"Ah." She looked around. "You're by yourself?"

"Yes." Baraka continued wiggling. "Except for him."

"But he wouldn't attack anyone, would he?"

"No." I gave up and let him go. "Other than to lick you to death."

Baraka bound down the stairs and ran to Sondra, sniffing her legs and the shoulder bag. When he started to jump, I yelled no and he stopped.

Sondra watched him for a minute, then rubbed his head and let him lick her hand. "Julia said he was friendly. She also said someone broke into your place last night, that it's happened several times since Punk was murdered."

"I think we've got that stopped." I pointed at my door. "New locks." I didn't mention the underground room, though if Lowe knew, probably everyone in Zenith did by now. "And there's going to be a sheriff's deputy here tonight, keeping an eye on the place."

"Oh that's good," she said. "But he's not here, yet?"

"No." The way she kept looking around, as if expecting someone to appear out of nowhere, made me nervous. "Why?"

Sondra slid the strap of her handbag off her shoulder and opened it. "Because of this." She pulled out a handgun.

TWENTY-FIVE

"Sondra?" I automatically took a step back and raised my hands. I couldn't believe this mild-mannered woman, mother of four, had a gun in her hand.

I do not like guns. I remember the time my father showed me his gun. I was nine, and he was on leave. He made me hold it. All I remember is it was heavy and it scared me.

I was scared now.

Sondra pointed the gun toward the sky. "What do you think? It's a Smith and Wesson AirLite. Lightweight and dependable."

"I think you should put it away. Don't you have to have a permit to carry something like that?"

She looked my way and frowned. "I have one. Well, not to carry a concealed weapon, but to own one. Why do you have your hands up?"

Why did I? I lowered them and tried to keep my voice calm. "So the gun is yours? What about your kids? Aren't you afraid they might get hold of it?"

"No. My kids have been taught that guns are not playthings. They've all shot it. My oldest prefers his shotgun to this. Calls mine a sissy gun. You know guys. No matter what age, they've got to have a bigger one."

She stepped closer and held the gun toward me, barrel pointed down and butt end my direction. "Here, take it."

"No." That sounded abrupt, so I softened my tone. "Thanks, but no."

"It will give you some protection."

"What I'd probably do is shoot myself or my dog. Maybe your kids know how to handle a gun, but I don't."

"I could show you."

I appreciated her offer, but I turned her down. I don't think she understood, but I grew up hearing my grandmother tell my father to keep his gun locked up. Guns around a person with a mental disease are not a good idea. And since I'm afraid I might one day be like my mother, I definitely don't want a gun around.

Once Sondra was sure I wasn't going to change my mind, she left. I don't think she was angry, just baffled. What I felt was depressed. I needed to talk to someone who would understand my fears.

And that someone would be Grandma Carter.

Thursday morning, I drove to Kalamazoo. First I delivered Sporbach's tax forms to them, then I dropped off completed tax forms to two other Kalamazoo businesses. Those tasks accomplished, I headed for Grandma's.

I arrived at her front door at eleven fifteen, Baraka by my side. Since I hadn't let her know I was coming, Grandma was surprised to see me. She gave me a hug, led me into the living room, sat me down, and said, "Okay, what's the matter?"

I tried to act nonchalant. "What do you mean, what's the matter? I was in town, and I decided to stop by and see you."

She said nothing, but her eyebrows rose, and I knew she could see through that excuse. Grandma knows me too well. I shrugged my shoulders and lowered my voice. "Is Mom around?"

"Upstairs." Grandma sat in the chair opposite me and leaned close. "Why?"

I glanced toward the stairs and continued to keep my voice low. "I wondered what her initial symptoms were? I mean, I know she saw things, but what other signs were there?"

"Other signs?" Grandma pursed her lips, then sighed. "Well, for one, right after she got pregnant with you, she wrote a letter to the editor about how we had to be nice to the aliens. Of course, back then, I thought she meant foreigners."

"Probably because she sees them as foreigners." Mom is sure she's been taken aboard a space ship and has talked to aliens. She swears she's been abducted three times.

"And then, there was the screaming." Grandma shook her head. "That day was wild. There she was in the bathroom, cowering in a corner, swearing bugs were coming out of the tub. For her they were real."

"What about paranoia?" I asked. "Did she think people were out to get her?"

"Not at first." Grandma gave me a quizzical look. "What's up, P.J.? What are you worried about?"

I told her the truth. "That I'm starting to show the signs."

"What have you noticed?"

As I'd expected, Grandma didn't dismiss the idea. We both knew this was a possibility. "A feeling that my neighbors are out to get me. I told you about Nora, that I'm sure she put poison in some stew she gave me. Then yesterday, at least for a moment, I thought another neighbor was going to shoot me. And what I didn't tell you is I thought Dad called me the other night."

"Your father?" Grandma sat back in her chair and stared at me.

"I know it's impossible. But the voice sure sounded like his."

"It's been eighteen years, P.J. You were a child when he died. How would you know if it sounded like him?"

"He called me Princess." That bothered me the most.

My mother must have overheard us, because from the top of

the stairs, I heard, "Paul's precocious princess picked purple peppers."

Slowly, she came down the stairs. Today she was dressed in a rose-colored silk blouse and tan slacks, a pair of stylish pumps covering her feet. Clothing and her appearance have always been important to Mom, even when she's at her worst.

She kept repeating the P words. It was a game Dad used to play with me. How many words could you string together that started with the same letter. Sometimes the sentences were totally ridiculous. Sometimes quite imaginative. Dad said it helped develop the mind. Anything to keep his daughter's mind from going bonkers. Right?

"Hi, Pumpkin," Mom said and sat on the couch next to me.

"Hi, Mom." I looked at her eyes and saw a clarity that had been missing four days ago. "How are you feeling?"

"Feeling great." She leaned over and gave Baraka a pat on the head, then grabbed a cigarette from the pack on the coffee table. "He's really growing. He's going to be a big dog," she said as she lit up. "So what did your dad have to say?"

I leaned away from the smoke. "I don't think it really was Dad. Whoever was on the phone simply sounded like Dad."

"Sure it was your dad," Mom said and leaned back on the couch, exhaling a breath of smoke. "After all, he said he'd be there if you ever needed help. And it certainly seems like you need help now."

She made it sound so logical, and as a child, I'd believed her. Now all I could think of were the reasons it wasn't him. "Problem is, he's dead, Mom. Remember? He was blown up by a bomb."

"They never found his body."

Grandma responded to that. "They didn't find a body, Flo, because he was blown to bits. They found his dog tags. They shipped back what they could."

"And what makes you think what they shipped back had anything to do with Paul? You can tell me I'm crazy, but I know he's not dead. I saw him after his funeral. He spoke to me. Maybe I wasn't in the best of shape that day, but I know what I saw and heard."

Mom definitely wasn't in the best of shape that day. And, in spite of my first impression, it didn't sound as if she was in the best shape today. "If he's still alive," I said, "where has he been these last eighteen years? We've had problems, needed help. That time we got kicked out of our apartment for not paying the rent. Why didn't he show up then?"

"Maybe he didn't need to," Mom said and looked at my grandmother. "Maybe he knew we'd be taken care of."

Grandma shook her head. "Flo, you are talking crazy. That man is dead."

"You thought you saw him once." Mom glared at Grandma. "Remember, back a few years ago? We were in Bronson Park, downtown. You swore you saw him coming out of the courthouse."

"And we checked, and no one in the building had a record of Paul Benson being there that day."

"Because he'd changed his name, or gave a false name. But soon after that, you received that letter and all of our problems were solved."

I remembered my grandmother's surprise when she received that letter. She'd been trying to get guardianship of my mother, but she'd run into dozens of legal roadblocks. Suddenly, everything was settled: Grandma had access to my father's trust, was appointed my guardian, as well as my mother's, and all of our medical bills were covered.

Because my father intervened?

I doubted it. Sure, I wanted my dad alive, but the idea was too far-fetched. Just as thinking my dad had called me was crazy. Either Grandma was right, someone was playing a trick on me, or I was showing the initial symptoms of the disease that plagued my mother.

I didn't like either possibility.

TWENTY-SIX

Grandma walked with me to my car. As I held the door open for Baraka to get in, she said, "You seem fine, P.J. Anyone who's gone through what you have would be a little paranoid."

I closed the door behind Baraka, then turned and hugged her. "Thanks. I'd needed to hear that."

Grandma sighed. "You know, up until your mother started talking about your father, I thought she was doing quite well today. I sure hope this new medication works."

"If she thinks Dad's alive—I mean, really thinks it—changing her medication might not make any difference."

"I suppose that's true. And your mother never has accepted your father's death. Almost from the day we received the message, she's said he's alive. It bothered me that she kept telling you he was. I hated seeing you get your hopes up. And, I can understand why this week would bring it up again. Stress can do funny things to a person."

"Stress?" The word hardly seemed adequate. "Like having someone die in my house? Having someone try to poison me? Break into my house?"

"And, if you're right, having someone pretend he's your father. That's worse than a simple trick of the mind. I think everyone, at one time or another, sees someone who looks familiar. As your mother said, I would have sworn I saw your father coming out of the courthouse. And the day you graduated from high school. . . ."

She didn't finish, and I urged her on. "What? What happened the day I graduated?"

"I thought I saw your father there. At the back of the room."

"You never said anything."

"I didn't dare. That wasn't one of your mother's better days. In fact, if you'll recall, I had to take her home early, and you had to get a ride from a friend."

"But you thought you saw my father there?" A giddy excitement flowed through me. "At my graduation?" Strange. I'd felt he was there. I'd finally convinced myself he was—in spirit. Could he have been there in the flesh, too? "But what made you think it was him? Mom said when she saw him, he didn't look the same."

"Well, both times these men were at a distance, so I never truly saw their faces. It was the way they stood and walked, their body language." She stared off into space, lost in her memories, then she shook her head and smiled at me. "I'm sure it was simply someone who moved like your dad. That, or we're both going crazy. You and me, P.J. Nutty as fruitcakes."

"Don't joke about it."

"I think I've got to."

I understood.

On the drive home, I stopped at the bank in Zenith. I needed to deposit the three checks I'd received today. That's one thing. I might be willing to deliver tax forms if I'm going to Kalamazoo, but I don't hand them over unless I'm paid.

Julia was at the bank. Working. She was helping the owner of our local grocery store, and I could see that transaction was going to take a while, so I went to the other teller's window.

Julia still had a customer at her spot, but she waved as I started out of the bank, and I waved back. Baraka was asleep on the back seat of the car, so I decided I'd get some stamps while in town. I looked both ways for cars—there were none—and crossed the street.

In Zenith, everything is close. Along one short block, you can buy stamps, pay your phone bill, by a soda pop at the local takeout, do your banking, and check a book out from the library. The grocery store is a little farther away—a quarter mile down the cross street—and if you want your hair done at the beauty shop, you have to cross the four corners and go past the Pour House. Of course, the men think that's just fine. While the wife gets her hair done, the husband has a beer or two.

Other businesses rim the village. There's the weekly news-paper, the funeral parlor, a Methodist church, and my competition . . . another tax service. I understand Zenith used to have a gas station and a Laundromat, but the potential cost of meet-ing EPA standards drove both out of business. Too bad, especially the lack of a gas station. However, I'd filled up in Kalamazoo and wasn't worried.

Just as I reached the post office, the door opened. Rose came out and walked past me without saying a word. I watched her head for her car, then I proceeded into the lobby of the post of-fice.

Carl stood by the boxes. Exactly the person I wanted to talk to. Except he spoke up first.

"Boy is she upset," he said.

"You mean Rose?"

"Yeah." He kept looking through the glass door, out toward the street. "I've never seen her so angry."

I heard a car door slam, and I turned and looked back out. I saw Rose behind the steering wheel. A second later, she had her car running and pulled away from the curb, tires squealing. I looked back at Carl. "What happened? You give her a poem, too?"

"Poem?" He shook his head. "No. Seems Nora got rid of all

of Rose's sleeping pills. Either flushed them down the toilet or did something, because when Rose went to take one last night, they were gone."

Carl's words sent a chill down my spine, and I forgot about the poem he'd left me. "Nora used a whole bottle of Rose's sleeping pills?"

"Didn't use, dumped. At least twenty of them according to Rose. She'd just gotten the prescription filled last week. Now she's afraid they might not fill it again. This is the second time she's run out before she should have. The first time she convinced the pharmacy they shorted her, but she doesn't think that will work again. Pharmacists worry about people hoarding pills, think they might be going to commit suicide."

Or murder, I thought. Now I knew what Nora put in the stew. Thank goodness I didn't like the taste . . . and hadn't fed more than I did to Baraka. One or both of us might be dead . . . and it wouldn't have been suicide.

I wondered about my grandfather. Did he die in his sleep of natural causes, or was that why Rose's pills came up short the first time?

That thought was on my mind when Carl left the post office. I never did ask him about the poem.

On the way home, I called Wade's cell phone number. I got his voice mail and left a message. He still hadn't called back by the time I unloaded Baraka, let him take a potty break, and went inside, so I tried again. Still no answer.

I was working on a tax form, trying to catch up, when Wade finally did call. "Hi. I was going to call you," he said right off the bat. "What's the problem?"

I detected a bit of reserve in his tone and suddenly felt cautious. "Tell me why you were going to call me."

"I got the toxicology report on you. They identified what

made you so sleepy the other day."

"Sleeping pills," I said. "And before you jump to any conclusions, no I didn't take them."

"Then how did you know what it was?"

"I just heard today that Rose is very upset because Nora threw away Rose's sleeping pills. Except, I don't think Nora threw them away. I think she put them in that stew she brought over to me."

"The stew that we couldn't find?"

"Wade, she did bring me a pot of stew. How she got the pot and my garbage out of here, I don't know. I just know what was here Monday night and what I ate."

"Maybe I'll go talk to this Rose."

"You do that." If he wasn't going to believe me, he could go talk to the Pope for all I cared.

"If you're thinking of prosecuting this Nora, you're going to have to prove she did put sleeping pills into the food and delivered it to you."

"And, of course, I can't." Somehow she'd made sure it was just my word against hers.

"This Rose is the one who lives on the road behind you?"

"Yes. Their house is almost directly behind mine."

"I know I have the address in the file on my desk, but I should be able to find it without any trouble."

I could hear traffic in the background. "You're in your car?"

"Heading south on Westnedge. We had a little fuss over here." He sounded distracted. "As soon as we're finished, I'll head out your way and talk to her."

I remembered Rose driving away from the post office. "She may not be home for a while. When I saw her, she was on her way to get her prescription refilled . . . if she could."

"I'll be tied up here for quite a while. Probably won't get out your way until late afternoon. You gonna be home?"

The official tone was gone. I was talking to a man now, not an officer of the law. And I responded like a woman trying to entice him. Even though he couldn't see me, I smiled and ran my fingers through my hair. "I'll be home. And if you're here around dinner time, I'm fixing goulash."

"Sounds better than anything I have at home. Oh, and before I forget it, we're a little shorthanded today. We won't be able to send a deputy out tonight."

"No problem." I was sure my intruder either had what he was looking for or had caught on that I knew nothing.

I put aside the tax form I'd been working on and did some housework. I straightened up in my living room, did the dishes in the sink, and made my bed. Not that I figured Wade would see it.

Or maybe I hoped he would.

Around four o'clock, I cleared one end of the table, set out two place mats, and turned on some music. As an old Rolling Stones CD blared away in the living room, I sautéed cubes of beef with onions and green peppers, then added carrots, corn, and a can of seasoned beef stock. I let the mixture simmer until five thirty, cooked the noodles, thickened the juice, and had everything ready by six o'clock.

Six thirty came and went. Seven o'clock. No word from Wade.

Disappointment takes different forms. In my case, I ate. Although there was enough goulash for two, I finished every bite of it. I didn't even share with Baraka. I did wash up the dishes afterward and cleaned the kitchen.

I'm the eternal optimist.

Darkness had fallen when I took out the garbage. Outside, the music from the CD was barely audible, the night eerily quiet. I carried the bag down the crumbling concrete back steps, Baraka bounding ahead of me.

I was almost to the garbage can when I heard a sound.

I might have missed the faint cry if Baraka hadn't halted his investigation of the grass and looked toward the woods. His complete attention captured mine. I listened and heard it again. A feeble cry for help.

The barely audible voice sounded masculine. It came from somewhere beyond the old chicken coop. Baraka started that direction, but I called him back. The yard light illuminated my back steps, the walkway between my house, and the garbage can, but not much beyond those points. I wasn't about to go dashing into the dark. As I said before, I'm not exactly scared of the dark, but if I can't see what's around me, I do get very edgy. I think it's a control thing . . . or maybe self-preservation.

I had to keep calling Baraka to make him come back and follow me into the house. Quickly I turned off my CD player, then grabbed a flashlight and my cell phone. I also slipped Baraka's choke chain and lead on him, and my jacket on me.

Feeling more prepared, I returned outside. With Baraka on his lead, I walked him past the bag of garbage I'd dropped when I first heard the sound. "Hello—" I called. "Anyone out there?"

Baraka heard the response first. Once again he alerted. Cocking his head to the side, he listened, then headed for the old chicken coop. I held onto the lead and aimed my flashlight in that direction. "Keep talking," I yelled. "So I can find you."

My stomach churned, and I wished I hadn't eaten all of that goulash. My courage decreased with every step I took away from the house. Even with a flashlight, it was dark. The old chicken coop loomed to the side like a monstrous creature, my light reflecting off the remaining glass in the broken window. Ahead of me the trees created a shadowy wall. I paused and checked my cell phone. I had it ready. All I had to do was punch the emergency key.

In the back of my mind, I wondered if this was another trick, another plot my neighbors had concocted to drive me crazy. And, of course, I remembered every scary movie I'd seen where the next victim goes haplessly into the dark to be stabbed, hatcheted, or sawed into parts by the villain.

Only Baraka's continuous pull toward the voice kept me going. If it was a trick, I wasn't the only one being fooled. My dog was heading for something.

I swung the light back and forth, illuminating as much of the woods as I could. My grandfather really was a slob, but not everything piled behind the chicken coop could be classified as junk. Julia told me my grandfather went to auctions and bought things he thought he'd use one day. Useable was intermingled with the throwaway, and off the trail lay boxes of old bottles, a roll of chicken wire, balded tires, and rusting barrels. I even had to work my way around an old bathtub.

I carefully bypassed each item and hoped Baraka didn't cut a pad. The cries were more audible but weaker. "Keep talking," I repeated when there was a pause. "I'm coming."

I think I heard him say "Hurry." The sound was so weak, I wasn't sure.

I scanned the area with my flashlight and felt Baraka pull me to my left. It took me three steps before I saw a body and even then I could only see parts. In front of me were the soles of a pair of brown boots and the trouser legs of tan overalls.

Baraka closed the distance, dragging me along. I held my breath as the rest of the body came into view. If this was the doing of my neighbors, I wasn't the only one being targeted. Lying in front of me, his plaid shirt soaked dark with blood, was Howard Lowe.

Twenty-Seven

I called for help. The nine-one-one dispatcher notified the appropriate people then kept me on the line. Turned out it was Martha, the same woman I'd talked to last Friday. I told her I didn't want to become a regular, and I certainly didn't want this to be a repeat of that call. I described Lowe's condition, which wasn't good, and she relayed instructions from the paramedics en route to my location.

I found a pulse along the side of Lowe's neck, described the wound in his chest, and applied pressure to stop the bleeding. I also took off my jacket and laid it over him, covering as much of his torso as I could. I know how shock can kill a person, and the temperature had dropped dramatically from earlier in the day.

Otherwise, there wasn't much I could do except mutter words of encouragement. "Help is on the way," I said. "Hang in there."

He tried to talk once, but started coughing. I told him to save his energy.

As soon as the paramedics arrived, I stepped back and let them take over. I kept Baraka by my side and moved closer to my driveway so I could direct others as they showed up. When Carl pulled his truck into the yard, I thought he was another volunteer fireman until he got out.

"What happened?" he yelled when he saw me.

"Lowe's been shot."

"Howard?" Carl came toward me. "You shot him for hunting

in your woods?"

"I didn't shoot him." For someone who doesn't own a gun, I certainly get blamed for a lot of shooting incidents. "I don't even know if he was hunting."

"His dog's loose," Carl said, stopping by my side. "I just came from his place. Jake came running up to my truck when I pulled into the yard. Howard never lets Jake off his chain except when he's hunting him."

"What would he have been hunting?" I didn't think anything was in season.

"Who knows?" Carl gave Baraka a pat on his head. "Maybe coon. Jake's a damn good coon dog."

"He shouldn't have been in my woods."

"You tell him that."

"I did." We both watched an ambulance pull into my yard. One of the volunteer firemen ran toward it.

"Is he dead?" Carl asked me, his tone somber.

"Not when I was with him. But he's not in very good shape. He's lost a lot of blood and had trouble breathing. I don't know how long he's been lying back there. If I hadn't taken the garbage out, I never would have heard him."

"If you didn't shoot him, who did?"

I lifted my hands in question. Rather than having no idea, I could think of several possibilities. John, if he thought Lowe had found his deadly ladybugs. Nora, if she thought Lowe was looking at Rose or trespassing on her property. The man in black.

The man in black. It had a mysterious lilt. The unknown. Dark. Sinister.

I was forming an image of this unknown person. Chuck, the bartender, had given a description. Medium height. Lean and muscular. Middle aged. Military type.

Someone who would kill a dog, run down an old lady, and shoot anyone who got in his way.

If Lowe was right, the man in black was a member of the CROWS. The attire fit, but not the tactics. Why would an organization devoted to curtailing bioengineering of the flora and fauna shoot and kill people? Sure antiabortionists killed doctors who performed abortions, but if that logic were applied, John should be the one in a grave, not Carroll "Punk" McDaniels.

"You ever heard of a group called the CROWS?" I asked Carl.

"Crows, capitalized?" he asked, suddenly interested in what I was saying. At my nod, he went on. "I heard about them from Howard. He said they're some sort of watchdogs for you and me. Keep big government and these crazy scientists from totally messing up our environment. I tried writing a poem about them once. Called it 'The Messengers.' " He looked toward his truck. "I never did finish it. Probably in there somewhere."

"Or maybe in my house?"

He gave me an odd look. "You have it?"

I nodded. "I found it on my dining room floor the other night."

"How'd it get there? It wasn't even finished."

"You tell me how it got there." I kept studying his face, looking for any signs that he was lying. "You didn't leave it?"

"Me? Why would I leave something I hadn't finished?"

Why indeed?

The ambulance left, taking Lowe to one of Kalamazoo's two major hospitals. I asked which hospital, but no one was sure. Either Bronson or Borgess. They did know he was still alive.

Wade showed up soon after that. He didn't give any excuse for not stopping by. Nor did he joke about my propensity for finding bodies on my property. Mostly he conferred with the officer in charge.

Carl left after giving a statement. A few of the volunteer fire-

men, now that the emergency was over, came up and asked me
about Baraka, each one petting him and touching his ridge as if
expecting it to be fake or bristly. They told me what I always
hear—that he is going to be a big dog.

One gave me back my jacket, but I didn't put it on. There
was blood on the lining and sleeve. Lowe's blood. I stood by my
house, shivering, until I realized how silly that was and asked if
I could go inside.

The sheriff's deputy in charge looked at me as if I were foolish to ask. Wade nodded, and I hurried up the back steps and
into the warmth of my kitchen.

I was about to put my jacket to soak in cold water when
Wade came inside. "Let me see that," he ordered, stopping me
mid-progress.

I handed over my jacket, and he held it by the collar. Slowly,
he looked at both sides, paying particular attention to the areas
covered with blood. "The victim's?" he asked, looking at me.

"Yes. They told me to keep him warm. So I put it over him."

Wade nodded, then asked to see my hands. Confused, I
showed him my palms. They, too, were bloody.

Suddenly, I realized what he was doing. "I didn't shoot him,"
I snapped. "Dammit all, when are you going to believe me?"

"I do believe you." Wade handed back my jacket. "Wash your
hands and pack a bag."

"A bag?" I glared at him. "Why?"

"Because I don't want you staying here. Your neighbor was
shot in your backyard. Last week you had a dead man in your
dining room. Until we find out who's doing these shootings, I
don't think it's safe for you to be here."

His argument made some sense, but I wasn't sure what I
wanted to do. I dropped my jacket into the washer and closed
the lid. "And where do you propose I go at this hour?"

"How about my sister's? She's in Detroit for two days. She

gave me a key to her place so I can feed her dog and cats. You can bring your dog. You can even bring your tax papers."

"Or I could stay at a motel." I wanted to see what he'd say to that.

He shrugged. "Motel's fine." But his glance toward Baraka, who lay at my feet, said "good luck."

Since I couldn't think of a good reason not to go to Ginny's place, and it would be cheaper and easier than a motel room—and going to Grandma's was out of the question—I agreed.

TWENTY-EIGHT

Wade drove me to Ginny's. "The boys" were not happy to see Baraka, but Spike was delighted. In spite of the differences in their sizes, it only took Spike a few minutes to establish dominance. They were chasing a ball when I left them in the fenced backyard.

Wade brought in my things. There really wasn't a lot of work I could do without my computer and tax program, but I had brought a couple of tax books and articles. As soon as Wade unloaded the Jeep, he said goodbye. "I need to stop by the station, but I'll be back later. To see if there's anything you need."

"Can you find out how Lowe's doing?" I asked. I might not like the man, but I didn't want him to die.

"Will do."

I watched Wade drive off, then stepped back into the house, feeling totally disoriented and displaced. I watched the dogs for a bit. Baraka found one of Spike's chew toys and demolished it in seconds. Spike took half and ran to the far side of the yard, guarding his fractured toy with a menace that taunted Baraka. My dog barked and growled, being as fierce as he could, but Spike ignored him until Baraka finally gave up and simply laid down and watched Spike.

Wade had said to make myself at home. I found some wine in Ginny's refrigerator and poured myself a glass, then I grabbed a couple of chocolate chip cookies from the cookie jar. My grandmother wrinkles her nose at the idea of mixing cookies and wine, but I love the combination.

When I took my treat into the living room, I discovered "the boys" were there, one on each side of the chair opposite the couch. They watched me, their almond-shaped blue eyes relaying their disapproval. "I'll make her some cookies and buy her another bottle of wine," I said, making a mental note to do so.

The cats continued staring.

I nibbled on the cookies and sipped the wine as I read through the books and bulletins I'd brought with me. When I was sure the dogs had tired themselves out, I let them in, losing more points with the cats.

"The boys" disappeared, and Baraka checked everything out, then lay down at my feet. Spike jumped up on the couch and curled up next to me. I must have dozed off because I lost track of the time until both dogs jumped to their feet, and I realized the front door was opening.

It took me a bit to remember where I was and what had happened. By the time my thoughts were clear, Wade was in the house being greeted by the two dogs. Seeing Baraka lick Wade's face as Wade kneeled to pet Spike created a warm feeling in me. For a moment I allowed myself to daydream, picturing Wade as my husband returning from work to be greeted by the family pets. He looked tired, yet he smiled my way as he stood.

"I thought you might be in bed," he said, the suggestion turning the warmth within me to a new desire.

"I think I did fall asleep." I couldn't look away from his face. Like the dogs, I wanted to go to him, to be touched and held. I wanted to draw from his quiet strength.

I don't remember rising to my feet and walking across the room. And I have no idea if I put my arms around him first or if he drew me to him. All I know is it felt right, that the warmth of his mouth was what I wanted, and the moan I gave was one of satisfaction.

Neither of us said anything, simply kissed and kissed some more. I knew when he began to back me toward the spare bedroom. In the far recess of my mind, the small voice of reason told me I was making a mistake and to stop while I could. I ignored the voice.

The dogs were shut out, clothes were removed, and I barely noticed that Wade took time to use protection. Primitive desires had taken over my thinking, a need to hold and be held, to bond and find a release more important than reason. I licked Wade's shoulder, the salty taste of his skin bringing me pleasure. His body smelled of scented soap and spicy aftershave and a maleness no manmade product could disguise.

The bed creaked when he positioned himself over me, and I cupped his face in my hands and looked deep into blue, blue eyes. Eyes that had fascinated me from the first day we met. "I can stop," he said, his voice heavy with desire. "If that's what you want."

I barely whispered, "Don't stop."

It wasn't until later, when he lay next to me, that I had second thoughts. Pregnancy wasn't a fear, yet I knew I'd made a mistake. For years I'd kept my emotions under control. I wasn't a virgin, but my experiences at lovemaking had been carefully orchestrated. I participated, but I didn't allow myself to get involved. No entanglements. No love.

It was safer that way.

This time, however, I was involved. Lying next to Wade, I knew it would not be easy for me to simply brush this off as a sexual release. In less than a week, I'd grown to like the man. He made me think of a future, dream of a long-term relationship, and that was dangerous. Here I was, unsure of my sanity, already acting insane.

I didn't want to cry, but the tears slid down my cheeks without my bidding. I tried to wipe them away without Wade noticing, but I should have known better. He levered himself up on one arm and used the corner of the comforter to wipe my cheeks dry. "I'm sorry," he said softly.

"Don't be." I knew he wouldn't understand.

"I took advantage of your emotions. I shouldn't have even come back. I stayed away from you earlier today because I knew I wasn't thinking straight. Then what do I do . . . ?"

I don't like being pitied, nor coddled. I poked a finger into his ribs. "You helped me relax, that's what you did. Don't go getting a big head over it. Tears are a way of releasing tension. And if anyone took advantage of emotions, I think I did. I walked across that room to you. Remember?"

For a moment he looked surprised by my comments, then he smiled. "Yeah, you did. So maybe you should be apologizing to me."

"Do I have anything to apologize for?" I hoped he hadn't found making love with me an inadequate experience.

"Not a thing," he said and leaned close and kissed me.

It was sometime after one o'clock in the morning when we came out of the bedroom and let the dogs outside for a while. We took a shower together, then Wade toweled me down. The way he looked, standing naked in front of me, I had a feeling we were going to have to take another shower . . . and we did.

Hunger finally took over and Wade slipped his clothes back on and went into the kitchen to find what he could in his sister's refrigerator. I'd gorged myself on goulash earlier, but the way I ate, you'd never have known it. Scrambled eggs and diced ham never tasted so good.

We'd finished eating when I thought about Howard Lowe. "Did you find out anything about Lowe?" I asked as Wade cleared the dishes from the table.

"He's at Bronson. They have him in intensive care, but the

nurse I talked to felt he'd make it. The bullet nicked one of his lungs and they're afraid of pneumonia. They have a tube down his throat, so he can't talk, but she said they should have that out tomorrow."

"So you have no idea who shot him?"

"Only one possibility has been suggested to us."

One was better than none, I supposed. "Who?"

Wade set the last of the dishes in the sink and came back to the doorway. "You."

"Me?" We were back to that. "I did not—"

Wade held up his hands, stopping me. "I know. I know. I'm just telling you what I've heard. Your neighbor, Carl Dremmer, told one of the officers that you'd threatened to shoot Lowe."

And here I was just starting to like Carl. "I never said that."

"If I recall correctly, Mr. Dremmer said you told Lowe he'd better stay out of your woods or else."

"Well, I didn't mean or else I'd shoot him."

"I told the others that." Wade smiled. "Funny, however, that you didn't hear the shot."

"Not funny at all. I had my CD player cranked up." I stood, ready to leave.

Wade stopped me with what he said next.

TWENTY-NINE

"That shot could have been meant for you, P.J., not Mr. Lowe."

I sank back into my chair. I hadn't wanted to consider that possibility, but I guess it had been in the back of my mind.

"He was in your backyard," Wade continued. "Not more than a hundred feet from your back door."

The proximity to my house had bothered me, but there were other factors. "Lowe and I aren't exactly similar in appearance."

"In the dark, maybe the shooter couldn't tell."

Not exactly reassuring. "Okay, let's say the bullet was meant for me. Why would someone want to shoot me?"

"You've said that the Wright woman wants your farm. You claim she tried to poison you. I never did get a chance to talk to her or her so-called sister."

After what I'd heard about Nora shooting at trespassers, and what happened to me with the stew she brought, I guess I wouldn't put it past her to take a shot at me.

"Or, what about your friend Julia?" Wade asked. "McDaniels's mother accused Mrs. Westman of killing her son. Maybe your neighbor didn't pull the trigger that day, but she might be involved."

I didn't hesitate with that suggestion. "No." I shook my head. "Julia's crime was telling others Mrs. McDaniels had gone to Florida. If Julia's in any way responsible for Punk's death, it's that she and John hired him. It's got to be the ladybugs, Wade. They're the reason Punk was shot."

"It's the reason you say he was shot. The Westmans are still denying the existence of these so-called lethal ladybugs. According to their testimony, nothing was taken from their pole barn."

"So you believe them and not me?" We were back to that.

"It's not a matter of who I believe. As I said—"

I cut him off. Once again, I rose to my feet. "Screw what you said. Either you believe me or you don't. I'm not crazy, Wade." That much I did feel sure about . . . at least tonight. "I know what John told me . . . and I know Nora brought me a pot of stew. That you can't prove it is your problem."

I started toward the bedroom. "What about the man dressed in black?" Wade asked.

"What about him?" I kept walking.

"We need to figure out who he is?"

I paused and looked back. "No, Wade, we don't need to figure out anything. You do. I'm tired, and I'm going to bed."

"Not a bad idea." He snapped off the kitchen light and started after me. "I'll do those dishes in the morning."

"No." I held up my hand, stopping him. "I said I'm going to bed. I mean alone. You can . . . Can—" I wasn't sure what he could do, but it wasn't going to be with me. "I don't sleep with a man who doesn't believe me."

In the morning, I heard Wade let the dogs out. A little later, I smelled coffee perking. It was then that I pushed back the covers.

My thighs ached from making love so many times, and I cursed myself for being a fool. What an idiotic thing to do. Talk about making love with the enemy. Wade didn't believe me about the ladybugs. He didn't believe me about Nora. He thought I was crazy.

Crazy like my mother.

Well, this whole situation was driving me crazy. I had to push it out of my mind. I had way too much work to do on taxes. No time for a man. No time for sex.

I slowly convinced my eyes to stay open, but it took a hot shower and two cups of coffee before I truly felt awake. By that time, Wade was dressed and had washed the dishes from the night before.

Neither of us said anything about our argument. I did see a blanket folded on the end of the couch and figured that's where Wade ended up sleeping. He commented on the weather and how well the dogs got along. I complimented him on his coffee.

When he slipped on his leather jacket, I realized he was planning on leaving without me. "Whoa," I said. "Wait for me. I need to go home."

"No. I want you to stay here. It's safer." Wade reached for his car keys.

"Forget it. I can't work here. I need my computer and the tax program that's on it. I need my files."

He frowned, glanced at the books I'd brought with me, then went to the phone. Two calls later, satisfied I could safely return to my house, he loaded everything up that we'd brought over.

I, meanwhile, made up the spare bed with fresh linens and dumped the ones Wade and I had made love on in the washing machine. I left a note for Ginny, letting her know the sheets would need to be put in the dryer. I also promised to replace the bottle of wine I'd finished.

Wade and I barely said a dozen words on the drive to my house. Less than a mile away, I twisted in my seat to look back at Baraka. He'd also been quiet for most of the drive. I found him sleeping on the floor, his head resting on my overnight bag.

"Is he okay?" Wade asked.

"Fine. Spike wore him out." I straightened in my seat, and as I did, my arm rubbed against Wade's shoulder. Immediately I remembered those muscular arms caressing my body. The way his mouth had felt on mine. The long, slow way he'd brought me to a climax.

Damn him. For those few hours, I'd been in heaven. Wade Kingsley knew how to arouse a woman . . . and how to satisfy her. I couldn't remember ever feeling so sexually content. As much as I wanted to regret what we'd done, I didn't.

My driveway and the grassy area around it showed the abuse of multiple cars and trucks. As soon as I let Baraka out of the Jeep, he sniffed the area, going from one spot to the next. I unlocked my front door and Wade brought in my things, then went through the house from top to bottom, including going into the underground room and passageway. I stood at the top of the cellar stairs, relieved when Wade finally came back into view.

"All clear," he said. "No signs of anyone being in there since we found it."

"That's good." Knowing someone had lived under me for a while was bad enough. I didn't want to think this person could return at will.

I thought Wade would simply say goodbye and leave. And he did say goodbye, but it wasn't simple. He cradled my face in his hands—those wonderful, strong, sexy hands of his—and gently kissed my lips. "We just need to get to the bottom of this," he said softly. "Then it will all make sense."

I didn't know what to say, and he kissed me again, gently, then left. I watched him drive away, Baraka by my side. I'd known Wade Kingsley less than a week, but the moment he walked out the door, my house seemed empty and my life incomplete. Too many emotions played inside my head, and I let the tears slide down my cheeks.

A cold water soak and a stain remover added to the washing machine took care of the blood on my jacket. I'd just pulled it out of the dryer when Julia called from the bank. She'd heard about Lowe and wanted to know how he was doing. I told her what I knew. Wade had checked with the hospital before we left his sister's house. Critical but stable were the words being used to describe Lowe's condition.

"Do you think he was looking for the box?" she asked.

"I don't know. He couldn't talk when I found him."

"You didn't see a box?"

"No. You really think it's still around?"

"People are still being shot, and Howard was on your property. There has to be a reason for that."

A reason I needed to discover.

After hanging up, I tried working on taxes, but after ten minutes, I knew I was too wound up to concentrate on 1040 forms. I needed some fresh air and time to clear my mind.

I didn't initially start out looking for John's box of ladybugs. A short walk with Baraka was my plan. I took him along the edge of the road, going to the corner, then headed north toward John and Julia's place. Everything was quiet, and with the leaves only in the bud stage, I could see quite a ways into my woods.

No man in black lurked about ready to shoot me. I didn't like being afraid to go outside; in fact, it made me angry to think someone was keeping me out of my woods. So I decided I wasn't going to live in fear. I let Baraka loose, and skirting the edge of John's field, headed for the path I knew would take me through my woods and back to my house.

I was almost to the path when I saw something white beneath one of the dead branches on the ground. It could have been something my grandfather dumped . . . or the corner of a box. I went over to check.

It was just a piece of paper—no box—but that was enough to start me looking again.

Where, I asked myself, would a man on the run—a man being shot at—enter my woods?

In addition to the junk my grandfather dumped in the woods, thickets of briars make some areas almost impossible to walk through. I wandered along the edge of the trees, trying to imagine the path Punk would have taken if he was running away from the pole barn toward my woods. With shots being fired at his back, where would he go into my woods?

A wide spot between two maples seemed a likely spot. And just past the maples was a fallen elm, its trunk half rotten. Would Punk have chosen that as a place to hide the box?

I leaned over to look.

Behind me, from somewhere in Nora and Rose's woods, I heard the excited cawing of crows. I started to straighten, to check on the disturbance, when I heard another sound. A thunk in the tree beside me.

Then came the crack of a rifle.

"What the—?"

I didn't have time to finish. A second shot hit the tree, and I knew what was going on.

I didn't fall to the ground this time. I ran. I didn't even think about my dog, not until he bumped into my leg, ready to play catch-the-running-person. I yelled at him, but didn't slow. All I wanted to do was get to my house.

Together Baraka and I reached my back door. I'd locked it. Now I wished I hadn't. I couldn't get my keys out of my pocket or into the keyhole fast enough. Blood pounded in my ears and my legs shook. Once inside, I locked the door. Gasping for breath, I stumbled into the dining room, then realized how easily I could be seen through the window.

I grabbed my cordless phone and scooted down the stairs to the cellar. I didn't go all the way down, only a step or two. There, my hand shaking, I punched nine-one-one.

I managed to stammer that someone was shooting at me.

Thank goodness it wasn't the same dispatcher that I'd talked to before. I didn't want any comments about becoming a habitual caller. For a week, when I was sixteen, my mother called nine-one-one. Grandma and I had to hide the phone from her.

A deputy came, then Wade. I sat in my living room, petting Baraka, drinking coffee and shaking. They asked questions, and I answered. Wade suggested I get a motel room and stay there for a while. I told him I'd think about it.

Other deputies combed the woods. They found the tree with the two bullets. Twenty-two rounds, they said. The rounds would be processed for evidence. They weren't the same as the slug taken out of Howard Lowe. Two shooters or simply two guns?

Wade stayed until the last deputy left, then he pointed a finger at me. "Pack a bag and get out of here."

Maybe it was his tone—or that finger. In the instant he said it, I made up my mind. "I'm staying. You do your job and figure out what's going on here. And I'll do mine. I run a business out of my home. People expect to find me here and this is where I'll be."

He argued with me, and I argued back. I'd made up my mind. Like Baraka and Spike facing off over a toy, neither of us gave in. Finally Wade growled, "Stay out of the woods."

"Gladly," I agreed.

I didn't cry when he left, but I paced the floor. I was tired of being afraid. For as long as I could remember, I'd been afraid of becoming like my mother. Now I was afraid of some lethal ladybugs, people shooting at me, and an unknown man in black.

"No more," I said aloud and walked over to the phone. I had to look up the telephone number, and I hoped she would be home. The phone rang three times before she answered, and I said, "Sondra, is that offer to borrow your gun still open?"

THIRTY

Sondra's children were at school, and she took an hour to instruct me on how to use the gun. The first time I pulled the trigger, my hand shook and the bullet hit the dirt, not the coffee can Sondra set up. By the end of the hour, I had three holes in the can, had used up dozens of bullets, and had provided Sondra with several good laughs.

I returned to my house wondering if I'd made a mistake. I had a gun and I knew how to use it—more or less. But could I? Earlier I'd decided I didn't want to be a victim. But shooting a coffee can was different from shooting a person. Could I take a life?

I slid the gun into my jacket pocket. Until the temperature warmed up, that would be as good a place to keep it as any. My jacket was usually close by and within easy access. Feeling just a little bit cocky and definitely more at ease, I sat down at my computer and once again started working on a tax form. I worked steadily until it was time for dinner. I fixed Baraka's food, then stared in the refrigerator, looking for something I could eat. Nothing looked good. I'd just pulled out a carton of cottage cheese when the telephone rang.

"You had dinner?" Wade asked.

I looked at the carton of cottage cheese in my hand. "I was about to."

"I thought you might like to drive into Kalamazoo with me, have dinner, then stop by the hospital and see your neighbor.

235

He wants to talk to you."

"He's all right?" I had wondered about Lowe and how he was doing. "He can talk?"

"They're still worried about pneumonia and complications, but he is talking. We won't be able to stay long, but he did ask specifically for you. I think he wants to thank you."

"I'll bet that's going to gall him." I was glad he was going to be all right, but the old buzzard was going to hear about hunting on posted land.

"I'm on my cell phone right now, about three miles from your place. I'll be there in five minutes or less," Wade said.

I put the cottage cheese carton back in the refrigerator.

Wade didn't take me to a fancy restaurant. In fact, if I hadn't been with him, I never would have stopped at the place. It was more of a bar than an eating establishment: the tables had paper place mats, there were TVs in every corner, and country-western songs competed with the heckling of the pool players in the back room. However, no smoking was allowed. That put the place a notch above a lot of other restaurants in Kalamazoo.

"I'm off duty," Wade said and ordered a draft. "What would you like?"

I ordered the same and decided on steak and potatoes. Today I was a gun-toting, macho woman, ready to take on the world. Of course, I didn't have the gun with me. I'd left it in my bedroom. I didn't think I'd need it while in the company of a sheriff's deputy, and Sondra had said I would need a permit to carry a concealed weapon if I took it off my property. Actually, she said I should be very careful and not let anyone know I had the gun since it was registered in her name, and she really shouldn't let anyone else use it.

With our beers in front of us and our orders given, Wade sprung his first bit of news. "We arrested your neighbor today."

"John?"

"No, Nora Wright. We probably won't be able to prove she tried to poison you the other day, but we found a twenty-two rifle in her garage, hidden under a pile of newspapers. It had been recently fired and ballistics matched it with the shot we dug out of that maple tree. I think the lab will also find gunshot residue on her jacket."

Nora. That made sense. The shots had come from the direction of her woods. Add the fact that Nora had tried to give me an overdose of sleeping pills and her animosity at the card party, and you had a pattern. "Did she give any reason why?"

"She didn't, but her partner told us that Ms. Wright sees you as an adversary."

"Did Nora shoot Punk?"

"She says no. She also claims she didn't shoot Mr. Lowe. We're looking into that, but she does have a good alibi for last Friday. We checked it out."

Wade took a long swig from his beer. I sipped at mine. "So today probably had nothing to do with what happened last Friday?"

"Not as far as we can tell, but she did say something interesting. Maybe it will make sense to you. It didn't to me."

I put down my beer. "What did she say?"

"That you were luckier than your grandfather. Mean anything?"

It did. "It means someone should have done an autopsy on my grandfather, that I don't think he died in his sleep of natural causes."

Wade nodded. "You give the okay, and we'll have the body exhumed."

"I'll give the okay." My grandfather might have been an old goat, as Nora called him, but he didn't deserve to die for ten acres of woods. "So it wasn't jealousy. It was good old greed that made Nora hate me."

"Perhaps mixed with a little jealousy. From a few things her live-in partner said, I have a feeling there's someone else. I wouldn't put it past her to let Nora think it was you."

"I bet it's that man I saw. Rose didn't want me to know he was there."

"It's a possibility. Of course, our job isn't to monitor relationships, just stop people from doing bodily harm to each other." He shook his head. "I've been in law enforcement since I was twenty-three. I'm constantly amazed by the things people do to each other."

"If people would only be honest with each other."

"Yeah, well, sometimes that's easier said than done."

"Speaking from experience, Detective Kingsley?"

I meant it jokingly, but from his expression, I knew I'd hit a sensitive spot. He cradled his beer mug in his hands and stared at the amber liquid. Someone in the back of the room at the pool tables gave a shout of glee, and someone at the bar laughed, but Wade said nothing.

I reached across the table and placed a hand on his arm. "I'm sorry. I didn't mean to get personal."

His gaze met mine, and he released his hold on his beer mug to take my hand in his. "I'd say, after last night, you have a right to get personal."

His fingers felt cool and slightly damp, but a warmth surged through my body. In his eyes I saw the spark of desire, and I looked away.

I didn't want to think about last night. What we did at his sister's house was definitely personal. I'd also list it as a mistake. A weak moment. Hormones taking over. Insanity.

"And you are right," he said before I had a chance to come back with anything smart and witty. "I wasn't honest with Linda, not when we first met. She's a looker, and I couldn't believe she'd be interested in me. I wanted her so much, I lied. I let her think I might one day work for her father. And maybe I would have, but not until I burned out on this job."

"Was she honest with you?" I'd discovered that most divorces weren't the fault of just one partner.

"No," he admitted. "She saw the glory of being a law officer's wife, not the reality. I couldn't talk about my job. Sometimes I get real moody, especially when a case isn't going well. I don't make a lot of money."

He sighed and shook his head. "Sure don't make what she was used to. When the time came that we couldn't afford the new car she wanted, and I complained about the money she spent on clothes, the glory vanished. That's why I want to be honest with you."

"And I want to be honest with you." I pulled my hand free from his. "Wade, I like you. You know that. And last night . . . Well, that was . . ." I didn't know how to explain what happened or why.

I was saved from going into reasons why a relationship between us wouldn't work by the waitress arriving with our salads. Somehow I managed to avoid the subject for the remainder of the meal.

The hospital was only a few blocks away from the bar and grill. Without Wade along, I wouldn't have been able to see Lowe. Tight security and protective nurses kept visitors away. With good reason, I decided, noting the array of tubes and machinery attached to Howard Lowe's body.

Lowe looked asleep, but when Wade spoke his name, he opened his eyes. "You found me," he said, looking at me. His voice was barely more than a rasp. "Thank you."

I wanted to tell him he shouldn't have been in my woods, but I merely nodded. For the first time since I'd met him, Howard

Lowe looked every day of his sixty plus years. The wrinkles in his face seemed deeper, his skin paler, and the fire was gone from his eyes, replaced by a drugged glaze.

He motioned for me to lean closer, then said two words. I straightened and stared at him.

Wade touched my arm. "What'd he say?"

"He said, 'Saw him.' That he saw the person who shot him."

"Who was it, Mr. Lowe?" Wade asked.

Lowe stared at my face. "I was right."

"Right about what?" I didn't understand what he was saying.

He stared at me. Just stared at me.

"Mr. Lowe," Wade said from my side. "We need to know who shot you."

A moment went by. Two. Three. I held my breath, waiting for Lowe's answer, a list of suspects running through my head. Nora, first. Then Carl, even though he'd acted concerned. A mysterious man in black. Possibly John.

I wasn't prepared for what Lowe said. His gaze flicked to Wade. "Her father."

"My father?"

Lowe coughed and gasped. I shook my head. "My father's dead."

Howard Lowe closed his eyes, and I looked over at the nurse standing at the end of the bed. The beep of his pulse continued at an even rate, but I was worried.

She came over and checked the monitors. "Asleep," she said quietly. "It's the medication. He'll be more alert tomorrow."

"He's crazy," I said as we left Lowe's room. "Delirious."

"Probably," Wade agreed. "From what the doctors say, it's a good thing you found him when you did. He nearly bled to death."

"My father died eighteen years ago."

"I'm not arguing with you." Wade put an arm around my

shoulders. "Had to be someone who resembled your father."

"Had to be," I repeated, but I wasn't sure. "My mother's always said he's alive. All they found were bits and pieces. No solid evidence. No DNA testing back then."

"There's a way we can prove it's not him."

"How?" I looked at Wade.

"Whoever was in that room under your house left fingerprints on the cot. I ran them, looking for a match, but didn't find anything. I'll ask for your father's records."

"Will they still be available?"

"I hope so."

"Good." Fingerprints would produce factual evidence, not some crazy idea.

"Until then, I think you should stay at my sister's."

"No way." I shook my head. "My dog's at my house. My work. And, I'm tired of being a victim."

"Then let me stay with you."

"You don't need to, Wade. I don't need a babysitter."

"I wasn't thinking of babysitting."

THIRTY-ONE

As Wade drove me home, I thought about what Lowe had said. The idea that my father was still alive was crazy, yet in a convoluted way, it did make sense. "My father would know about that underground room," I said, needing to express my thoughts aloud.

"Probably," Wade agreed.

"He'd know about the passageway from the woodshed to the house."

"More than likely."

"And the other day, Lowe said this rogue working for the CROWS was a local. My father grew up in Zenith."

"Years ago."

"It hasn't changed much."

Wade glanced my way. "P.J., do you really believe your father's alive?"

"No. I mean, I don't know." That was the problem. "That one caller did sound like my father."

"You were only ten years old the last time you heard your father's voice. Memories can play tricks."

"My mother and grandmother think they've seen my father. Not lately, but at times in the past."

"And you consider your mother a reliable witness?"

"Okay, so she's talked to aliens." I smiled, in spite of everything that had happened. "Are you going to hold that against her?"

"Wouldn't someone recognize your father?"

"Not if he changed how he looks." I knew I was groping. "Some people do that. Have plastic surgery."

"And why would he do that?"

"You tell me." None of it made sense to me, and I wouldn't have even considered the idea if Lowe hadn't suggested the possibility. "All I know is my father was exactly the sort of person who would belong to this CROWS group. He didn't like what scientists were doing to the environment. I remember him telling me they were going to screw everything up."

"So you think your father came to Zenith to destroy ladybugs, forced McDaniels to help him, then shot McDaniels, broke into your house—not once, but several times—bugged it, and shot Lowe." Wade shook his head. "It just doesn't make sense, P.J."

I stared out into the darkness. Maybe I was crazy because it did make sense to me.

"I'll check the house," Wade said as soon as we stepped through the front door. "You stay here."

"I need to take Baraka out."

Wade looked at the dog crate. Baraka stood, patiently waiting, but I knew what that slight wag of his tail meant.

"Stay right out in front, and don't be too long."

I was about to unlatch the crate, when I remembered Sondra's gun. I'd left it on my dresser when I took it out of my pocket. I didn't want Wade seeing it and asking questions. Being a sheriff's deputy, he'd ask if I had a permit to own a handgun. Which, of course, I didn't. Then he would probably confiscate the gun. That wouldn't do at all.

He'd gone downstairs to check the cellar. I scooted into my bedroom, grabbed the gun, and slipped it into my jacket pocket. As I did, I felt a crumpled piece of paper.

I pulled the wad out of my pocket, intent on throwing it into the wastebasket beside my dresser. The moment I saw the twenty-dollar bill, I remembered why it was in my pocket and how I'd found it in the underground room, wedged between the springs and mattress of the cot.

Stuffed in my jacket pocket, it had gone through a wash and dry cycle. What I held was laundered money.

I smiled at the idea and straightened out the bill, being careful not to tear the paper. The overhead light in my bedroom gave me a better look than the quick glance I'd gotten with a flashlight. What I had in my hand looked like a twenty-dollar bill, but something wasn't quite right. The picture of the White House? The feel?

I held the bill up to the light and looked for the watermark that these are supposed to have . . . and the colored thread. Both were there, still . . .

I work with money every day, but only in the form of numbers. The abstract. Intangible.

Julia works with the tangible. As a bank teller, she'd know if the color on this bill was right. The design. Texture of the paper. Weight. Finish. She could tell me if this was a counterfeit. Bank tellers take classes in that.

I heard Wade coming up the cellar steps, and I decided I wanted to talk to Julia before I showed him the money. The wrinkled twenty went back into my pocket, next to the gun, and I quickly grabbed the flashlight on my night stand.

Wade caught me coming out of the laundry room. "You were in your bedroom?"

"I wanted to get this." I held up the flashlight, but kept my other arm by my side to hide the bulge in my pocket.

"You shouldn't have gone in there until I checked if it was safe."

I walked by him. "Well, I did. Nobody there."

I felt his gaze on me, and I hoped he couldn't hear the thud of my heart. I felt like a thief. Here I probably had a fake twenty along with an illegally possessed gun in my pocket.

I opened Baraka's crate door and gave him the release command. He went straight for the front door. I followed him out onto the porch, and leaned against one of the porch columns while Baraka began his search for that perfect spot.

The night was cool but comfortable with my jacket on. I tapped my pocket, once again making sure the gun was there. Funny how having a gun in my pocket made me feel braver. Sondra was right, every woman should have one.

I watched Baraka wander around, then I closed my eyes. In the next few minutes, I needed to come up with a good reason why Wade couldn't spend the night at my house. If I didn't, I knew we would end up in bed together.

Priscilla Jayne, you are crazy, I thought. Here I had a good-looking, hot-blooded male that I knew was great in bed, and I was trying to think of ways to keep him out of my bed. What was wrong with me?

I certainly didn't have any qualms about making love with Wade last night. So, if he ended up in my bed tonight, would it be so bad?

Yes. I knew it was illogical, but he couldn't stay. That's all there was to it. He could check my house, then he had to leave. I needed him out of my life before I cared too much.

I sighed and looked around the yard. In my musings, I'd lost track of Baraka. Normally he stays close to the porch, especially at night. His reddish brown coat isn't easy to see in the dark, so I snapped on the flashlight.

"Baraka," I called and stepped off the porch. "Baraka, come."

I waited, expecting to see him dash around the corner of the house. But no dog came. I listened for the click of his toenails on stones or the panting of his breath. Nothing.

"Baraka," I called again. Louder . . . more frantic.

When he wandered, he normally went toward the west end of the house. He liked to go number two over there, just off the lawn area. Which was fine with me. Less chance of me stepping into a surprise.

I walked that direction, swinging the flashlight beam back and forth in front of me. Clouds covered the moon, trees and bushes looming ominously all around. I really needed to get a yard light. I was scaring myself.

Baraka wasn't where I thought I'd find him, and, not knowing what else to do, I stepped around the rhododendron bush growing at the end of the house, its branches heavy with buds that would open in the next month. A light came on in one of the upstairs bedrooms. Wade checking for an intruder. I almost yelled for him to come down and help me look for Baraka, then decided against it. Baraka couldn't be far.

I panned my light over the field where Wade's son, Jason, and Baraka had played. In my mind, I could hear the boy's laughter and my dog's playful growls. Baraka did love to play growly. Most of the time he would stop when I yelled at him, but not always. I was going to have to work on that. When Baraka reached his full growth, if he started growling and grabbing at sleeves, someone might actually think he was trying to attack.

I passed the beam of my flashlight over the rock pile where Jason found his arrowhead. No dog. Slowly I moved the light on to the old chicken coop.

There I stopped.

The door was open.

"Dang it all." Every time the sheriff's deputies were here, they left that door open.

"Baraka," I called. "What are you into now?"

I started that direction. No telling what my dog had found. Another newspaper to tear up. An opossum or raccoon. Ridgebacks do like to hunt. They were bred to hunt lions, but just about anything that moves will do.

"Baraka," I said again, stopping at the coop's doorway.

I aimed my light into the shed. I saw my dog standing on top of a pile of boxes by the broken window, his tail wagging as he showed me his find.

It wasn't an opossum, and it wasn't a raccoon. My light illuminated shards of glass . . . and a man.

In a second, I took in the dark leather boots, black jeans, black turtleneck pullover, and black leather jacket. The man was physically fit, medium height, and clean shaven. His face was covered with camouflaging soot, and a black knit cap hid his hair.

I stared at him, saying nothing and not moving. I barely took a breath.

"Hello, Princess," he said softly.

Thirty-Two

I recognized the voice. Some memories never fade. The face, with or without camouflaging soot, however, wasn't one I knew. More than age had changed the features. What was once a rounded jawline was now square. An upturned and wide nose had become straight and narrow.

I knew the answer, still I asked. "Dad, is that you?"

"You grew up nice," he said, petting my dog as he looked at me. "Very pretty. Like your mother. How is your mother?"

"About the same," I answered, too numb to think.

"And your grandmother?"

"Fine."

I kept staring at him. Grandma was right. The way he stood was the same. The way he cocked his head just slightly to the side. The shrug of his shoulders. Those things hadn't changed.

"Why, Dad?" I asked. "Why fake your death? Why disappear for eighteen years?"

"Seemed like a good idea at the time." He smiled. A cold, unfeeling smile. "Got me out of a hellish marriage and gave you and your mother the medical coverage you needed."

"We needed you."

"You did fine without me."

"It wasn't easy."

Again, that familiar shrug. "Wasn't easy living with her."

"So you just walked away?"

"I joined a greater cause."

"The CROWS?"

"Not initially, but yes." He looked smug. "Actually, I've lent my talents to several groups over the last eighteen years. Well, not actually lent. I do get paid. Damn good money."

"You're a mercenary?"

"I like to think of myself as a man who takes advantage of opportunity when it presents itself."

I thought of other words to describe what he did but said nothing, just kept my flashlight focused on him. It must have made him nervous. He added, "I did miss you."

"Not enough to call or visit." And that hurt.

"I kept track of you. I attended your high school and college graduations. You did well. But then, you were always smart, even as a baby. No signs of . . ." He tapped his head. "You know."

"No, not so far." I understood now. My heroic father had deserted his wife because she had a mental problem. He kept his distance from his daughter because he feared she would inherit that problem.

Acknowledging my hero had feet of clay wasn't easy. I didn't know what to say or do. Baraka must have sensed my distress. He started toward me, picking his way over the pile of boxes, knocking one over and scattering the magazines inside. Baraka gave it a glance, then proceeded to my side.

"By the way, nice dog," my father said. "We've become pretty good buddies in the last week."

"Yeah, well that doesn't make me happy. He's supposed to be a watchdog."

"He watched. Watched me search your house and plant those bugs. He really likes doggy biscuits. You should get him some."

"How long did you live in that room under the house?"

"Live?" He shook his head. "I never lived there. I have a motel room where I've been staying. Much better bed than that old cot. But the room did come in handy. Brought back some memories."

He smiled. "I remember when my folks kept it stocked with supplies, just in case of a bomb attack. Then, after years with no attack, we decided to eat the food, only to end up in the hospital with food poisoning. And there was the time my mother took me down there when we had a tornado warning and she forgot to bring the radio with her, so we ended up staying down there until Dad got home. But my worst experience was when I stole a pack of Dad's cigarettes and went there to smoke them. I should have realized smoke rises. I didn't make that mistake this time. If I needed a smoke, I went into the woods."

"You never showed me the room. I didn't even know about it."

"No need to tell you about it. You couldn't get into it when you were little. Your grandma kept food on the shelves in the cellar, so that door couldn't be opened. And after fuel oil prices went up, your grandfather filled the woodshed, covering up that entrance, just like you did when you had that wood delivered."

I didn't see any reason to tell him I hadn't asked for the wood to be delivered. I had more important questions. "Why did you kill Punk McDaniels?"

"He tried to double-cross me."

"How? By taking the ladybugs so you couldn't sell them to some terrorist organization?"

"Ladybugs?" My father gave a harsh chuckle. "Hell no. I was sent to destroy them and that's what I did. This was what I was after." He held up a box about the size of a brick. It might have been cream-colored once, but it was now a muddy brown.

"I've been looking for this damn thing all week. Even checked in here once, but I missed it, same as those deputies must of. Not that it was easy to find. Either one of them or your dog knocked some magazines over it."

I stared at the box in my father's hand, and Julia's warning flashed through my head. "Don't open it."

"Why not? Don't you want to know what all of this has been about?" My father lifted the lid from the box and angled the bottom half so I could see inside.

I aimed my flashlight toward the box. What I saw was a rectangle of steel with scratches on it. No beetles, dead or alive. Nothing but the sheet of steel. Either he had the wrong box, or Julia and John had lied about what was stolen.

"Do you know what I have here?" my father asked.

I shook my head, yet the size and shape of the metal gave me a clue. If I could see closer . . .

"Your friend Julia made these. She's very good at what she does."

"Julia's a bank teller."

"And also an artist. Think about it, P.J. She has prints hanging in her pole barn. She did that etching on your dining room wall, didn't she?"

She had. And he'd used it to cover his listening device.

"Her artwork isn't very original, but she is great at making copies. She showed our friend Punk one of her etchings. Even gave him a print. The fool actually tried to pass it one night at the Pour House."

"But you stopped him, didn't you? You paid the bill." What Chuck the bartender had said made sense now.

"Paper's all wrong. He would have gotten caught. But I saw the potential, and I now have the plates. On the right kind of paper and with a little doctoring, most people won't be able to tell the difference from the real thing. Hundreds and fifties, you look at. Check closely. But a twenty?" He shook his head. "Most people just stuff a twenty into their wallets or purses."

I'd stuffed the one I found in my pocket. It was the feel of the paper that had made me look closer. On the right kind of paper would I have done that?

I touched the pocket with the bill and felt the bulge of Sondra's gun. For a moment I considered pulling it out, then decided to wait and see what my father did. "Why kill Punk?"

"Why?" He chuckled. "I couldn't have him telling others I was still alive. I think, as we were getting ready to leave, he realized that. He took those plates and ran. Ran like a scared rabbit, but I knew I'd hit him." He looked at me. "I didn't figure on you being in those woods. Or that he'd end up in the house. He must have tossed the box through the window when he went by."

"I think he tried to tell me it was here."

"I kept hoping he had, that you'd say where it was and I could get to it before anyone else did. That's why I took a chance and used that entry from the woodshed, so I could get close enough to hear what was being said. I thought for a while they were going to haul you off for his murder."

Kingsley had made it clear I was a suspect. I wondered how closely the other deputies searched my outbuildings. Did they miss the trapdoor because they never truly thought there was anyone else involved?

My father's confession that he'd hidden in the cellar explained one thing. "You stayed down there Friday until Julia and I left, didn't you? Then you went through my house."

"I had to make sure Punk hadn't stashed the box somewhere in there."

"And you kept coming back, breaking into my house and shooting people."

"Ran right into Lowe." My father snorted. "Never did like him. Thought he was Mr. Tough Guy."

"One man dead, another almost. All for some counterfeit money."

"Money makes the world go round, Princess." My father

moved away from the window toward me.

Again, I thought about the gun in my pocket. But could I shoot my father?

He carefully maneuvered his way over and past boxes, not even worrying about the cobwebs he walked through. I grimaced as I watched a spider the size of a quarter scurry up to the ceiling.

My father stopped in front of me. I didn't move, but I wasn't sure where to aim my flashlight. To the side seemed best. That gave enough light for me to see him clearly.

He wasn't as tall as I remembered, and crow's-feet etched the edges of his eyes. Blue eyes, not brown. Colored contacts, I supposed.

"It surprised me that Dad gave you this place," he said. "I'm not sure he did you any favors. You've got a lot of cleaning up to do.

"And the neighborhood's gone to pot. Nora's always been a nut. I remember her as a kid. Even then you could tell she was a lezzie. Was kinda fun playing Rose against Nora. Of course, I didn't think Nora would go and try to kill you. The night I phoned, you sounded so strange, I thought I'd better come over. I almost pulled into the yard when I saw Nora leaving the house, carrying something. I waited until she was clear, then I went inside."

I remembered thinking I saw crows in my house that night. Considering I'd ingested several sleeping pills and had crows on my mind, I imagine seeing Nora then my father in my house could trigger that image. "How'd she get in?"

"Probably picked the lock. Your back door was open when I tried it."

"You called nine-one-one, didn't you?"

He shrugged. That old, familiar shrug. "Someone had to."

I stared at him. My dad had been there when I needed him,

just as he'd promised. I owed him my life. He started to move, and I swung the flashlight beam up to his face. "Where are you going?"

"South America." He paused and tweaked my chin. "Nice talking to you kid."

"You can't just leave."

"Sure I can. Nobody's going to believe you if you tell them a dead man showed up in your chicken coop and walked off with a box containing counterfeit plates for twenty-dollar bills. You say that and you'll be visiting the same doctors your mother's been visiting for the last twenty-nine years."

"Someone will believe me."

He looked at me, the coldness back in his eyes. "Do you really want to tell me that?"

For the first time, I felt fear. I was talking to a man who had killed Punk and shot Lowe to keep his identity secret, had probably killed many men.

But would he kill his daughter? The daughter he'd rushed to save when he realized she was in trouble? I didn't think so.

I stared at him, my mind racing through options. I could pretend he never was here and let him go, or I could pull out Sondra's gun and make a citizen's arrest. Yeah, right, I thought. He could easily overpower me, even with a gun.

As I debated my alternatives, my father walked out of the chicken coop. I followed, still not sure what to do. He stopped, and I nearly ran into him. "You can't," I said.

He scowled at me.

It was then that I heard my name being called.

Thirty-Three

I'd forgotten about Wade. Again, he called for me. Baraka took off at a run, heading for the front of my house. I watched him go, then looked back at my father.

In his hand, he held a gun. Where it came from, I don't know. I hadn't seen it before. Both his gaze and the gun were pointed toward the corner of the house.

My mind raced. I had to do something. If Wade came around that corner looking for me, his life would be in danger. He wouldn't know what awaited him, wouldn't have his gun out.

I might be able to knock the gun out of my father's hand, but I doubted it. The way we were standing, it would be difficult to dislodge a gun. And if I moved to a better position, I'd lose the advantage of surprise.

Or maybe I should pull out Sondra's gun. It would be a standoff. Father against daughter. An expert against a person with about twenty minutes actual shooting time.

Not a good idea.

My last alternative was avoidance. "I'm coming," I yelled as loud as I could and started to move toward the house.

"Stay where you are," my father demanded and aimed the gun at me.

I didn't think about how foolish it was to argue with a man with a gun. I just thought my idea was a good one that he didn't understand. "Let me go to him," I said. "I'll stop him, and you can get away."

"No," my father said firmly.

I could barely see his face, but his smile erased all hope. He wanted Wade to come around that corner and see him. He wanted to shoot him.

The realization triggered a response. "Wade, he's here," I yelled as loud as I could. "It's—"

I didn't get a chance to finish. My father whacked me with the side of his fist and his gun, the metal striking my skull. A black haze clouded my eyes, and I stumbled back. Gravity took over, and I hit the ground with a jarring thud.

"P.J.?"

Through the pain, I heard Wade's confused question. I turned my head toward the sound and saw him. He stood at the corner of my house, looking my way. In his hand, he held a gun.

"Drop it, or I shoot her."

Once again, I turned my head, ignoring the pain. My father stood by my feet, his gun pointed down at me. Looking into the barrel of a semiautomatic, I fought an urge to vomit.

Baraka came bounding toward us, and for a moment I thought he was going to attack my father. I should have known better. Maybe in the movies Rin Tin Tin and Lassie would save the day, but my puppy only had one thought in mind.

Tail wagging, he pounced on me.

"Go away," I demanded. "Stop. We're not playing."

But he was. He nipped at my jacket, then licked the side of my face. I pushed him aside with my hand, my gaze on my father, not my dog. The gun was still pointed at me, my father's attention directed toward the corner of my house.

"Drop it, Sheriff," my father said.

Still fending off Baraka, I looked toward Wade. I saw him bend and place his gun on the ground, then straighten and raise his hands.

"What do you plan on doing, Benson?" Wade asked. "Shoot us both?"

"If necessary." My father glanced down at me, then back at Wade. "Though maybe she'll be the one who shoots you."

"She doesn't own a gun."

"If they find her fingerprints all over this gun, she'll have a tough time proving that. And by the time a jury decides she is innocent—that is, if they do—I'll be long gone."

I listened, the nausea slowly subsiding and my head clearing. My father figured no one would believe me. He didn't realize Lowe was still alive.

Baraka continued trying to get me to play. He grabbed at my jacket with his teeth and growled. I tried to ignore him and think.

I'd fallen on my right side, and I could feel the outline of Sondra's gun under my hip. To get to it, I would have to roll over to my left side, reach in, pull it out, and aim. With my father standing over me, I didn't see much chance of doing that.

As if reading my mind, he looked down at me. Baraka growled and tugged on my left sleeve. Irritated, I grabbed for him and yelled "No!"

"Great watchdog you have there," Dad said and focused his attention back on Wade.

I realized then that he saw both my dog and me as ineffectual. In his eyes, I was still the child, the offspring that needed to be disciplined on occasion but one who didn't really pose a threat. Just as I'd held onto an image of him for eighteen years, he had one of me.

I decided to play on that. "You don't have to kill him, Dad. You can tie him up and get away. He'll say it was you and I'll tell the others he's crazy, that it couldn't have been you since you're dead."

"You think like me, P.J." He gave an approving nod. "But I can't chance it. Too bad, too. I think the guy likes you."

Either my father hadn't noticed that I'd shifted position or he didn't care, again proving he thought of me as ineffectual. And maybe I was. I now had my right hand down by the right pocket of my jacket, but could I pull out Sondra's gun and aim it at the man I had idolized all of my life?

I glanced in Wade's direction. From the way he stood, I knew he was ready to move. But would he be able to drop to the ground, grab his gun, and shoot before my father shot him?

Did I want him to?

My head ached, the nausea continuing to churn in my stomach. I needed time to think, a chance to plan my move. If I could keep my father talking, maybe we could work something out.

Wade ruined that hope. "You won't get away with this, Benson," he said. "You left a print on the cot downstairs. They're running it against yours. Even if you shoot the two of us, they'll know you're not dead."

"Will they?" My father gave him a smug smile. "Don't forget, I visited here often up until my untimely demise in Beirut. Without you around to tell anyone you saw me, a print could easily be discounted. Of course, you have brought up a point. A fingerprint would give more validity to P.J. saying I was alive."

The way he looked at me, I knew he'd changed his mind about letting me live. He'd fathered me, but he'd been gone when I was born, off serving his first stint in the Marines. Maybe the bonding process never occurred. Maybe all of those times he told me he loved me had been lies.

Maybe I was waking up to reality.

"Howard Lowe saw you," Wade said, bringing my father's attention back to him. "You won't get away with this, Benson."

"Sure I will. Once I finish up here, I'm on my way to Chile."

He aimed his gun toward Wade.

Baraka saw him move and reacted. Still growling in play, he grabbed the sleeve of my father's jacket. The gun went off, the gunshot deafening my ears. I heard Baraka yelp, and from the corner of my eye, I saw Wade fall.

Again, my father raised his gun. This time he aimed at Baraka. "Damn dog," he swore.

"No!" I screamed.

In one motion, I pulled the gun out of my pocket, and aimed it at my father. I don't remember pulling the trigger, but I felt the gun jerk, the recoil slamming my hand against the ground.

And I heard the shot.

In all, I heard three shots, all happening at almost the same time.

And then there was silence.

My father looked down at me, his eyes cold and empty and his gun pointing directly at my chest. I closed my eyes and waited.

I expected a loud bang, but had no idea how it would feel to be shot. I'd read that some people don't even realize when they've been shot, not right away. Would I die before I even knew it? Or would it be a slow, painful death? I hate pain. Grandma was right. Guns are bad.

The shot never came, only a heavy thud. I opened my eyes and looked at the man lying on the ground beside me.

THIRTY-FOUR

Hours later, one thought played through my head. I killed my father. Over and over, the words tormented me. The man I'd adored, idolized and revered all of my life, was dead. And I was the one who had killed him.

I must have voiced my feelings aloud as Wade and I drove toward Julia's house because Wade suddenly looked at me and said, "You didn't kill him, I did."

"I heard them say there were two bullets in him."

"True, but yours didn't hit anything vital."

"I think you're trying to make me feel better." And, in a way, hearing him say it wasn't my bullet that ended my father's life did help. Nevertheless, I knew I'd wanted to kill my father. At the moment I pulled that trigger, murder was on my mind.

"If we hadn't shot him, we'd be dead."

More consoling words. Wade had been consoling me from the moment he checked my father's pulse, then removed the gun from his hand. Wade helped me through the long moments as we waited for his fellow officers to arrive, through the interviews with the detective who took charge of the case, and through the call I made to my grandmother. We felt she needed to know before the news was on television or in the papers. She could prepare my mother, though my mother might not need any preparation. After all, Mom had always said my father was alive. She wouldn't be surprised.

Wade even talked the detective in charge into letting the two of us give John and Julia Westman the news that we'd found their missing box. Not that we would be doing that on our own. Five patrol cars accompanied us on our short journey around the corner to John and Julia's house, and before Wade and I were allowed to go to the front door, we had to wait until more than a dozen deputies positioned themselves front and back.

I held the box, though it had been photographed and its contents removed. The sheriff's department wasn't bending the rules that much. Evidence was evidence. And I wore latex gloves, just in case fingerprints were needed to prove the case against Julia Westman. There is a fine line between artwork and counterfeiting. Julia had crossed that line.

Their house was dark, and we'd arrived without sirens or lights. "What time is it?" I whispered.

Wade snapped on a small flashlight and looked at his watch. "Two a.m."

"It's later than I'd thought." Not that I cared. Not after what they'd put me through.

Wade looked over at the detective in charge. I saw the two men exchange nods. "Showtime," Wade said, and we started up the walk.

I rang the doorbell. Mr. Stubs, their Jack Russell terrier, began barking. I heard John yell at him, then the porch light came on and the front door cracked open. "P.J.?" he asked, groggy with sleep. Then he looked at Wade. "What's up?"

"What is it?" Julia asked from somewhere behind him.

"We need to talk to the two of you," I said, not sure if the giddy sensation in my stomach was due to excitement or disappointment.

"It's P.J. and that detective," John said, opening the door just a little more. "They want to—"

I knew when he saw the patrol cars parked by the side of the road. He opened the door wider and stood there, wearing just the bottoms of a pair of blue and gray striped flannel pajamas, staring out at the road.

"They want to what?" Julia asked, coming up beside him.

She'd slipped a red terrycloth robe over her nightgown, just the bottom edge of something creamy and silky-looking showing below the robe's hem. She looked at me first, then Wade . . . then at her husband. "What—?"

I spoke up before she had a chance to finish. "We found your missing box," I said and held it out in front of me. "Punk must have dropped it. It got a little muddy."

Both John and Julia looked down at what I held. I watched their faces. Under the porch light, I could see John blanch. Julia looked at Wade. She still hadn't noticed the patrol cars or the sheriff's men, but she understood. "You opened it, didn't you?"

"I didn't, but someone else did." I smiled. "I don't think you need to worry about ladybugs."

I heard one of the deputies recite the Miranda warning as Wade and I left John and Julia's house. I returned the box to the detective in charge and slipped off the latex gloves. Wade drove me back to my house, and we went inside together. I'd already given Baraka a treat, but I gave him another, then put him in his crate.

Then Wade and I went to bed—together.

ABOUT THE AUTHOR

Maris Soule graduated from U.C. Davis and U.C. Berkeley and taught art and math for four years in California. She was attending U.C. Santa Barbara when she met the blue-eyed redhead who became her husband and talked her into moving to the small town of Climax, Michigan. There they raised a son and a daughter, several Rhodesian Ridgebacks, and a slew of farm animals. Although she taught art for four more years, a love of reading led Soule to writing. She started with romances (twenty-five published, several winning awards) but over time found murder and suspense equally intriguing. Melding the two genres, she's now writing mystery/suspense with a touch of romance. In addition to novels, she's had several short stories published.